D1501647

THE NEW PROPHECY

WARRIORS

SUNSET

WARRIORS

WARRIORS: THE NEW PROPHECY

THE NEW PROPHECY

WARRIORS

SUNSET

ERIN
HUNTER

HARPERCOLLINS*PUBLISHERS*

Library of Congress Cataloging-in-Publication Data

Hunter, Erin.

Sunset / Erin Hunter. — 1st ed.

   p.   cm. — (Warriors, the new prophecy ; bk. 6)

Summary: Amidst ongoing strife within and between the Clans of
warrior cats, Brambleclaw is tempted by the dark plans of his father and
brother, and the meaning of Leafpool's ominous visions becomes clear.

   ISBN-10: 0-06-082769-6 (trade bdg.)

   ISBN-13: 978-0-06-082769-4 (trade bdg.)

   ISBN-10: 0-06-082770-X (lib. bdg.)

   ISBN-13: 978-0-06-082770-0 (lib. bdg.)

   [1. Cats—Fiction. 2. Fantasy.] I. Title.

PZ7.H916625Sun 2007   2006019548

[Fic]—dc22   CIP

                                            AC

Typography by Rob Hult

1 2 3 4 5 6 7 8 9 10

First Edition

To Rod Ritchie,

who first figured out what really goes on beyond the garden fence . . .

Special thanks to Cherith Baldry

ALLEGIANCES

THUNDERCLAN

LEADER
    FIRESTAR—ginger tom with a flame-colored pelt

DEPUTY
    GRAYSTRIPE—long-haired gray tom

MEDICINE CAT
    LEAFPOOL—light brown tabby she-cat with amber eyes

WARRIORS
    (toms, and she-cats without kits)

    DUSTPELT—dark brown tabby tom

    SANDSTORM—pale ginger she-cat

    CLOUDTAIL—long-haired white tom

    BRACKENFUR—golden brown tabby tom
    APPRENTICE, WHITEPAW

    THORNCLAW—golden brown tabby tom

    BRIGHTHEART—white she-cat with ginger patches

    BRAMBLECLAW—dark brown tabby tom with amber eyes

    ASHFUR—pale gray (with darker flecks) tom, dark blue eyes
    APPRENTICE, BIRCHPAW

    RAINWHISKER—dark gray tom with blue eyes

    SQUIRRELFLIGHT—dark ginger she-cat with green eyes

    SPIDERLEG—long-limbed black tom with brown underbelly and amber eyes

APPRENTICES (more than six moons old, in training to become warriors)

WHITEPAW—white she-cat with green eyes

BIRCHPAW—light brown tabby tom

QUEENS (she-cats expecting or nursing kits)

FERNCLOUD—pale gray (with darker flecks) she-cat, green eyes, mother of Dustpelt's kits

SORRELTAIL—tortoiseshell-and-white she-cat with amber eyes

DAISY—cream-colored, long-furred cat from the horseplace

ELDERS (former warriors and queens, now retired)

GOLDENFLOWER—pale ginger coat, the oldest nursery queen

LONGTAIL—pale tabby tom with dark black stripes, retired early due to failing sight

MOUSEFUR—small dusky brown she-cat

SHADOWCLAN

LEADER BLACKSTAR—large white tom with huge jet-black paws

DEPUTY RUSSETFUR—dark ginger she-cat

MEDICINE CAT LITTLECLOUD—very small tabby tom

WARRIORS (toms, and she-cats without kits)

OAKFUR—small brown tom
APPRENTICE, SMOKEPAW

CEDARHEART—dark gray tom

ROWANCLAW—ginger tom

TAWNYPELT—tortoiseshell she-cat with green eyes

QUEENS (she-cats expecting or nursing kits)

TALLPOPPY—long-legged light brown tabby she-cat

ELDERS (former warriors and queens, now retired)

BOULDER—skinny gray tom

WINDCLAN

LEADER **ONESTAR**—brown tabby tom

DEPUTY **ASHFOOT**—gray she-cat

MEDICINE CAT **BARKFACE**—short-tailed brown tom

WARRIORS (toms, and she-cats without kits)

TORNEAR—tabby tom

WEBFOOT—dark gray tabby tom

CROWFEATHER—dark gray tom

OWLWHISKER—light brown tabby tom

NIGHTCLOUD—black she-cat

WEASELFUR—ginger tom with white paws

QUEENS (she-cats expecting or nursing kits)

WHITETAIL—small white she-cat

ELDERS (former warriors and queens, now retired)

MORNINGFLOWER—tortoiseshell queen

RUSHTAIL—light brown tom

RIVERCLAN

LEADER

LEOPARDSTAR—unusually spotted golden tabby she-cat

DEPUTY

MISTYFOOT—gray she-cat with blue eyes

MEDICINE CAT

MOTHWING—dappled golden she-cat
APPRENTICE, WILLOWPAW

WARRIORS

(toms, and she-cats without kits)

BLACKCLAW—smoky black tom
APPRENTICE, BEECHPAW

HAWKFROST—dark brown tom with a white underbelly and ice-blue eyes

VOLETOOTH—small brown tabby tom

SWALLOWTAIL—dark tabby she-cat

STONESTREAM—gray tom

REEDWHISKER—black tom
APPRENTICE, RIPPLEPAW

QUEENS

(she-cats expecting or nursing kits)

MOSSPELT—tortoiseshell she-cat with blue eyes

DAWNFLOWER—pale gray she-cat

ELDERS

(former warriors and queens, now retired)

HEAVYSTEP—thickset tabby tom

THE TRIBE OF RUSHING WATER

BROOK WHERE SMALL FISH SWIM (BROOK)—brown tabby she-cat

STORMFUR—dark gray tom with amber eyes

OTHER ANIMALS

SMOKY—muscular gray and white tom who lives in a barn at the horseplace

FLOSS—small gray and white she-cat who lives at the horseplace

PIP—black and white terrier who lives with Twolegs near the horseplace

MIDNIGHT—a stargazing badger who lives by the sea

THE NEW PROPHECY

WARRIORS

SUNSET

PROLOGUE

Night lay heavily over the forest. No wind stirred the long grass at the edge of the path where a massive tabby cat stalked through the shadows. He paused, ears pricked, amber eyes narrowed. No moon or stars shone in the sky above his head but tree trunks thick with fungus shed an eerie glow on the bare earth beneath his paws.

The huge tom opened his jaws to draw in air, though he did not expect to taste the scent of prey. He knew that the twitching of the ferns meant nothing, and the flickering scraps of darkness that he could see from the corner of his eye would vanish like mist if he pounced on them. There was no hunger in this place, but he longed for the sensation of claws sinking into prey and the first warm bite of fresh-kill after a successful hunt.

The fur on his neck and shoulders rose as a new scent drifted toward him: the scent of cat, but not the two he had met here before. This was a different cat, a cat he knew from long ago. He stalked forward, following the scent, until the trees thinned out and he stood at the edge of a clearing washed by sickly light. The other cat came bounding across the open space to meet him, ears flattened and eyes wild with terror.

"Tigerstar!" he gasped, sliding to a halt and cowering to the ground. "Where did you come from? I thought I was alone here."

"Get up, Darkstripe." The tabby tom's voice was a rumble of disgust. "Stop cringing like a terrified kit."

Darkstripe rose to his paws and gave his fur a couple of quick licks. Once sleek like a well-fed fish, his pelt was now thin and tangled with burrs. "I don't understand this place," he meowed. "Where are we? Where are StarClan?"

"StarClan do not walk here."

Darkstripe's eyes stretched wide. "Why not? And why is it always dark here? Where is the moon?" A shiver ran through him. "I thought we would be hunting across the sky with our warrior ancestors, and watching over our Clanmates."

Tigerstar let out a faint hiss. "That way is not for us. But I don't need starlight to follow my path. If StarClan think they can forget about us, they're wrong."

He turned his back on Darkstripe, shouldering his way through the ferns without waiting to see whether the other cat followed him or not.

"Wait," Darkstripe panted, scrambling after him. "Tell me what you mean."

The massive tabby glanced back, his amber eyes reflecting the pale light. "Firestar thought he won when Scourge took my nine lives. He is a fool. What lies between us is not over yet."

"But what can you do to Firestar now?" Darkstripe protested. "You can't leave this forest. I know—I've tried. But however far I walk, the trees never end, and there's no light anywhere."

Tigerstar did not reply at once. He padded on through the undergrowth with Darkstripe following close behind. The smaller cat started at every rustle among the ferns and every flickering shadow that fell across his path. Once he halted, eyes staring, jaws open to taste the air.

"I can scent Brokenstar!" he exclaimed. "Is he here too? Brokenstar, where are you?"

Tigerstar stopped and looked back. "Save your breath. Brokenstar won't answer you. You will sense traces of many cats here, but seldom will you meet one face-to-face. We may be trapped in one place, but we are trapped alone."

"Then how do you expect to deal with Firestar?" Darkstripe asked. "He doesn't even walk this forest."

"I won't deal with him." Tigerstar's voice was a soft, threatening growl. "My sons will. Together, Hawkfrost and Brambleclaw will show Firestar that the battle is far from won."

Darkstripe's gaze flickered to his former leader's face and away again. "But how can you make Hawkfrost and Brambleclaw do what you want?"

Tigerstar silenced him with a single lash of his tail. His claws flexed in and out, scoring the earth beneath his paws. "I have learned to walk in the paths of their dreams," he hissed. "And I have time. All the time in the world. When they have destroyed that mangy kittypet, I'll make them leaders of their Clans, and show them what true power is."

Darkstripe flinched back into the shelter of a clump of bracken. "They couldn't have a better teacher," he meowed.

"They will learn the best fighting skills in the forest," Tigerstar went on, as if the other cat had not spoken. "They will learn to have no mercy on any cat who tries to oppose them. And in the end, they will divide the entire territory around the lake between them."

"But there are four Clans—"

"And soon there will be only two. Two Clans of purebred warriors, not weakened by kittypets and halfClan cats. Firestar has already taken in that useless lump of fur from the horseplace, and her whining kits. Is that any way to lead a Clan?"

Darkstripe bowed his head, ears flattened in agreement.

"Hawkfrost is fearless," Tigerstar growled approvingly. "He proved that when he drove a badger out of RiverClan's territory. And he showed great wisdom when he helped his sister become a medicine cat. Her support will smooth his path to leadership, and Hawkfrost knows that. He knows that power comes only to those who want it most."

"Yes, he's truly your son." The words spilled out of Darkstripe like rainwater from an upturned leaf, but if Tigerstar was aware of any edge to them, he ignored it.

"As for Brambleclaw . . ." Tigerstar narrowed his eyes. "He has courage too, but he is troubled by his loyalty to that fool Firestar. He must learn to allow *nothing*—not his leader, not the warrior code, not StarClan themselves—to stand in his way. He earned the respect of every cat when he made the journey to the sun-drown-place and led the Clans to their new home. His reputation alone should make it easy for him to take control." He straightened, his powerful shoulder muscles rippling. "I will show him how."

"I could help you," Darkstripe offered.

Tigerstar turned on him with a look of cold contempt. "I need no help. Did you not hear me say that every cat walks this dark forest alone?"

Darkstripe shivered. "But it's so empty and silent. . . . Tigerstar, let me come with you."

"No." There was a hint of regret in Tigerstar's voice, but no hesitation. "Don't try to follow me. Cats have no friends or allies here. They must walk their path of shadows alone."

Darkstripe sat up, curling his tail over his forepaws. "Where are you going now?"

"To meet my sons." He bounded away down the path, his fur gleaming in the pale yellowish light. Darkstripe was left behind, crouching in the shadow of the ferns.

Before Tigerstar vanished into the trees he glanced back to make one last promise. "Firestar will learn that my time is not yet over. He may have seven lives left to lose, but I will stalk him through my sons until every one has been ripped from him. This is one battle that he will not win."

CHAPTER 1

❧

Brambleclaw stood in the middle of the clearing, gazing at what was left of the ThunderClan camp. A crescent moon, thin as a claw, drifted above the trees that surrounded the stone hollow. Its pale light revealed the dens trampled down, the thorn barrier at the camp entrance broken and tossed aside, and the wounded cats of ThunderClan slowly creeping from the shadows, their fur bristling and their eyes stretched wide with shock. Brambleclaw could still hear the trampling of the badgers as they lumbered away. The undergrowth beyond the entrance quivered where they had pushed through, driven off with the help of Onestar and the WindClan warriors who had come just in time to help ThunderClan.

But it wasn't the sight of devastation that pricked Brambleclaw's pelt and kept his paws frozen to the ground. Two cats he had never thought he'd see again were picking their way carefully among the scattered thorns of the entrance barrier. They were uninjured, their pelts sleek and their eyes alight with alarm.

"Stormfur! What are you doing here?" Brambleclaw called.

The powerful gray tomcat paced forward until he could

touch noses with Brambleclaw. "It's good to see you again," he meowed. "I . . . I wanted to see if you'd found a place to live. But what has happened here?"

"Badgers," Brambleclaw replied. He glanced around, wondering where to begin helping his wounded and frightened Clanmates.

Beside Stormfur, the slender brown tabby she-cat brushed her tail against a long scratch on Brambleclaw's shoulder. "You're hurt," she mewed.

Brambleclaw twitched his ears. "It's nothing. Welcome to ThunderClan, Brook. I'm sorry you had to travel so far to find us like this." He paused and looked from one to the other. "Is everything all right in the Tribe of Rushing Water? I never expected you to come visit us so soon."

Stormfur shot a glance at Brook, so swift Brambleclaw almost missed it. "Everything's fine," he meowed. "We just wanted to be sure you had found a new place to live, like StarClan promised."

Brambleclaw looked around the devastated camp, the stricken cats stumbling through the remains of their home. "Yes, we found it," he murmured.

"You said *badgers* attacked you?" Brook prompted, sounding puzzled.

"They came here on purpose," Brambleclaw explained. "StarClan knows where they came from, more badgers than I've ever seen in my life. They would have killed us all if WindClan hadn't turned up." His paws trembled, and he sank his claws into the bloodstained earth to keep himself steady.

Stormfur nodded. "Don't worry about telling us every-thing now. What can we do to help?"

Brambleclaw sent a silent prayer of thanks to StarClan that they had chosen this moment to send his old friend back to the Clans. He and Stormfur had been through a lot together on the first journey to the sun-drown-place, and he could think of few cats he'd rather have beside him now.

He turned his head as a thin wail came from a trampled clump of ferns at the edge of the hollow. "We need to find all the cats that have been badly wounded. Some will be on their way to join StarClan," he warned, glancing at Brook. "The badgers came to kill, not drive us out."

Brook met his gaze steadily. "Whatever they have done, I want to help. I have seen this kind of savagery before from Sharptooth, remember?" Sharptooth was a giant mountain cat that had terrorized the Tribe of Rushing Water for many moons, until the cats from the forest arrived. Stormfur's sis-ter, Feathertail, had died in the fall that killed the savage ani-mal.

"We'll do whatever we have to," Stormfur promised. "Just tell us what to do. Are you ThunderClan's deputy now?"

Brambleclaw studied a fragment of moss that was trapped under his front paw. "No," he admitted. "Firestar has decided not to appoint another deputy. He wants to give Graystripe more time to come back."

"That's tough." There was a note of sympathy in Stormfur's voice that made Brambleclaw wince. He didn't want any cat's pity.

Suddenly Brook froze. "I thought you said the badgers had gone," she hissed.

Brambleclaw whipped around, then relaxed as he saw a familiar, pointed, black-and-white face pushing its way out of a clump of dead bracken.

Stormfur touched Brook's shoulder lightly with his tail. "That's Midnight," he meowed. "She wouldn't hurt any cats." He bounded forward to meet the elderly badger.

Midnight peered at Stormfur with shortsighted eyes. Then she gave a small nod. "Cat friend from journey," she rumbled. "Good it is to see you again. And this cat from mountain Tribe, is she not?" she added, gesturing with her snout toward Brook.

"That's right," Stormfur meowed. "This is Brook, a prey-hunter from the Tribe of Rushing Water." He beckoned Brook forward with his tail; she went over reluctantly, as if she couldn't quite believe this badger was friendly. Brambleclaw understood her feelings; he knew Midnight as well as any cat, but it was hard not to look at her bulky shape without remembering snapping jaws, fierce gleaming eyes, and claws that shredded cats' fur like leaves in newleaf. . . .

There was the sound of heavy paws, and he looked up to see Midnight standing beside him. Grief and anger sparked from her berry-bright eyes. "Too late my warning," she rasped. "Not enough could I do."

"You brought WindClan to help us," Brambleclaw pointed out. "Without you, our whole Clan would have been wiped out."

Midnight bowed her head, the white stripe that ran the length of her snout gleaming in the faint moonlight. "Shame for my kin I feel."

"Every cat knows this attack had nothing to do with you," Brambleclaw told her. "You will always be welcome in this Clan."

Midnight still looked troubled. Behind her, Brambleclaw spotted his Clan leader near the center of the clearing, with Onestar and the WindClan warriors. He padded toward them, motioning with his tail for Stormfur and Brook to follow. A fox-length away, in the shelter of an upturned thornbush, Leafpool was bending over the limp body of Ashfur. For a heartbeat Brambleclaw wondered if the gray warrior was dead, until he saw Ashfur's tail twitch. *StarClan shall not take all our warriors tonight*, he thought determinedly.

Firestar's chest still heaved from the effort of fighting. His flame-colored pelt was torn, and blood was oozing from a long scratch along his flank. Brambleclaw felt a flash of concern. Had his leader lost another life? Whether he had or not, he was badly hurt. *I will help him until my last breath*, Brambleclaw vowed. *Together, we can bring the Clan through this until we are even stronger than before.*

In spite of his injuries, Firestar's eyes were bright and he sat up straight as he faced the WindClan leader, Onestar. "The thanks of all ThunderClan go with you," he meowed.

"I doubt you'll have any more trouble with the badgers," Onestar replied. "But I can leave a couple of warriors behind to keep watch, if you like."

"No thanks, I don't think we'll need them." The warmth in Firestar's eyes revealed the long friendship between these two cats. Brambleclaw silently thanked StarClan that the tension between them, which everyone had felt since Onestar became WindClan leader, seemed to be over at last. "Do your warriors need the help of our medicine cat before you go?" the ThunderClan leader added. "If any of them are badly injured, they're welcome to stay here."

Brambleclaw glanced across at Leafpool, who was still crouched beside Ashfur. When she heard Firestar, she raised her head and stared across the clearing at the WindClan warriors. Brambleclaw felt a stab of sympathy as her gaze sought out one in particular. Two days ago, Crowfeather and Leafpool had abandoned their Clans so that they could be together, but news of the badger attack had brought them home again. Brambleclaw hoped that Leafpool had come home for good; ThunderClan needed her more than ever now that so many cats had been wounded in the badger attack.

Crowfeather was staring down at his paws as if he was deliberately avoiding Leafpool's gaze. Fur was missing from a broad scratch on his flank, but the wound had stopped bleeding and he stood with his weight on all four paws. Webfoot had a torn ear, and the WindClan deputy Ashfoot was bleeding from one shoulder, but none of the wounds looked serious enough to stop the warriors from returning to the WindClan camp.

"I think we're all fit to travel, thank StarClan," Onestar

answered the ThunderClan leader. "If you're sure you don't need our help anymore, we'll return to our own territory now."

Crowfeather raised his head and shot one despairing glance at Leafpool. She scrambled to her paws, leaving Ashfur, and padded across to meet the WindClan warrior. They stood a little way from the other cats, their heads close together. Standing in the shadows, Brambleclaw couldn't help overhearing, but he didn't want to disturb them by moving.

"Good-bye, Crowfeather," Leafpool murmured, sounding choked with pain. "We . . . we'd better not see each other again."

Crowfeather's eyes flashed, and for a heartbeat Brambleclaw thought he was going to protest. Then he shook his head. "You're right," he meowed. "It would never have worked. I will never mean enough to you."

Leafpool sank her claws into the ground. "You mean more to me than you will ever know."

The tip of Crowfeather's black tail twitched. "You're a medicine cat. I understand what that means now. StarClan go with you, Leafpool. I'll never forget you."

He and Leafpool touched noses, a delicate contact that lasted less than a heartbeat. Then Crowfeather turned back to his Clanmates. Leafpool watched him go, her eyes clouded with loss.

Webfoot gave Crowfeather a dark look, and Weaselfur pointedly turned his back on him, but Onestar said nothing, only gathering all his warriors together with a sweep of his tail before leading them out of the camp.

"Thank you again!" Firestar called after them. "May StarClan light your path."

Leafpool stood motionless until Crowfeather's gray-black figure had vanished into the shadow of the trees, then padded across the clearing toward Cinderpelt's den. On the way she flicked her tail to summon Brightheart, who had helped Cinderpelt with medicine cat duties in the past.

"Are you sure?" Brightheart asked hesitantly.

"Of course I'm sure." Leafpool's voice was ragged with exhaustion and grief. "Every cat in the Clan is wounded. I'll be glad of your skills."

Brightheart's eyes gleamed, and she seemed to shake off some of her own weariness as she followed Leafpool to the den.

"Is that Stormfur and Brook?"

Brambleclaw jumped as a hoarse voice spoke in his ear. Squirrelflight had appeared beside him. Her dark ginger fur was matted with blood and the tip of one ear was torn.

"Can't you see that it is?" Brambleclaw replied, realizing too late how abrupt he sounded. "Sorry—" he began.

Squirrelflight took a pace forward so that her pelt brushed his. She touched the tip of her tail to his mouth to silence him. "Stupid furball," she whispered.

Brambleclaw tensed, wondering if he was imagining the affection in her green gaze. Glancing past her, he saw Ashfur glaring at him with narrowed eyes.

Squirrelflight didn't notice Ashfur. She limped past Brambleclaw to touch noses with the visitors. "Thank

StarClan you have come," she meowed, echoing Bramble-claw's thoughts. "We need all our friends right now."

Brambleclaw felt his shoulders droop in exhaustion just thinking about how much had to be done. Injuries to treat, dens to rebuild, fresh-kill to gather . . . "We'll speak to Firestar and then get started."

As they approached the Clan leader, Thornclaw staggered up to them. Blood trickled from a deep gash above one eye. "Stormfur?" he muttered, shaking his head in confusion. "No, it can't be." The golden brown warrior slumped to the ground, where he lay panting.

Squirrelflight rested her tail on his shoulder, urging him to lie still until his injuries could be treated. Brambleclaw led Stormfur and Brook up to Firestar.

The Clan leader's eyes stretched wide in surprise. "Stormfur . . . and Brook! What are you doing here?"

"There'll be time to explain later," Stormfur meowed. "For now, Firestar, put us to work."

Firestar stared around the clearing as if he wasn't sure where to start. "We should sort out the warriors' den so the cats who have been hurt most can get some sleep . . . but we need to get the entrance barrier back in place, too."

The whole camp was devastated, and few of the ThunderClan cats were in any shape to start rebuilding. Ashfur was slumped on the ground, bleeding from flank and foreleg, while Leafpool patted cobwebs onto his wounds. Cloudtail limped up to her, holding one forepaw off the ground; blood trickled from where a claw had been torn out.

"Hi, Stormfur," he mewed as he passed, as if this had been such an extraordinary night, the sight of an old friend was no longer a surprise. "Leafpool, can I have a piece of that cobweb?"

Sandstorm was close behind him, her head bent with exhaustion and her tail dragging in the dust. She stopped dead when she spotted Leafpool, then swung around to face Firestar, her green eyes questioning.

"Leafpool's here?" she meowed. "What happened?"

Firestar shook his head to silence her. "We'll talk to her later," he promised. "For now, she's home, and that's all that matters."

"Firestar!" A yowl came from across the clearing. "Firestar, have those crow-food eaters gone?"

Brambleclaw turned to see the three elders, Mousefur, Goldenflower, and Longtail. In the darkness they had to pick their way carefully down the tumble of rocks that led to the ledge where Firestar had his den. They had taken shelter there while the battle raged below. It was Mousefur who had called out; she had lost some fur from one shoulder, Longtail's tail was bleeding, and Goldenflower had a deep scratch down one side. She was guiding Longtail with her tail across his shoulders.

"Are you all right?" Brambleclaw asked, going to meet them.

"Fine," Mousefur growled. "A badger tried to climb up to the Highledge, but we sent it back down the rocks faster than it intended."

"What if they come back?" Goldenflower sounded distraught.

"They'd better not." Longtail flexed his claws, and Brambleclaw saw dark tufts of badger fur caught in them. "I don't need to see to fight badgers. I can find them by their disgusting scent."

"Better let Leafpool look at those scratches," Firestar meowed.

"Leafpool?" Mousefur's voice was sharp as she swung around to stare at the medicine cat. "She's back, is she? For good—or until that WindClan warrior starts sniffing around again?"

Brambleclaw bit back a sharp retort. He knew Mousefur sounded so harsh only because she was shocked and hurt.

"And who's this?" Mousefur padded up to Stormfur and examined him with narrowed eyes. "Stormfur? What's he doing here?"

"Just paying a visit." Stormfur sounded uncomfortable at the brown elder's suspicious tone.

Mousefur grunted, as if she wasn't completely convinced that Stormfur was a friend. "You were a RiverClan warrior before you left us. Why are you here and not over there?"

"Mousefur, don't be so ungrateful!" Squirrelflight meowed indignantly. "We need every cat who's prepared to help. Besides, Stormfur is half ThunderClan, remember?" Stormfur's father was Graystripe, the ThunderClan deputy who had been captured by Twolegs before the cats left the forest.

Mousefur bristled at Squirrelflight, but before she could reply she was interrupted by a cry from Ferncloud, racing through the broken thorns that were strewn across the entrance to the hollow. "Dustpelt, where are you?"

Brambleclaw bounded over to her as she stopped just inside the entrance, gazing around the dark camp and yowling her mate's name.

"Brambleclaw, have you seen Dustpelt?" she demanded.

"No, not yet," he admitted. "Come on, I'll help you look."

"I should have stayed with him!" Ferncloud wailed. "I never should have left the camp!"

"But Daisy needed you," Brambleclaw reminded her. "She couldn't have coped without a warrior to look after her, and it was much safer for you both to stay hidden outside the camp. Remember, Daisy hasn't been in the Clan long, and she can't fight well enough yet to defend herself and her kits."

Ferncloud shook her head distractedly. "Dustpelt *can't* be dead," she mewed.

"We'll find him," Brambleclaw promised. Silently, he hoped StarClan had not chosen this warrior to join their ranks tonight. He began to search, padding back and forth among the scattered remains of the entrance barrier, gradually working his way back toward the center of the camp. His breath caught in his throat when he picked up Dustpelt's scent and almost stumbled over a heap of tabby fur lying in the shadow of the rock wall. Dustpelt's eyes were closed, but as Brambleclaw stared at him his ears twitched and he let out a sneeze.

"Ferncloud—over here!" Brambleclaw called. "Dustpelt! Dustpelt!"

At the sound of his mate's voice Dustpelt opened his eyes and started to struggle to his paws. Ferncloud bounded up to him, brushing her pelt against his and covering him with licks. Dustpelt let out an unsteady purr.

Brambleclaw decided that if Dustpelt could stand up, he could wait a while before Cinderpelt or Leafpool saw him. He was heading back to the clearing, anxious to start work on the wrecked camp, when he saw that Birchpaw had followed Ferncloud into the hollow. The young apprentice had lost almost all the fur from his haunches, and one eye was closed. With his good eye he darted nervous glances from side to side, as if he still expected to see the camp full of invading badgers.

Behind him, Daisy, the cat from the horseplace, picked her way through the thorns with her three kits scrambling after her. They stared with huge eyes at the devastated dens and the weary, wounded cats. Spotting Midnight standing in the shadows, Berrykit drew back his lips in a snarl. He took a pace forward, his legs stiff and his fur bristling.

With a squeak of alarm, Daisy rushed to his side. "Berrykit! What are you doing? Come away before the badger hurts you."

"Nothing to fear, small one," Midnight rumbled gently.

Daisy just glared at her, sweeping her tail around Berrykit and drawing him away toward the other cats. Brambleclaw realized she had no idea who Midnight was.

"It's all right!" he called.

Leafpool reached the horseplace cat before him. "Don't worry, Daisy," she meowed. "Midnight's a friend. Crowfeather and I met her when we were up in the hills. She warned us that her kin were going to attack, and she brought WindClan to help us."

"But she's a badger!" Daisy exclaimed.

Brambleclaw padded over to help Leafpool explain. "We met Midnight on our journey to the sun-drown-place. She wouldn't harm us."

"There's nothing to be scared of," Berrykit assured his mother. "*I'll* look after you."

"I bet you would, too." Cloudtail limped up and gently flicked Berrykit's ear with the tip of his tail. "It takes enough courage for a full-grown cat to face up to a badger. You'll make a great warrior one day."

Berrykit's tail went straight up with pride. "Race you to the nursery!" he yowled to his littermates.

"No—wait!" Cloudtail called after the three kits. "You can't go in there yet."

"Why not?" Daisy asked, puzzled. "My kits need to rest."

"Cinderpelt's body is in there," Leafpool mewed quietly. "A badger broke in while she was helping Sorreltail give birth." Her voice quavered and she swallowed hard. "I tried to save her, but she was already on her way to StarClan."

Brambleclaw stared at her in disbelief.

Cinderpelt was dead?

CHAPTER 2

Brambleclaw felt as if every drop of his blood had turned to ice. It was bad enough that any warrior should have gone to join StarClan tonight, but losing the Clan's medicine cat was a cruel blow. He suddenly realized why Leafpool had asked Brightheart to help her treat the injured warriors.

Mousefur let out a shocked yowl. "She was only a young cat! She had her whole life ahead of her."

Squirrelflight padded up and brushed her muzzle against Leafpool's shoulder. "We won't forget her," she murmured.

Brambleclaw nodded, too shocked to speak. Leafpool stood with head bowed for a heartbeat, then nudged Thornclaw to his paws. "Come to my den." Her voice sounded thin, as if she was keeping it tightly under control. "I have more cobwebs there." She padded away, glancing back just once to be sure Thornclaw was following.

Movement in the darkness at the edge of the hollow caught Brambleclaw's eye, and he turned to see Spiderleg and Whitepaw heading slowly toward them. Spiderleg beckoned with his tail; Brambleclaw had to force his numbed legs into action.

"What is it?" he asked.

"Come and see." Spiderleg led the way to the wall of the hollow, near the escape route where Daisy and her kits had climbed to safety. A limp bundle of gray-black fur lay in the shadows.

"It's Sootfur," Whitepaw whispered. "I think he's dead."

Brambleclaw's belly twisted. Even though he was afraid that Whitepaw was right, he nosed the young warrior's body in the faint hope of rousing him. Sootfur didn't move, and his glazed eyes stared at nothing.

"May StarClan light his path," Brambleclaw murmured. Sootfur's sister, Sorreltail, had only just given birth; how would she cope with the loss of her brother?

Both the younger cats were staring at Brambleclaw as if they were waiting for him to tell them what to do. With a massive effort he forced himself to think.

"Carry him into the center of the camp, so we can have a vigil," he meowed. "I'll go and look for Rainwhisker." Sootfur's brother would have to be told; perhaps he could help their sister, Sorreltail.

Brambleclaw waited until Spiderleg and Whitepaw had lifted Sootfur's body, then began to search. He couldn't remember seeing Rainwhisker since the end of the battle. Anxiety sank sharp claws into him; surely Rainwhisker couldn't be dead too?

Then he spotted the gray warrior half buried under the torn-up thorn branches that had once sheltered the warriors' den. He lay without moving, but as Brambleclaw dragged a branch off him he managed to lift his head.

"The badgers—have they gone?" he asked hoarsely.

"It's all over," Brambleclaw replied. "But I'm afraid there's sad news. Can you get up?"

With a grunt, Rainwhisker brought his paws under him and scrabbled at the prickly twigs until he had hauled himself upright. He balanced precariously on three legs; the fourth hung at an awkward angle, and Brambleclaw was afraid it had been broken. Giving Rainwhisker his shoulder for support, he guided him toward the center of the camp where Sootfur now lay. Firestar, Squirrelflight, and several other cats stood around him, their heads bowed.

Rainwhisker let out a yowl of dismay at the sight of his brother's body. Limping forward, he bent his head to thrust his nose into the gray-black fur. He stayed still for a few heartbeats, then looked up, his eyes filled with grief.

"I should tell Sorreltail," he meowed.

Firestar twitched his tail to stop him. "Your leg needs to be seen to first. Some other cat—"

"No," Rainwhisker interrupted stubbornly. "Let me do it. Sootfur was our brother. She will want to hear this from me."

The Clan leader hesitated, then nodded. "Okay, but go to see Cinderpelt as soon as you can."

"Firestar, you mean Leafpool," Sandstorm gently corrected him.

Firestar blinked, stupefied by shock and exhaustion. "Sorry," he murmured. "I still can't believe Cinderpelt's dead."

Brambleclaw gazed at him sympathetically. The Thunder-Clan leader had been very close to Cinderpelt. He was sure to be badly shaken by her death.

He's going to need my help. Brambleclaw braced himself. Touching Squirrelflight on her shoulder with his tail, he murmured, "Let's go and bring Cinderpelt's body into the clearing."

"Right," Squirrelflight mewed. "Rainwhisker, come with us if you want to speak to Sorreltail."

The three cats made their way to the nursery. The bramble thicket, growing close to the wall of the hollow, was the least damaged part of the camp. Squirrelflight, Ashfur, and Brackenfur had stayed there throughout the battle, defending the entrance while Sorreltail's kits were born. Only part of it had been trampled down where the badger that killed Cinderpelt had swatted Brackenfur aside to break in.

Daisy and her kits were standing outside the entrance. Cloudtail and Ferncloud were with them, and Birchpaw, who lay splayed out on the ground beside his mother. For a dreadful instant Brambleclaw thought that the apprentice had died of his wounds, until he saw the rapid rise and fall of his chest. Ferncloud crouched over him, gently licking his shoulder.

Leafpool and Brightheart approached at the same time. Leafpool was carrying a wrap of herbs in her jaws, which she set down as Brambleclaw came up.

"Thank StarClan, Cinderpelt's den was too small for the badgers to get in," she meowed. "All her herbs and berries are still intact." Her voice shook as she added, "Please can we move her body, so the Clan can sit in vigil for her?"

"We've come to do that," Brambleclaw told her.

Leafpool blinked gratefully. "Thank you. Brightheart," she

went on, "please fetch some marigold for Birchpaw. Then tell all the cats who are able to walk to go to my den. It'll be easier to treat them there. And let me know if there's any cat who can't manage it. I'll need to see them first."

Brightheart gave a brisk nod and left.

Leafpool led the way into the nursery, followed closely by Brambleclaw, Squirrelflight, and Rainwhisker. Hardly any moonlight penetrated through the brambles, making it shadowy as a cave inside, and Brambleclaw winced as he stepped on a thorny tendril. He could just make out Cinderpelt lying on her side in a nest of soft moss. Her tail was curled over her nose, and she looked as if she were asleep.

Brambleclaw padded up to her. "Cinderpelt?" For a heartbeat he thought she might raise her head and answer him, but when he touched his nose to her fur it felt deathly cold.

Sorreltail was lying on the other side of the dead medicine cat, in the farthest corner of the nursery. Her body was curled away from Cinderpelt's body, sheltering her kits. Her mate, Brackenfur, crouched beside her, his fur bristling; as the other cats entered he bared his teeth in a snarl.

"It's all right, Brackenfur," Brambleclaw meowed. "It's only us. There's nothing to be afraid of."

Brackenfur relaxed, though he still looked wary, and shifted even closer to Sorreltail. Leafpool squeezed past Brambleclaw and began nosing carefully over the young tortoiseshell. Brambleclaw blinked, waiting for his eyes to get used to the gloom until he could see Sorreltail's four kits burrowing blindly into her fur. Sorreltail was gazing up at

Leafpool, her eyes blank with shock.

Rainwhisker edged up beside Brambleclaw. "What can I say to her?" he whispered. "She's suffered enough already. Knowing about Sootfur could kill her."

"Not when she has Brackenfur and Leafpool to look after her," Brambleclaw reassured him. "Come on—it's better for her to hear it from you than some other cat."

Rainwhisker nodded, though he still looked uncertain. "Sorreltail . . ." he began, gently nuzzling his sister's shoulder.

"Rainwhisker, is that you?" Sorreltail mewed, twisting her head around to look at him. "Are you hurt?"

"I'll be okay," Rainwhisker replied. "But I've got some bad news. It's Sootfur. He's . . . dead."

Sorreltail stared at him for a couple of heartbeats as if she hadn't understood. Then she tipped back her head and let out a high-pitched wail. "No! Oh, no!"

Her body twisted in a spasm of grief; Brambleclaw heard a faint mewling of protest from the kits as they were dislodged from her belly.

"Sorreltail, it's all right!" Brackenfur mewed. He pressed himself to her side, covering her face and ears with licks until she shuddered and buried her head in his shoulder. "Sorreltail, I'm here," he went on. "Think of the kits. You have to care for them."

"How did he die?" Sorreltail's voice trembled, but she shifted until her kits were tucked once more in the curve of her body. The babies scrambled back into place and kept suckling, pressing into her belly with tiny soft paws.

"The badgers killed him," Rainwhisker told her.

"Sootfur was a brave warrior," Brambleclaw meowed. "He's safe with StarClan now."

Sorreltail nodded and reached out to give Rainwhisker a comforting lick. "Thank you for telling me."

Leafpool nudged her leaf wrap closer to the young tortoiseshell. "That's borage," she meowed. "It will help your supply of milk." She hesitated and then added, "If you can't sleep, I'll get you some poppy seed, but it would be better for the kits if you can manage without."

"It's all right, I can do without it." Sorreltail bent over and chewed up the borage, wincing at the taste but swallowing until it was all gone.

"Brackenfur, can you find some fresh-kill for her?" Leafpool suggested. "As for you, Rainwhisker, you'd better stay right here while I have a look at that leg."

Brackenfur touched his nose to Sorreltail's ear, promised, "I'll be right back," and slipped out of the nursery past Cinderpelt's body.

Sorreltail's gaze followed him. "It's my fault Cinderpelt died." Her voice rasped with grief. "She could have escaped the badger, but she stayed to help me."

"It's *not* your fault." Leafpool sounded unusually fierce, and Brambleclaw glanced at her in surprise. "Cinderpelt was doing her duty as a medicine cat. That was the choice she made."

"That's true," meowed Squirrelflight. "Sorreltail, just think—if Cinderpelt had left you, the badger might have killed you too, and your kits. You wouldn't want that, and neither would she."

Sorreltail shook her head, shuddering.

"They're beautiful kits," Brambleclaw said, trying to distract her. He got a good look at the newest members of ThunderClan for the first time. "Have you given them names yet?"

Sorreltail nodded. "This one is Molekit." She touched the biggest kit's head with the tip of her tail. "He's the only tom. Then this is Honeykit and Poppykit." She touched in turn a pale bracken-colored tabby and a tortoiseshell-and-white kit who looked like a tiny copy of Sorreltail. "And this is Cinderkit."

Brambleclaw heard a gasp from Squirrelflight. The fluffy gray kit looked hauntingly familiar, and he couldn't help casting a rapid glance at the body of Cinderpelt behind him. Leafpool, bent over Rainwhisker's injured leg, froze for a heartbeat. "I think Cinderpelt would like that," she mewed softly, then carried on with what she was doing.

"They all look strong and healthy," Brambleclaw meowed. "Come on, Squirrelflight, we have a job to do for Cinderpelt now."

Squirrelflight paused and touched Leafpool lightly on the shoulder with the tip of her tail. "You should get some rest soon," she mewed. "You look awful."

"I don't have time to rest," Leafpool responded, not looking at her. "What are all these wounded cats going to do if I take a nap?"

Squirrelflight's gaze was troubled. "But I'm worried about

you. I can feel how tough it is for you right now."

This time Leafpool didn't reply. Brambleclaw could see that she just wanted to be left alone to take care of Rainwhisker. He nudged Squirrelflight's shoulder. "Come on," he repeated, lowering his voice to add, "give her a bit of space. She can cope; she just needs time."

Squirrelflight still looked uncertain, but she turned around in the tight space and helped Brambleclaw carry Cinderpelt's limp body out of the nursery. Daisy and the kits were still huddled by the entrance with Cloudtail and Ferncloud. Brightheart had brought the marigold and was treating Birchpaw's wounds.

"You *can't* leave," Cloudtail was protesting. "You and the kits belong here."

Daisy shook her head, her gaze falling on the dead medicine cat. "My kits could have been killed," she mewed. "Or I could have died, and then what would happen to them? They'll be safer back at the horseplace."

All three of her kits let out meows of protest.

"But what about the Twolegs?" Cloudtail pressed. "You came here in the first place because you were afraid they would take your kits away from you."

Daisy flexed her claws, her eyes clouded with indecision. Before she could speak, Brightheart meowed, "The kits might be safe from the Twolegs by now. After all, they're nearly old enough to make themselves useful, catching rats and mice in the barn."

"But we don't want to go back there," Berrykit wailed. "We want to stay here."

Daisy flicked him with her tail. "You don't know what you're talking about. Do you *want* a badger to come and get you?"

"But none of you are hurt," Squirrelflight pointed out. "The Clan made sure you were safe."

"Please stay," Ferncloud urged. "Life will be much easier now that newleaf is here."

Daisy gave her a doubtful look. "Can you promise me the badgers won't come back?"

"No cat can promise that," Cloudtail replied, "but I'll bet we won't see anything of them for a good long time."

Daisy shook her head and pushed her kits in front of her into the nursery. "Come along. You need to rest after such a dreadful night."

"But we're not tired," Mousekit complained.

Daisy didn't reply. She cast one more glance back at Cloudtail, full of fear and uncertainty, before she vanished.

Ferncloud followed her. "I'll just see her settled."

"Daisy could be right, you know," Brightheart meowed, without looking at Cloudtail. "She knows what's best for her kits, and maybe they would all feel safer back at the horse-place."

Cloudtail opened his mouth to protest, then closed it again.

"You'd better get over to Leafpool's den," Brightheart told him, as if she didn't want to talk about the horseplace cat anymore. "That torn claw is bleeding again. You need more cobwebs."

Cloudtail glanced at the nursery entrance and muttered, "Right, I'll be off, then."

Brambleclaw turned back to Cinderpelt, his heart twisting with grief as he gazed at the sleek gray body, the blue eyes glazed and empty. Squirrelflight stood beside him with her head bowed; Brambleclaw saw a shiver pass through her and he pressed himself against her side, hoping she wouldn't pull away. When she didn't move, he stood for a moment with his eyes closed, breathing in her sweet, familiar scent.

"Come on," he mewed softly. "The night will be over soon. It's time for her vigil."

He and Squirrelflight picked up Cinderpelt's body again to carry her across the clearing and lay her beside Sootfur. Spiderleg and Whitepaw were crouching with their noses pressed into the gray-black warrior's pelt.

"Good-bye," Brambleclaw murmured, touching his nose to Cinderpelt's fur. "StarClan will honor you."

"We'll miss you," Squirrelflight added. "And we'll never forget you."

Brambleclaw would have liked to crouch beside the dead medicine cat and keep a proper vigil for her, but there was too much to do. He padded across to Firestar, who was still in the center of the camp with Stormfur, Brook, and Midnight.

"I think we should start on the warriors' den," he meowed.

Midnight dipped her head to Firestar. "I go now," she announced. "By night is travel well."

"But you must be as tired as the rest of us," Firestar protested. "Stay until you have slept for a while."

Midnight's white-striped head swung around as she surveyed the shattered camp. "No more here for me to do. I go back to sea cave, hear beating of waves on shore, rustle of wind in grasses."

"ThunderClan would have been destroyed if you hadn't brought WindClan to help us. We can never thank you enough."

"No need is thanks. Too late warning come. My kin not hear talk of peace."

"But *why?*" Brook asked, her eyes wide with distress. "In the mountains, we've never had trouble with badgers. Are they like Sharptooth, wanting to kill cats for their prey?"

Midnight shook her head. "My kin not eat cats. But cats drive them from territory, first from RiverClan on other side of lake, then from here. Revenge they want, and take territory back."

"I remember Hawkfrost reporting that at the Gathering," Firestar meowed. "He was the RiverClan warrior who drove the badger out."

Brambleclaw drew a sharp breath, ready to defend his half brother. Were his Clanmates going to blame Hawkfrost for the badger attack?

"We drove a badger out of our territory too," Squirrelflight pointed out. "With her kits. And to think I felt sorry for her!"

"I wonder if that means they'll come back," Firestar murmured thoughtfully. "The patrols will have to keep a sharp lookout."

"I also," Midnight added. "When know anything, I come, or send word. But now I go, say farewell to cat friends."

"Good-bye, Midnight," mewed Stormfur. "It was good to see you again."

Midnight's small eyes rested on him for a moment. "Spirits

watch over you," she told Stormfur. "StarClan and Tribe of Endless Hunting also. Hard the path you walk, but not finished yet."

The gray warrior dipped his head. "Thank you, Midnight."

"I wish you didn't have to leave," Brambleclaw meowed to Midnight. With a glance at his Clan leader, he added, "Couldn't you make a set in the woods here and stay with us?"

"Please!" Squirrelflight urged.

The old badger shook her head, her eyes deep with wisdom. "This not my place," she warned. "But StarClan may lead us meet again."

"I hope so," meowed Brambleclaw.

"Then it's good-bye." Firestar lowered his head to Midnight in the deepest respect. "ThunderClan will always honor you." He escorted her to the entrance, as if he didn't want to see her go either. Dustpelt and Sandstorm, gathering up the thorns from the damaged entrance barrier, stopped work briefly to add their own farewells.

With Squirrelflight and Stormfur beside him, Brambleclaw watched Midnight leave the hollow, her broad, flat paws tramping across the remains of the thorn barrier. For the second time now, ThunderClan had needed Midnight's help to survive. How could they be safe when she was so far away, at the sun-drown-place? Brambleclaw wasn't even sure he could find the sandy cliff again.

I must go on, he told himself. *I'd give my last breath to help my Clan, and ThunderClan needs me now more than they ever have before.*

Stormfur turned away from the dark forest where the

badger had disappeared. "Right," he meowed, "what needs doing next?"

"I think every cat has been accounted for, and Leafpool and Brightheart are taking care of the injuries. But we all need to rest and recover," Brambleclaw meowed. "That means we need to sort out places to sleep. And do something about fresh-kill."

"Brook and I will hunt for the Clan in the morning," Stormfur promised. "For now, I'll work on the warriors' den. Where is it?"

Good question, thought Brambleclaw. He pointed with his tail at the trampled thorn tree beneath the far wall of the hollow. "Over there," he meowed. The branches had been dense and low-growing, providing good protection against the cold winds and rain of leaf-bare. But the badgers had broken through the canopy to get at cats trying to shelter inside, and it didn't look much like a den now.

Stormfur blinked. "Okay, I'll get started." He bounded off in the direction Brambleclaw had pointed.

"Brook, you could check on the elders," Squirrelflight suggested. "Their den's under that twisted hazel over there. Come and find me if you need any help."

Brook nodded and bounded off into the shadows.

Brambleclaw was about to follow Stormfur when Ashfur padded up. "Are you going to sit vigil for Sootfur and Cinderpelt?" he asked Squirrelflight.

"You go ahead," Squirrelflight mewed. "I want to help rebuild the dens right now, but I'll try to sit with them later.

Cinderpelt and Sootfur would understand."

Ashfur blinked at her with hurt in his blue eyes, as if he was taking her refusal personally. "Okay, I'll see you later, then." He padded off and settled down beside the other cats circled around the two still bodies.

Squirrelflight flicked her tail lightly over Brambleclaw's ears. "Don't you think you should go to Leafpool's den and get those scratches looked at?"

In spite of everything that had happened, the expression in Squirrelflight's eyes made something in Brambleclaw's heart purr like a kit. "Not yet," he told her. "Leafpool has enough to do, and there are plenty of cats hurt worse than me. I'll help Stormfur with the warriors' den. Every cat is exhausted, and it'll be dawn soon."

"Then I'll do something about fresh-kill. The pile must have been scattered, but the badgers wouldn't have had time to eat our prey. I might be able to salvage enough to keep us going until we can send out hunting patrols. If I find anything fit to eat, I'll bring you some."

"Thanks." Brambleclaw watched the ginger warrior as she padded across the clearing, then made his way to the remains of the warriors' den. Every muscle in his body was aching, the scratch on his shoulder throbbed, and he felt almost too tired to put one paw in front of another. But his Clanmates needed him. He *had* to find the strength to help them.

The thorn tree where the warriors had made their den grew close to the highest part of the cliff, not far from the tumble of rocks leading up to the Highledge. As he approached, Brambleclaw saw that although the outer branches were broken and trampled down, farther in, toward the trunk, there seemed to be less damage. He hoped that there might be enough shelter left untouched, even if the warriors were a bit cramped until the tree put on fresh growth in newleaf.

As he drew closer, sniffing cautiously at the wrecked outer branches, Stormfur appeared, hauling a tangled mass of thorns behind him.

"Hi," he panted, setting the thorns down to catch his breath. Narrowing his eyes, he added, "Shouldn't you be resting? You look very battered, you know."

"We're all battered," Brambleclaw pointed out. "I can't rest now; there's too much to do."

Stormfur's gaze traveled around the clearing. "There certainly is."

Brambleclaw rested his tail against Stormfur's gray flank. "I'm glad to see you," he meowed. "StarClan couldn't have chosen a better time to bring you here."

"Well . . . the Tribe of Endless Hunting watch over me now."

"Some ancestors sent you to us. I don't care whose, I'm just thankful."

Squirrelflight trotted up just then, carrying a couple of mice by their tails. She dropped the fresh-kill at their paws. "There you are," she mewed to Brambleclaw. "Eat. You need your strength." She patted the second mouse toward Stormfur. "You too, Stormfur."

"No thanks," the gray warrior meowed. "Brook and I ate

on the way here. I'm not hungry right now."

"Okay, if you're sure, I'll take it to the elders. I've found plenty of fresh-kill," she added to Brambleclaw. "It's a bit trodden on, but it'll do until tomorrow." With a whisk of her tail she picked up the spare mouse and headed for the elders' den.

While Stormfur went back inside the den, Brambleclaw crouched down to eat the mouse. It was flattened and covered with earth, as if a badger's huge paw had trampled it into the ground, but he was too hungry to care. He devoured it in a few famished gulps. Then he went to help Stormfur shift the damaged thorns. Blood began oozing again from the scratch on his shoulder as he struggled to drag the broken branches away from the rest; thorns pricked at his paws and scraped against his side, adding fresh scratches to his pelt.

As he was backing out of the den, tugging a particularly stubborn branch, Squirrelflight's scent drifted around him. He dropped the end of the branch and turned to see her standing behind him with a dripping wad of moss.

She set it down and meowed, "I thought you might need a drink."

"Thanks." As he lapped water from the moss, he thought he had never tasted anything so delicious. It seemed to soak into every part of him, giving him new energy.

When he had drunk as much as he wanted, Squirrelflight picked up the moss and gently dabbed it against his shoulder wound. Her eyes met Brambleclaw's; he shivered at the closeness of her.

"Squirrelflight, I'm sorry for everything—" he began.

She swept her tail-tip across his mouth. "I know," she murmured.

Brambleclaw thought he could have stood like that forever, drowning in the depths of her green gaze. But a movement beyond her distracted him, and he looked up to see Ashfur staring at him.

The gray warrior had left the vigil for his dead Clanmates and was crossing the clearing. After a few moments, he turned away and disappeared behind the brambles that screened the medicine cat's den.

Brambleclaw stepped back and faced Squirrelflight. "What about Ashfur?" he meowed. He didn't need to say any more—Squirrelflight and Ashfur had become very close in recent moons, and the gray warrior might have good reason to feel that Brambleclaw was treading on his paws.

Squirrelflight dropped the moss. "Don't worry about Ashfur. I'll talk to him." There was regret in her eyes, but no uncertainty. Briefly she touched her nose to Brambleclaw's. "I have to fetch water for the elders now. I'll see you later."

Dazed, Brambleclaw watched her go before starting to tug at the branch again. He could hardly believe how quickly everything had changed, and how little he and Squirrelflight had needed to say to each other. Their quarrels, the way they had deliberately tried to hurt each other, all that was gone in the wake of the badger attack, now that they realized how much they cared about each other. They didn't even have to apologize; they could just look forward to all the moons ahead of them.

As he finally yanked the branch free, Stormfur emerged

from the den, pushing a tangle of moss and thorns in front of him.

"It's good to see you and Squirrelflight are still getting on so well," he meowed.

"Yes, she's a terrific cat," Brambleclaw mumbled. He didn't want to tell Stormfur that the closeness he shared with Squirrelflight had melted away for a time. "Why don't we take some of these thorns over to Sandstorm for the entrance barrier?"

"Okay." Stormfur looked faintly amused, as if he could tell Brambleclaw was deliberately changing the subject away from Squirrelflight. "You know," he added, "I feel just the same about Brook."

He picked up the end of a long branch, but before they had gone more than a couple of paces Brambleclaw spotted the young Tribe she-cat heading toward them with a huge bundle of moss in her jaws.

"The elders are going to be fine," she reported, after setting her burden down beside Brambleclaw. "Leafpool has put cobwebs on Mousefur's scratches, and given them all a few poppy seeds to help them sleep. Squirrelflight has gone to fetch them some water."

"Thanks for your help, Brook," Brambleclaw meowed, nodding at the ball of moss.

"I took it out of the elders' den because it's full of thorns. No cat could sleep on that. Can you tell me the best place to find some more moss?"

"Are you sure you're not too tired?" Brambleclaw asked.

"You've traveled a long way."

Brook's ears twitched. "I'm in better shape than you. Besides, we took it easy on the journey. It's been more than a moon since we left the Tribe."

"We thought we would never find you," Stormfur meowed.

"How did you?" Brambleclaw asked. He jumped at a flicker of movement behind him, but it was only Brackenfur, padding across to the nursery with fresh-kill in his jaws. "Did the Tribe of Endless Hunting show you the way?"

A glance flashed between Stormfur and Brook.

"I wish they had," Stormfur replied. "We might have got here sooner. We wandered around in the hills until we came across a rogue who knew some cats who live with horses. Do you know them?"

"Oh, yes, the horseplace cats," Brambleclaw mewed. "We've met them—in fact, one of them is here now, with her kits."

Stormfur looked surprised. "Well, the rogue said they told him a huge number of cats had moved into their area. We knew that had to be you, and the rogue told us which way to come."

"So you haven't been to RiverClan yet?"

Stormfur shook his head, but before he could say anything else, Brook prodded Brambleclaw in the shoulder with one paw. "Moss? Your elders will be waiting."

"Oh, sure. Let's take these thorns over to the camp entrance, and I'll show you."

Brambleclaw and Stormfur dragged the branches across to where Sandstorm, Dustpelt, and Firestar were working on the barrier. Brook followed with her bundle of moss.

"Over there." Brambleclaw pointed with his tail into the forest. His pelt prickled with horror as he remembered how the badgers had come roaring out of the shadows with death in their eyes. "Keep going straight on, and you'll find plenty of moss around the tree roots."

"I'll come with you, Brook," Stormfur meowed. "You never know, there might still be badgers around."

"I've posted guards," Firestar called across. "It should be safe." He flicked his ears toward the top of the hollow, where Brambleclaw could just make out the shadowy shapes of Cloudtail and Thornclaw.

Stormfur followed his gaze, then turned back to Brook. "I'm still coming with you. We'll need more moss for the warriors' den."

He and Brook headed into the forest. As Brambleclaw turned back into the camp, he spotted Leafpool emerging from her den. When she reached Cinderpelt's body she stopped, bowed her head, and rested her nose in her mentor's soft fur.

"Forgive me, Cinderpelt." Brambleclaw was just close enough to hear her murmured words. "I want to sit vigil with you, but there's too much to do. I know you would want me to care for your Clan."

Leafpool lifted her head, seemed to brace herself, and padded on toward Brambleclaw. "I want you in my den *now*," she meowed. "Your wounds need treatment."

"But—"

"Don't argue, Brambleclaw. Just do it." For a moment Leafpool sounded as forceful as her sister, Squirrelflight. "How much use will you be if your shoulder gets infected?"

Brambleclaw sighed. "All right. I'm on my way." As the young medicine cat brushed past him, he rested the tip of his tail on her shoulder. "Thanks, Leafpool. I mean, thanks for coming back. ThunderClan needs you."

Leafpool flashed him a glance filled with sorrow before padding on toward her father and mother by the camp entrance. "Firestar!" he heard her call. "I haven't had a chance to look at your wounds yet."

As Brambleclaw was approaching Leafpool's den, he spotted Ashfur emerging from behind the bramble screen. His torn ear was wrapped in cobwebs, and more of them were plastered along his flank and on his foreleg.

"Are you okay?" Brambleclaw asked as Ashfur padded past him.

Ashfur didn't look at him. "Fine, thanks," he mewed curtly.

Brambleclaw watched him cross the clearing to the nursery, where Brackenfur and Spiderleg were dragging out the broken bramble tendrils. Ashfur set to work beside them.

Just outside the cleft in the rock wall where Leafpool had her den, Birchpaw was curled up asleep in a nest of bracken, one paw over his nose. Though he was only an apprentice, he had fought bravely in the battle and helped to protect Daisy and her kits as they escaped from the hollow. The wounds on his haunches, where fur had been ripped away, were covered with a poultice of marigold; Brambleclaw's nostrils twitched at the sharp scent of chewed-up herbs.

On the other side of the cleft, Rainwhisker lay among more bracken. As Brambleclaw appeared around the screen of brambles he raised his head and blinked drowsily. "Hi, Brambleclaw." His voice sounded blurred with sleep. "Is everything okay?"

"It will be. How's your leg?"

"Not broken, thank StarClan. Just dislocated." He let out a sleepy purr. "Leafpool put it back in place." His eyes closed again and he rested his nose on his paws.

Brightheart emerged from the cleft in the rock with a mouthful of herbs. She nodded to Brambleclaw, then bent over Rainwhisker and Birchpaw to give each a quick sniff.

"They're doing fine," she meowed. "Brambleclaw, when Leafpool comes back, tell her I've taken some marigold to Brackenfur. He's working on the nursery so he doesn't have to leave Sorreltail."

"Okay," Brambleclaw agreed.

He sat down beside the two sleeping cats. Leafpool arrived a few moments later with Firestar following her. Carefully she looked Brambleclaw over, then gave the deep scratch on his shoulder a lick.

"That's the only serious wound," she meowed. "I want to take a look at it every day, okay? Wait there while I fetch you some marigold." She paused, staring into the distance for a couple of heartbeats before taking a deep breath and disappearing into the cleft.

"Will she be all right?" Brambleclaw murmured to Firestar. "No medicine cat is looking after *her*."

"I'll tell Squirrelflight to keep an eye on her."

Leafpool came back with the marigold leaves, and began chewing them up for a poultice.

"We're down to the last scraps," she mewed, glancing up with the end of a leaf poking out of her jaws. "Some cat will need to fetch more first thing tomorrow."

"I'll see to it," Firestar promised. "Or—Brambleclaw, maybe you could organize that? Find a cat who isn't too badly hurt."

Brambleclaw dipped his head. "Okay, Firestar."

Leaving the cleft in the rock, he spotted Stormfur beside the warriors' den, beckoning to him with his tail.

"I think we're done for tonight," the gray warrior meowed. "We've shifted the worst of the thorns, and I've put down some fresh moss. It might be a bit cramped, but you can all get some rest now."

"What about you?" Brambleclaw asked.

"Brook and I are still fresh. We'll guard the camp for the rest of the night."

"Thanks." Suddenly Brambleclaw felt his legs start to give way beneath him; the prospect of curling up to sleep made him realize just how exhausted he was. He touched Stormfur on the shoulder with his tail-tip, then slid past him into the warriors' den.

There was a clear space near the trunk of the tree, good enough for cats who were too tired to be fussy about where they slept. Spiderleg and Ashfur were already asleep; just beyond them, Dustpelt and Ferncloud were drowsily sharing tongues. Brambleclaw muttered a greeting to them, and sank into the moss and bracken. A heartbeat later, sleep crashed over him like a black wave.

CHAPTER 3

❧

Leafpool opened her eyes, sticky with sleep, and blinked. She was crouched in the middle of the stone hollow beside Cinderpelt's body. Next to her, Firestar lay with his nose pushed deep into his friend's gray fur, his eyes narrowed to slits as if he were lost in memories of the cat who had once been his apprentice. Above the hollow, the sky was milky pale with the first light of dawn.

Opening her jaws, Leafpool tried to draw in the last of her beloved mentor's scent, but all she could taste was death. She had come to sit vigil with Cinderpelt after all the injured cats had been treated. But exhaustion had overwhelmed her and she had fallen asleep. *I couldn't even stay awake for you,* she thought despairingly.

She would never forget the dream she had had on her journey with Crowfeather, in which she had heard Cinderpelt's terrible cry of pain as the badger struck its killing blow. *I should have stayed here,* she told herself, guilt tearing at her sharper than a badger's claws.

But even though she had come back to her Clan, her thoughts were still haunted by Crowfeather. The glow in his amber eyes when he told her how much he loved her. The pain in his voice when he realized that her heart lay here, as ThunderClan's medicine cat, and not with him. Leafpool had been faced with a terrible choice, but in the end she knew her place was here, in the stone hollow. She had given up Crowfeather, and had lost Cinderpelt too. All that remained was her duty to her Clan.

As she sat up, stretching cramped limbs, careful not to disturb her father at his vigil, she saw Stormfur keeping watch just outside the warriors' den. Brook guarded the camp with him, sitting closer to the entrance. Other cats were beginning to stir now; Brackenfur put his head out of the nursery, then vanished back inside. A moment later, Brambleclaw and Dustpelt emerged from the warriors' den and stood tasting the air.

Soon it would be time for the elders to carry the bodies of Cinderpelt and Sootfur out of the camp for burial. Leafpool bent her head over Cinderpelt, touching her muzzle to her mentor's shoulder and brushing against her soft gray fur. She closed her eyes to try to sense Cinderpelt's spirit, but above her the warriors of StarClan were disappearing as the sky grew brighter.

Cinderpelt? Tell me you're still with me!

Leafpool tried to imagine herself padding through the stars with silvery pelts brushing against her on either side, but she couldn't smell any trace of Cinderpelt's familiar scent. Had Cinderpelt rejected her because she left ThunderClan with Crowfeather? Would she never hear her mentor's voice again, not even in dreams?

Cinderpelt, I'm sorry, I'm sorry! she cried. *Don't leave me alone like this.*

"I can manage. I don't need to be able to see to carry my Clanmates."

Longtail's voice interrupted Leafpool's desperate prayer. She opened her eyes to see the three elders approaching, Mousefur in the lead and Goldenflower guiding Longtail.

"Of course you don't," Mousefur agreed. "We'll carry them together, don't worry."

Firestar rose from Cinderpelt's side, his movements stiff from wounds and weariness. Whitepaw crept out of the remains of the apprentices' den, glancing around nervously as if she wanted to make sure no more badgers had appeared. Thornclaw, who had been Sootfur's mentor, padded up to him and pushed his nose one last time into the cold, gray-black fur.

"You taught him well," Leafpool mewed softly, sharing his grief for the young warrior. "He died bravely, fighting for his Clanmates."

Rainwhisker slid between the cats who were clustering around the bodies. Leafpool saw that he was able to put weight on his injured leg, though it would be a while yet before the torn muscles were fully healed.

"Take it easy," she warned him. "You'll be limping permanently if you strain that leg."

Rainwhisker nodded and spoke to Mousefur. "I want to help, please. Sootfur was my brother."

Mousefur dipped her head. "Very well."

She and Rainwhisker took up the body of Sootfur, while Goldenflower and Longtail carried Cinderpelt. With a wrench of grief, Leafpool had to step back and let them take her mentor away. Her sister's scent drifted around her and she felt the warmth of Squirrelflight's pelt against her side. Leafpool leaned against her shoulder, grateful for the comfort of her presence.

The rest of their Clan stood with bowed heads as the elders made their way past the shattered thorn barrier and into the trees beyond.

Once they had disappeared, Firestar began to organize the patrols. Squirrelflight turned to Brambleclaw and the two cats headed back toward the warriors' den, their flanks brushing.

Leafpool's ears pricked. She had thought her sister and Brambleclaw weren't close anymore. She looked around for Ashfur and saw that he was watching too; she was shaken by the look of fury in his eyes.

Sudden fear for her sister swept through Leafpool like an icy wave. She recalled the dream where she had found herself wandering in a dark, unfamiliar forest with no sign of StarClan. There she had hidden on the edge of a clearing, watching while Tigerstar trained his sons Brambleclaw and Hawkfrost and urged them to seek power within their Clans. Brambleclaw had a fearful inheritance, and Leafpool was not sure he was strong enough to resist his father's treacherous promptings.

Should she tell Squirrelflight about the dream? She took a step toward her sister, then stopped. She had enough to do already, caring for the injured cats, and it was no part of a medicine cat's duties to interfere in the friendships of other cats. Besides, that had not been a dream from StarClan, so she couldn't be sure what it meant, or whether it was a warning about the future.

She padded across to Ashfur. "I need to check your wounds," she meowed. "Especially that torn ear."

Ashfur's eyes glittered with anger, still staring after Squirrelflight. "Okay."

He stood without flinching while Leafpool sniffed the wounds on his flank and foreleg, and gave his ear a careful examination. "They're healing well," she told him. "I'll give you some poppy seed to help you sleep, if you like."

Ashfur shook his head. "No, thanks. I'll be fine." With a last glance across the clearing, he padded over to join Dustpelt and Spiderleg, who were rebuilding the thorn barrier.

As Leafpool turned toward her den, she spotted Brightheart trotting rapidly across the stone hollow with her daughter, Whitepaw, just behind her.

"Leafpool, do you want me to gather herbs?" she offered. "Brambleclaw said I could take Whitepaw to help me."

"That would be great," Leafpool replied.

She gave the apprentice a friendly nod. Whitepaw was looking nervous. *She probably imagines the forest is crawling with badgers*, Leafpool guessed. *I don't blame her.*

"We need marigold more than anything," she went on to Brightheart. "You'll find plenty beside the stream."

Brightheart nodded. "I know a good place. Thank StarClan it's newleaf."

Leafpool felt a sudden flood of gratitude toward her Clanmate. She winced with guilt when she remembered how she had been convinced that Brightheart was trying to take her place with Cinderpelt. "It's a good thing Cinderpelt taught you so well," she meowed. "I really need your help now."

Brightheart's good eye glowed with pleasure. "Let's go, then. Come on, Whitepaw." With a flick of her tail she bounded away to the camp entrance, the apprentice scurrying behind her.

Leafpool padded back to her den. Birchpaw, roused from sleep as she brushed past the screen of brambles, struggled to stand up, then flopped back into his nest of bracken.

"Don't try to get up yet," Leafpool warned. "I want to take a look at your eye."

She was more worried about Birchpaw than any of the other cats. He was very young to have fought in such a fierce attack; he didn't have the strength of a full-grown cat to help him recover from serious wounds.

The scratch around Birchpaw's eye was red and puffy, only a faint gleam escaping past the swollen flesh. He was very lucky not to have lost the eye, Leafpool thought privately, shuddering as she pictured a badger's blunt claws ripping at the apprentice's face.

Slipping inside her den where her supplies were kept, Leafpool found the last two leaves of marigold. Thank StarClan Brightheart was fetching more. Leafpool took the leaves outside and chewed them up, but when she tried to lay the pulp on Birchpaw's eye, he ducked away.

"It stings," he complained.

"I know, and I'm sorry. But it'll hurt worse if the scratches get infected. Come on." Leafpool tried to encourage him. "You're not a kit anymore."

Birchpaw nodded; his whole body stiffened as he braced himself. Leafpool patted on more of the marigold pulp, and this time breathed a sigh of relief to see the healing juices trickle into his eye.

"Try to get some more sleep," she suggested once she had checked the wounds on his haunches. "Do you need poppy seed?"

"No, I'll be fine," meowed Birchpaw, curling up again. "Will you tell Ashfur that I won't be able to train today?"

"Sure," Leafpool replied.

She waited until Birchpaw was asleep again, then set off for the nursery with more borage for Sorreltail. On her way she spotted Stormfur and Brook returning to the camp with jaws full of fresh-kill and realized how hungry she was. She could hardly remember the last time she had eaten: it must have been before her desperate dash back from the hills with Crowfeather to warn her Clan.

She made her way over to Stormfur and Brook. A small fresh-kill pile was already there, showing how hard the visitors had been working that morning.

"Hi," Brook meowed. "I was going to bring some fresh-kill to your den."

"No need, thanks, I'll eat here," Leafpool replied, after setting down the borage. "If you're sure there's enough. Have Sorreltail and the elders had some?"

"I'm seeing to them now," Stormfur mewed. "You take what you want, Leafpool. There's plenty of prey, and Sandstorm and Cloudtail are out hunting as well." He grabbed a couple of mice and headed for the nursery.

Brook took more fresh-kill for the elders, while Leafpool chose a vole for herself. As she crouched to eat it, Spiderleg and Ashfur came over.

Spiderleg shot Leafpool a swift glance, dipping his head awkwardly. "It's good to have you back," he muttered.

Leafpool felt as embarrassed as he looked. She didn't want to talk to any cat about why she had left the Clan. "It's good to be back," she told him. It was a relief to turn to Ashfur and give him Birchpaw's message. "It'll be a few days yet before he's fit to start training again," she finished.

Ashfur nodded. "I'll come and see him later," he promised.

Leafpool ate her vole in a few rapid bites, then headed for the nursery to visit Sorreltail. The sun had cleared the trees at the top of the hollow, shining down from a blue sky dotted with a few white puffs of cloud. Leafpool was grateful for the warmth on her fur. The injured cats would be able to bask in the open while their nests were cleaned out.

The damaged brambles had been dragged out of the nursery the night before, leaving a few ragged holes where the sun shone in. Daisy's three kits were playing around her, pouncing on the bright spots of light.

"Take *that*, you horrible badger!" Berrykit squealed.

"Get out of our camp!" Hazelkit growled, while Mousekit spat and showed his teeth.

"That's enough." Daisy swept her tail around the three kits, drawing them closer to her. "If you want to play rough games, you must go outside. You're disturbing Sorreltail. Remember how tiny her kits are."

"Yeah, we're not the youngest anymore," Berrykit boasted. "We'll be apprentices soon."

Daisy didn't reply, but Leafpool thought she saw uncertainty in the horseplace cat's eyes.

Berrykit's head popped up from behind Daisy's protective tail. "Hi, Leafpool!" he meowed. "Where have you been? We missed you. Is your friend from WindClan going to stay with us?"

"Shhh," Daisy mewed, giving Berrykit's ear a flick with her tail-tip. "Don't bother Leafpool now. Can't you see she's busy?"

Leafpool dipped her head gratefully to Daisy, her mouthful of borage giving her the perfect excuse not to answer. She slid farther into the nursery to find Sorreltail.

The young tortoiseshell was curled up in a deep nest of moss and bracken, her four kits burrowing close to her belly. Brackenfur was beside her while the two cats finished off the fresh-kill Stormfur had brought them.

"Hi, Leafpool." Sorreltail blinked drowsily. "Is that more borage?"

"That's right." Leafpool put the leaves down where her friend could reach them. "You need to make sure you have plenty of milk, with four kits to feed."

"They're worse than famished foxes," Brackenfur purred, beaming proudly at his offspring. Leafpool was glad to see he was calmer now, beginning to recover from the shock of the attack, so that he could care for his mate and kits.

"They're fine, healthy kits," meowed Leafpool. "Just what the Clan needs."

As she watched Sorreltail chew up the borage, she remembered the adventures the two of them had shared in the old forest, when she was still an apprentice and Sorreltail was a carefree young warrior. They could never be as close as that again. Now Sorreltail was a mother, while Leafpool was ThunderClan's medicine cat. When she left with Crowfeather, she had briefly glimpsed what it would be like to turn her back on her duties—but her heart had brought her back to her Clan.

Leafpool felt distance yawning between her and Crowfeather like a mountain gorge. Pain twisted inside her, but she pushed it away. She had chosen the life of a medicine cat; there was no going back.

"Try getting some sleep now," she mewed to Sorreltail. "Brackenfur, make sure she rests."

Brackenfur gave Sorreltail's ears an affectionate lick. "I will."

Leafpool turned away and blundered out into the bright sunlight, where she stood blinking. She had given up Crowfeather, her mentor was dead, and her best friend had a mate and kits to care for. Even her sister, Squirrelflight, who had once shared everything with Leafpool, was together with Brambleclaw again. Leafpool wanted her sister to be happy, but she missed being closer to her than any other cat.

Oh, StarClan! she murmured. *I have given up everything for you. I hope this is what you wanted.*

For the rest of the day she buried herself in her duties. Brightheart and Whitepaw worked tirelessly to collect supplies, and by the time the sun went down the stocks of herbs and berries had been replenished, and Leafpool had treated the wounds of every cat in the Clan. As they withdrew to their dens for the rest they badly needed, she looked around the clearing and saw that the terrible scars of the attack were beginning to fade. Dustpelt and his helpers had piled up thorns for a new entrance barrier that was already half completed, while Sandstorm and the other hunters had brought in plenty of prey to build up the fresh-kill pile.

Leafpool was exhausted, but she knew she would be unable to sleep. Instead of going back to her den, she padded across the clearing and out past the partly rebuilt barrier of thorns. Unbidden, her paws carried her toward the lake, until she reached the open ground at the edge of the trees and could gaze out over the starlit water.

Memories flooded back of the nights she had sneaked out

of camp to meet Crowfeather. Then her paws had felt as light as air; she had raced through the bracken to their meeting place.

Now everything was changed. Grief and loss weighed her down like stone. She settled into a drift of dry leaves, letting her gaze rest on the starry surface of the lake.

Not many heartbeats passed before she saw that the stars in the water were moving. At first she thought it was just wind ruffling the surface, but all around her the air was still. Her pelt prickled. Above her the stars of Silverpelt blazed down as they had always done, cold, white, and unmoving; but in the lake, some patches of water were dark and empty, while the reflected stars swam sparkling across the surface until they were clustered together in two slender paths.

Leafpool gasped. The stars had become two sets of paw prints, twining together across the indigo water.

Was this a message from StarClan? Was she dreaming? A movement at the far end of the starry paw prints caught her eye, and she peered across the lake. Two cats had appeared, walking away from her with more stars spooling out after them. At first they were indistinct, shadowy shapes; Leafpool strained to make them out, expecting to see warriors from StarClan. Then as the shapes grew clearer she saw that one was a dark tabby with broad shoulders, while the other was smaller, lighter-framed, with dark ginger fur.

Leafpool's heart thudded harder. It was Brambleclaw and Squirrelflight. They were padding away from her side by side, so close that their pelts brushed together and their tracks merged into a single glittering path. On and on went their paw prints, sparkling across the dark water. Then the cats faded into the shadows, and the reflected stars spilled across the surface of the lake until they matched the stars in the sky once more.

Leafpool shivered. StarClan knew she had been anxious about Brambleclaw, that her trust in him had been shaken by her sinister dream of Tigerstar. They must have sent this sign to let her know that his destiny was so closely intertwined with Squirrelflight's, no cat could separate their paths.

Surely this meant StarClan approved of Squirrelflight's choice for her mate? If that was the case, Leafpool had no need to worry about her dark vision of Tigerstar training his sons. She didn't have to warn Squirrelflight about her relationship with Brambleclaw. Their future rested in the paws of StarClan.

Comfort crept over her like a warm breeze, and she curled up among the rustling leaves and drifted out on a wave of sleep.

Her eyes blinked open what felt like moments later. She still lay in the hollow; shadows of leaves danced over her as the branches of the beech tree moved in a gentle breeze. A sweet scent drifted around her, and she lifted her head to see Spottedleaf sitting on a root a tail-length away.

"Spottedleaf!" she exclaimed, knowing that she was dreaming. Suddenly she remembered the last time she had spoken to the beautiful tortoiseshell and she sprang to her paws, trembling with anger. "You lied to me! You told me to

leave ThunderClan and go away with Crowfeather. Cinderpelt *died* because I left my Clan!"

"Peace, dear one." Spottedleaf jumped lightly down from
the tree root and came over to brush her muzzle against
Leafpool's shoulder. "I told you to follow your heart—and
your heart lies with your Clan. So you have followed your
heart after all."

Leafpool gazed at her, bewildered. Crowfeather had said
exactly the same thing before he left her to go back to
WindClan. "Then why didn't you tell me that's what you
meant?" she protested.

"Would you have listened?" Spottedleaf's gaze was full of
pained love. "You needed to make the choice to go with
Crowfeather. It was the only way you could find out that it
was the wrong path for you to follow."

Leafpool knew she was right. She hadn't understood how
committed she was to her Clan until she had tried to leave.
"But Cinderpelt *died*!" she repeated miserably.

"Cinderpelt knew what was going to happen," Spottedleaf
meowed. "She knew there was no way to escape it. Not even
StarClan can turn aside the paws of fate. That's why she
didn't try to stop you from going. Do you think things would
have been different if you had stayed?"

"I know they would," Leafpool insisted. "I would never
have left her if I'd known!"

"That is a weight you will carry for a long while, but I
promise you could not have done anything to change what
happened to Cinderpelt." Spottedleaf pressed close against

Leafpool's side. Her comforting warmth was still not enough to ease Leafpool's pain.

"Since she died, I haven't seen her in my dreams," Leafpool whispered. "I haven't felt her presence, smelled her scent, or heard her voice. She must be angry with me, or she would come to me."

"No, Leafpool. Cinderpelt loved you; do you think she would abandon you, even in death? Her paws walk another path for now."

Fresh anxiety surged up inside Leafpool. She had thought she understood the links between a medicine cat and the spirits of her warrior ancestors. What was this "other path"? Did Spottedleaf mean that Cinderpelt was wandering in the dark forest where Leafpool had seen Tigerstar?

"What do you mean?" she demanded, her neck fur bristling. "Where is she?"

"That I cannot tell you. But she is well, I promise you, and you *will* see her again, sooner than you think."

Spottedleaf's voice faded away. The warmth against Leafpool's side melted into the breeze, and the StarClan cat's tortoiseshell fur blended into the dapples of light and shadow until Leafpool couldn't see her anymore. Only her scent remained a heartbeat longer.

Leafpool opened her eyes to see the peaceful lake water still dappled with the reflections of countless stars. Fresh grief for Cinderpelt swept over her. Why did she have to die? Why hadn't she come to Leafpool in her dreams like Spottedleaf? Leafpool wanted to cry like an abandoned kit.

Instead, she rose and stretched. "Wherever you are, Cinderpelt," she mewed out loud, "if you can hear me, I promise that I will never leave our Clan again. I am their medicine cat now, and I will follow in your paw steps until it's my turn to walk with StarClan." Hesitating, she added, "But please, if I ever meant anything to you, come to me when you can and tell me you forgive me."

CHAPTER 4
❧

A cold breeze ruffling his fur woke Brambleclaw. Stretching his jaws in an enormous yawn, he looked up. A patch of pale sky was visible through a ragged hole where once thorn branches had sheltered the warriors' den. Dawn was breaking; it was time to get to work. Brambleclaw felt more hopeful after a good night's sleep, undisturbed by dreams.

Around him the other cats were beginning to wake. Cloudtail got up, wincing as he put weight on the paw that had lost a claw. "Badgers!" he snorted. "If I never see another, it'll be too soon." He brushed between two branches, out into the clearing.

Brambleclaw had gone to sleep with Squirrelflight curled up by his side, her sweet scent in his nostrils. But now she was gone, leaving only a flattened patch of moss. His pelt prickled when he saw that Ashfur was gone too. He sprang up, making his wounded shoulder protest with a shriek of pain, but before he could follow them into the clearing he heard Squirrelflight and Ashfur just outside; he stood without moving, screened by a branch, to listen.

"Look, Ashfur." Squirrelflight's voice told Brambleclaw

that she was trying hard to hold her temper. "I really care about you as a friend, but I don't want any more than that."

"But I love you!" Ashfur protested. More hesitantly, he added, "We'd be great together, Squirrelflight, I know we would."

Brambleclaw felt a stab of sympathy for the gray warrior. He remembered how he had felt when he thought he had lost Squirrelflight's affection.

"I'm sorry," Squirrelflight went on. "I never meant to hurt you, but Brambleclaw—well, I think StarClan has destined us to be together."

"I don't know how you can say that!" There was the hint of a snarl in Ashfur's voice. "You said yourself that it's impossible to trust a cat with Brambleclaw's heritage. He's a great cat, I know, but he is still Tigerstar's son."

Brambleclaw's feelings of sympathy vanished instantly. He unsheathed his long, curved claws and sank them into the ground. Would he never be judged for what *he* was, instead of who his father had been? Worse, would Squirrelflight be unable to trust him because Tigerstar was his father?

"I'll judge Brambleclaw by his own actions," she retorted hotly, "not by something that other cats did long before I was born."

"I'm only thinking of you, Squirrelflight," Ashfur meowed. "*I* can remember Tigerstar. His paws were red with the blood of innocent cats. You know that he murdered my mother to lure a pack of dogs to our camp?"

Squirrelflight murmured something Brambleclaw couldn't

catch, then went on more clearly, "But that doesn't mean Brambleclaw will turn out like his father."

Movement behind Brambleclaw distracted him, and he realized that more of the warriors were stirring. Not wanting to be caught eavesdropping, he slid quickly between the branches and into the clearing.

Squirrelflight turned to him as he appeared. "Hi, Brambleclaw!"

The light was strengthening and the sky was clear, promising sunlight later to drive off the dawn chill. But for Brambleclaw the warmth in Squirrelflight's eyes was even better. He padded over and touched noses with her, trying to ignore the frosty look Ashfur gave him.

As he stretched to ease the stiffness in his shoulder, Brambleclaw saw Firestar emerge from his den onto the Highledge and taste the morning air.

"Firestar!" he called. "Has the dawn patrol left yet?"

"No, would you like to lead one?"

Brambleclaw dipped his head. "Of course. Coming with me?" he asked Squirrelflight.

She nodded. Ashfur mewed abruptly, "I'm going to check on Birchpaw," and stalked off toward Leafpool's den without waiting for a reply.

Squirrelflight watched him walk away, her green gaze troubled. "I'm sorry he's been hurt," she meowed. "I thought he was the right mate for me, but he's not. I don't know how I can make him understand."

Brambleclaw knew there was nothing he could say to make

her feel better, so he just pressed his muzzle briefly to hers. But would the Clan side with him or with Ashfur? The gray warrior was popular with all their Clanmates, while Brambleclaw had forged his strongest friendships with the cats who had traveled to the sun-drown-place, and all but Squirrelflight were in different Clans.

A rustle sounded behind him as Brightheart pushed her way into the open. She glanced around as if she was looking for Cloudtail, then pricked her ears when she spotted him outside the nursery. He was talking to Daisy while her three kits tried to scramble over him. Brambleclaw saw sadness shadow Brightheart's gaze, and felt a stab of anger. Cloudtail had bees in his brain if he couldn't see how he was hurting Brightheart with the attention he was giving to the horseplace cat!

"Hey, Brightheart," he meowed, pretending he hadn't noticed anything. "Do you want to come with the dawn patrol?"

Brightheart shook her head. "Thanks, but I've promised to help Leafpool this morning. Can we have Whitepaw again?"

"Sure. It's a good idea to keep her busy while Brackenfur's in the nursery with Sorreltail."

"Thanks. I'll go and call her." Brightheart took a pace toward the apprentices' den, then paused to look back. "It's really great to see you and Squirrelflight back together again," she added softly. Surprise kept Brambleclaw silent, while Brightheart bounded away, calling for Whitepaw.

Impatient to be off, Brambleclaw stuck his head back through the branches into the den. Dustpelt was just getting up, shaking scraps of moss from his brown tabby fur.

"Dawn patrol?" Brambleclaw meowed.

Dustpelt twitched his whiskers. "I'll be right with you. If ShadowClan have heard about the badgers, they might be getting ideas about helping themselves to our territory while we're still recovering."

Brambleclaw had been thinking exactly the same thing. The border with WindClan should be secure. Onestar had brought his warriors to help drive out the badgers; he wouldn't be so two-faced as to take advantage of ThunderClan's weakness. But Blackstar, the ShadowClan leader, was a different cat altogether. He would take any chance he could to extend his territory.

Calling Spiderleg to complete the patrol, Brambleclaw retreated into the clearing again. Once the other warriors joined him, he led the way out through the tangle of thorns at the entrance and down toward the lake.

By the time the trees thinned around them, the sun was rising over the hills. The lake glittered so brightly that it dazzled Brambleclaw's eyes. A breeze blew across the water, ruffling his fur. As he padded along the lakeshore toward the stream that marked the boundary with ShadowClan, he realized how good it felt to have Squirrelflight at his side again. Quarreling with her always made him feel as if his fur were being brushed the wrong way.

"You go ahead," he ordered Spiderleg. "Check the ShadowClan scent markers as far as the dead tree. Make sure they're all where they should be and wait for us there." As

Spiderleg raced off, he added to Dustpelt and Squirrelflight, "We'll renew our own scent markers and check for ShadowClan scent on our territory."

He led his patrol upstream until they reached the point where the stream veered away, deeper into ShadowClan.

Dustpelt let out a hiss. "I still can't believe we let ShadowClan set their markers here," he meowed with an irritable twitch of his tail. "The stream should be the boundary. Any cat can see it."

Squirrelflight's tail curled up with amusement. "Try telling that to Blackstar. You *might* get away with both your ears."

Her former mentor snorted and stalked on, following the line of the border. Before they had gone many paw steps farther, Brambleclaw heard the sound of a cat hurtling through the trees ahead of them. He raised his tail for the others to stop, then tasted the air, but the only scent he could detect was ThunderClan's.

A clump of bracken waved wildly and Spiderleg dashed into the open.

"What are you doing?" Brambleclaw scolded. "I told you to wait by the dead tree. You haven't had enough time to—"

"I know," Spiderleg interrupted, his chest heaving. "But I found something really weird. You have to come and look."

"What now?" Dustpelt sighed, rolling his eyes. "Not more badgers, I hope?"

"Trouble from ShadowClan?" Brambleclaw asked sharply.

"No, some Twoleg thing," Spiderleg panted. "I've never seen anything like it."

He waved his tail for them to follow. Brambleclaw exchanged a glance with Squirrelflight and padded after Spiderleg, still checking carefully for any ShadowClan scent on the ThunderClan side of the border. He scented nothing but the usual markers, until Spiderleg brought them to a small clearing. The ground was almost covered with a thick growth of ferns, the fresh green fronds unfurling in the pale sun.

Brambleclaw felt the fur on his shoulders bristle as he picked up a new scent. "Fox," he growled.

"Stale, though," Squirrelflight added. "There hasn't been a fox here for the last couple of days, at least."

Brambleclaw wasn't reassured. He had spotted a track through the ferns, a narrow path dimpled with many paw marks. The scent of fox was strongest there; the vile creatures must use it regularly. He reminded himself to check the area later to see if there was a den nearby.

Spiderleg had stopped a little farther up the fox track, a few tail-lengths from the ShadowClan border. "Here's the Twoleg thing," he meowed, pointing with his tail.

Brambleclaw pushed his way through the ferns to avoid setting a paw where the foxes had been. There was something gleaming near the young warrior's paws. It was a length of thin, shiny stuff, curved into a loop and fastened to a stick that was stuck in the ground.

"You're right, it must be a Twoleg thing," he mewed. "They use that shiny stuff to make fences for their sheep."

"And there's Twoleg scent all over it," Dustpelt added, catching up to them. "What's it doing here? What's it for?"

Spiderleg bent his head to sniff it more closely, but Dustpelt shouldered him aside before he could touch it. "Mousebrain!" he snapped. "Didn't your mentor ever tell you not to stick your nose in before you know what you're dealing with?"

"Sure, Mousefur taught me everything," Spiderleg retorted, glaring at the older warrior.

"Remember it, then."

Squirrelflight stood beside Brambleclaw while they both studied the loop and stick closely.

"What happens if we touch it?" Squirrelflight asked, cautiously advancing a paw.

Brambleclaw's tail struck her paw aside. "We don't want to find out the hard way," he warned her.

"But we have to do *something*," Squirrelflight protested. "Hang on, let's try this." She grabbed a long stick in her jaws.

"Careful," Brambleclaw warned.

Squirrelflight flicked her ears at him, then crept cautiously up to the Twoleg thing and poked the stick into the shining loop. At once, the loop snapped tight, gripping the end of the stick. Spiderleg let out a squeak of alarm and leaped backward, his pelt bristling and his ears flattened.

Brambleclaw stood his ground, but a shudder went through him from ears to tail-tip. He closed his eyes, imagining a cat loping along the track, unaware of any danger, until it thrust its head into the loop and . . . "That could snap a cat's neck," he meowed.

"Or choke it to death," Dustpelt agreed grimly.

Squirrelflight dropped the stick. "This isn't meant for us," she pointed out. "The Twolegs put it on a fox track. They must mean to trap foxes with it."

"But *why*?" meowed Spiderleg.

Dustpelt shrugged. "They're crazy. All Twolegs are crazy."

Brambleclaw looked again at the length of shiny stuff, thinner than an ivy tendril, wrapped so tightly around the stick that it had crushed the pale green bark. "It's harmless now," he mewed, "but there might be more of them. We'll have to report it, and make sure every cat knows what to watch out for."

"At least we know what to do with them." Dustpelt dipped his head to his former apprentice. "Good thinking, Squirrelflight."

Squirrelflight's green eyes gleamed; Dustpelt didn't give praise lightly.

"Spiderleg, too. That was well spotted," Brambleclaw added. But his belly clenched at the thought of how easily the young warrior could have run straight into the trap. "We'd better finish the patrol," he ordered. "And let's all be careful where we put our paws. The forest could be full of these things."

As they made their way along the ShadowClan border, Brambleclaw let Dustpelt take the lead. He and Squirrelflight padded along, side by side, at the rear of the patrol. Brambleclaw tried not to let her closeness distract him from tasting the air and keeping his eyes open for any more of the sinister shining loops.

"Do you think we ought to warn the other Clans about these fox traps?" he asked her.

Squirrelflight glanced at him, her green eyes wary. "You're thinking of Hawkfrost, aren't you?"

"No, not just RiverClan," Brambleclaw meowed, trying not to let his neck fur bristle. "WindClan probably haven't much to worry about, except for that patch of woodland on the other side of the stream. But there must be traps on ShadowClan territory; the one we found was right on the border."

"Firestar will have to decide whether we tell them or not," Squirrelflight pointed out. "He'll probably announce it at the next Gathering."

Brambleclaw halted and faced her. "Squirrelflight, can we talk this through without clawing at each other? Did you really think I just wanted to warn RiverClan because of Hawkfrost?" Hawkfrost—his half brother, Tigerstar's son, the cat Squirrelflight refused to trust. If he and Squirrelflight were to be together now, they had to sort this problem out once and for all.

"Yes, I did think that." To his relief Squirrelflight was direct, but didn't sound angry. "You know how I feel about Hawkfrost."

"But he's my brother," Brambleclaw reminded her. "I can't ignore that, any more than I can ignore that Tawnypelt's my sister, even though she is a ShadowClan warrior."

He wondered if he was being entirely honest. He had never walked in dreams with Tawnypelt, as he did with

Hawkfrost, following twisting paths to their meetings with their father, Tigerstar. Tawnypelt had never joined in these meetings, where he and Hawkfrost were taught to lead their Clans. He knew he could never tell Squirrelflight, or any other cat in ThunderClan, about that dark forest and the dark warrior who waited for him.

But there's no need, he argued with himself. *They'd never understand. There might be things Tigerstar can teach me, but that doesn't mean I'd do what he did to gain power.*

"Tawnypelt's different," Squirrelflight persisted. "She journeyed with us, for one thing. And she's half Thunder-Clan."

Brambleclaw bit back a protest. He wanted to settle the quarrel, not start it up again. "Think of it like this," he began. "If Leafpool had gone to WindClan with Crowfeather, would you care for her any less?"

"Of course not!" Squirrelflight's eyes stretched wide. "She could go off with the whole of WindClan, and she'd still be my sister."

"And Hawkfrost is still my brother. Like Tawnypelt's still my sister. We'll always be kin, even though we are in different Clans. You're lucky that you have your sister in the same Clan. I'd give anything to have my kin with me."

Squirrelflight searched his face with a penetrating green gaze. "Okay," she mewed. "I guess I can understand that. I just don't like to feel that Hawkfrost is as important to you as your Clanmates."

"He's not," Brambleclaw replied at once. "My first loyalty

will always be to my Clan."

"Brambleclaw!" Dustpelt's voice interrupted them. Brambleclaw whipped around to see the brown tabby warrior shouldering his way through a clump of bracken; Spiderleg peered out of the ferns just behind him. "Are we on a patrol, or aren't we? Do you plan to stand there all day gossiping?"

"Sorry," Brambleclaw meowed, bounding toward Dustpelt and taking the lead to head farther along the border.

As Dustpelt, Spiderleg, and Squirrelflight padded hard on his paws, he hoped that his arguments about Hawkfrost had convinced Squirrelflight more thoroughly than they had convinced him. He hoped that if he ever had to choose, he really would put his Clan before his brother.

CHAPTER 5

❧

"Let all cats old enough to catch their own prey join here beneath the Highledge!"

Firestar's yowl halted Leafpool on her way back from the elders' den, where she had been checking Mousefur's wound. The brown-furred elder was still complaining of stiffness, but the claw marks had begun to heal, and there was no sign of infection.

Leafpool made her way toward the edge of the clearing, stopping beneath the ledge where Firestar stood looking down at his Clan. Sandstorm and Thornclaw got up from the fresh-kill pile and padded over, while Cloudtail and Rainwhisker left their work on the thorn barrier. Uneasiness gnawed in Leafpool's belly. The dawn patrol had just returned and gone straight to Firestar; had they discovered more badgers, or maybe signs that ShadowClan were trying to take over part of the territory?

Trying to stifle her anxiety, Leafpool sat down beside Ferncloud, who mewed a greeting and asked anxiously, "How's Birchpaw?"

"He'll be fine," Leafpool replied. Birchpaw was

Ferncloud's kit, the only one of his litter to survive the famine in the old forest; she could understand how worried his mother must be about his injuries. "The swelling around his eye is going down. But I'll keep him with me for a few more days until I'm sure there's no infection."

Ferncloud gave Leafpool's ear a grateful lick. "You're a wonderful medicine cat, Leafpool. I'm so glad you came back."

I haven't been wonderful, Leafpool thought. *I abandoned my Clan!*

The elders emerged from their den and settled down near the rock wall, glancing nervously at one another like they expected bad news. Stormfur and Brook hovered on the edge of the clearing, as if they weren't sure whether they were meant to be there or not.

Leafpool beckoned to them with her tail. "Come and sit here," she invited them. "You're welcome to join in while you're staying with us."

Nodding gratefully, Stormfur and Brook came over to join her. Daisy brought her three kits out, and Brackenfur sat in the entrance to the nursery, where he could listen and still be close to Sorreltail.

Brambleclaw and the rest of the dawn patrol were standing together at the foot of the tumbled rocks. Leafpool saw their tails were fluffed out and their eyes alert, as if they could sense danger on its way.

"Cats of ThunderClan," Firestar began, "Brambleclaw and the dawn patrol found something you need to know about. Brambleclaw, will you tell them?"

Brambleclaw leaped up onto one of the rocks. "We found a Twoleg trap on a fox track," he meowed. "It's a loop of thin, shiny stuff, fastened to a stick driven into the ground. When you touch the loop, it pulls tight. Any cat who got their head stuck in it could be killed."

Before he had finished speaking, wails of dismay began to rise from the cats who sat around him. Ashfur crouched down with his neck fur bristling as if he were about to leap onto an enemy, while Whitepaw pressed her belly to the ground in terror. Beside her, Cloudtail lashed his tail and bared his teeth in a snarl.

Mousefur's voice rose above the rest. "Are these traps all over the territory?"

Brambleclaw waved his tail for silence so that he could reply. Leafpool thought how commanding he looked, standing on the rock. It wasn't difficult to imagine him becoming Clan deputy. *Is Firestar right to keep on hoping that Graystripe will return? Would it be better for the Clan to accept that he has gone, and appoint a new deputy?*

"We only found one trap," Brambleclaw was meowing. "But it makes sense there would be more."

"Why?" Rainwhisker demanded. "Why would Twolegs want to trap foxes, anyway?"

The cats glanced at one another, murmuring in bewilderment. Then a new, trembling voice spoke up. "I can tell you why."

Leafpool glanced over her shoulder and saw that Daisy had risen to her paws. It was the first time the horseplace cat

had spoken in a Clan meeting, and she looked almost as terrified as when the badgers had broken into the camp.

"Go on, Daisy," Firestar mewed encouragingly.

"The Nofurs—I mean, the Twolegs—keep birds on their
farms for fresh-kill. Not little birds like the ones we eat, but
bigger. But foxes come and steal them, so the Twolegs want to
kill the foxes to protect their birds." She sat down again, blinking in embarrassment, and wrapped her tail around her paws.

"Thanks, Daisy," Firestar told her. "At least now we understand what's going on."

"But what are we going to do about it?" Cloudtail
demanded.

"What can we do?" Goldenflower challenged him. "No cat
can stop Twolegs from doing what they want. We saw that in
the old forest, and this place is worse!"

"That's not true." Ferncloud spoke gently to the elder.
"Even if it was, we can't go back. There'll be nothing left of
the old forest by now. Here we have to learn new things.
StarClan wouldn't have brought us somewhere that's too
dangerous for us to live."

"Then maybe StarClan can tell us what to do about the
traps!" Goldenflower flashed back at her.

"We can do that," Brambleclaw meowed. "Squirrelflight
worked it out. Squirrelflight, come up here and tell them."

Leafpool watched her sister leap up onto the rock beside
Brambleclaw. The sunlight gleamed on her dark ginger fur,
turning it to flame, and for an instant she looked just like
their father. "It's easy," she meowed. "You get a stick—as long

as you can manage—and poke it into the loop. The loop snaps tight around the stick, and there you are—no more problem."

Pride flooded over Leafpool. Their mother Sandstorm's green eyes shone with admiration too.

"The real danger," Firestar warned, "is that cats will come across these things when they aren't expecting it. All patrols will have to keep a lookout, and report back if they find anything."

"And if we spring a trap with a stick," Brambleclaw added, "we should check it regularly in case the Twolegs set it again."

"Good thinking," Firestar meowed. "We'll do that. Every cat who goes outside the clearing should watch their paws and check for scent. Fox scent and Twoleg scent together means danger."

"How are we supposed to hunt, then?" Rainwhisker muttered. "We can't watch and scent and chase prey all at the same time."

Leafpool knew he was partly right. She shivered at the thought of a cat racing along, intent on bringing down fresh-kill for the Clan, only to run into one of the shining loops. *StarClan help us!* she thought. *Sooner or later, some cat is going to be killed.*

Her worries had distracted her briefly from the meeting and when she started listening again, Firestar was talking about hunting patrols.

"Stormfur and Brook, ThunderClan thanks you," he meowed. "Feeding the Clan after the attack would have been a lot tougher without you."

Stormfur dipped his head in acknowledgment, while Brook studied her paws, looking embarrassed to be praised in front of the whole Clan.

"I want all cats who are fit to go out on hunting patrol," Firestar went on. "By sunset I'd like all the Clan to be well fed and the fresh-kill pile stocked up."

"Cloudtail and I went out yesterday," Sandstorm meowed, rising to her paws. "I'll go again, but I think Cloudtail should rest that injured paw. I spotted you limping," she added to Cloudtail as he sprang up with a yowl of protest, "and your pad is bleeding again."

Cloudtail sat down again, the tip of his tail twitching.

"I'll come with you," Brambleclaw offered.

Instantly Ashfur was on his paws. "So will I." He spoke to Sandstorm, but he was glaring at Brambleclaw.

Stupid tomcats! Leafpool thought. She got up, signaling with her tail to Firestar that she wanted to speak.

"Yes, Leafpool?" her father mewed.

"Brambleclaw's shoulder is badly hurt, and he's already been out on patrol today," Leafpool explained. "And Ashfur's injuries are some of the worst in the Clan. I want to check them both before they set paw outside the camp."

"Quite right," meowed Firestar. "In that case, I don't think either Brambleclaw or Ashfur should go. And Leafpool, please check all the other cats. No cat should leave camp until Leafpool approves it. Sandstorm, will you see to the patrols?"

Sandstorm agreed, and the meeting broke up.

"Hey, Leafpool," Thornclaw meowed, "take a look at my

injuries first, will you? I want to go hunting."

"And mine," Spiderleg added, thrusting forward to stand beside his Clanmate. "Look, the scratches are healing. I'm fine, honestly."

"You're fine if I say you are," Leafpool retorted. She began rapidly checking wounds, sending the worst-injured cats to her den for more treatment, while Sandstorm organized the others into patrols.

In the end, two patrols left camp: Thornclaw with Dustpelt and Ferncloud, and Sandstorm leading Squirrelflight and Spiderleg.

"Wait!" Firestar called, climbing down the tumbled rocks to join Sandstorm in the clearing. "I'll come with you."

Sandstorm looked at him with narrowed eyes. "I suppose it's no good telling you to go back to your den and rest?"

"No good at all," Firestar agreed, giving her shoulder an affectionate flick with his tail. "Every cat is injured, and my scratches aren't as bad as most."

"That should be for Leafpool to say," Sandstorm mewed, turning to their daughter.

Leafpool sniffed the scratches on Firestar's flanks and shoulders. She knew she had to forget he was her father and Clan leader, and treat him like any other injured cat. He wouldn't thank her for trying to keep him safe by insisting that he stayed in the hollow. Fortunately, though his body was laced with scratches, none of them was very deep. She had treated them with marigold right after the battle, and they were beginning to heal.

"You should be okay," she meowed at last. "I'll fetch you some more marigold before you go, and if the scratches start bleeding again, come straight back."

Firestar gave a grunt of acknowledgment. StarClan only knew whether he would actually do as he was told.

Leafpool went back to her den to fetch the marigold. As she emerged with the leaves in her jaws, she saw Firestar had followed her, meeting her a couple of fox-lengths from her den.

"You've noticed how Squirrelflight and Brambleclaw have been since the battle?" he asked as she chewed up the leaves and began patting them on his wounds. "They seem to be getting over their fight."

Leafpool went on working for a moment; she didn't particularly want to discuss her sister, but Firestar was obviously waiting for a response. "Yes," she mewed after a busy pause. "I think the badger attack made them realize what's important."

"Ashfur must be disappointed."

"I suppose he is." Leafpool wondered whether to tell her father about her dream of Tigerstar with his sons in the dark forest. Wasn't that what a medicine cat was for? To warn her Clan leader of possible trouble?

"I used to find it hard to have a cat in the Clan who looks exactly like Tigerstar," Firestar went on. Leafpool knew he meant Brambleclaw. "But when Tawnypelt left to join ShadowClan, I realized that she and Brambleclaw belonged by birth to ThunderClan. Whoever their father was, that doesn't change. Besides, StarClan wouldn't have sent Brambleclaw on the quest to the sun-drown-place if they didn't trust him."

Leafpool murmured agreement, moving around Firestar to trickle the healing juices onto the scratches on his other side.

"I need to trust Squirrelflight's judgment. She's not a kit anymore," Firestar continued. "She values Brambleclaw for the warrior he is now. Judging him for being Tigerstar's son would be like judging me for being a kittypet."

"You haven't been a kittypet for many seasons!" Leafpool protested. She still found it hard to imagine her father, of all cats, eating the hard kittypet food and letting Twolegs handle him.

"And Brambleclaw hasn't seen his father for many seasons," Firestar countered.

That's where you're wrong! Leafpool wanted to say, but before she could speak, her father went on more gently, "I'm glad you came back, Leafpool. I think you made the right decision, and I hope you think so too. Cinderpelt had great faith in you."

"I know," Leafpool meowed humbly. "I owe it to her to be the best medicine cat I can be."

When she had finished dabbing on the marigold, Firestar thanked her and padded away to join Sandstorm, who was waiting near the thorn barrier with the rest of the hunting patrol.

Frustrated, Leafpool watched him go. She couldn't tell him

about the dream or voice her fears about Brambleclaw now. It might sound as if she were jealous of her sister's happy relationship, because she had been forced to give up Crowfeather.

Sighing, she turned back to her den and the cats who were waiting for her.

It was almost sunhigh by the time Leafpool had finished treating the injured cats. Most of them had gone back to their dens to rest. Apart from Birchpaw, only Cloudtail remained, holding out his paw while Leafpool put a poultice of horsetail on the wound.

"You have to stay off it as much as you can," she scolded him. "No wonder the bleeding won't stop. Going hunting yesterday was mousebrained."

Cloudtail mutinously twitched his tail. "The Clan needs to be fed."

"The Clan is being fed. Now, do you want to stay here where I can keep an eye on you, or will you rest in the warriors' den?"

"I'll rest in the warriors' den," Cloudtail promised with a sigh. "And thanks, Leafpool. You're doing a fantastic job."

"It would be easier if some cats had the sense of a newborn kit," Leafpool retorted. "And if I see you—"

She broke off as Squirrelflight brushed past the screen of brambles in front of the den, a vole in her jaws.

"Here—fresh-kill," she meowed, after dropping it at Leafpool's paws.

She turned to leave again, but not before Leafpool had seen the misery in her eyes. She hardly needed to see it; she could feel her sister's churning emotions like the crackles in the air before a thunderstorm.

"Wait, Squirrelflight. What's the matter?" she asked.

For a moment she thought Squirrelflight would stalk off without replying. Then her sister turned back, cast a rapid glance at Cloudtail, and mewed in a low voice, "It's Ashfur. I passed him just now, and when I said hi he stared through me as if I wasn't there. Rainwhisker was with him," she went on as Leafpool laid her tail comfortingly on her shoulder. "The whole Clan must be talking about me!"

"You can hardly blame Ashfur," Leafpool told her. "He really cares for you."

"I never meant to hurt him!" Squirrelflight's voice, though quiet, was anguished, and her green eyes were filled with guilt. "He's a great cat, and I thought it would work out, being with him. But Brambleclaw . . . Oh, Leafpool, do you think I'm doing the right thing?"

Leafpool moved closer to her so that their pelts brushed. "Last night I went down to the lake," she meowed carefully. "StarClan sent me a dream: two sets of starry paw prints on the water, wound so closely I couldn't tell which was which. And then I saw you and Brambleclaw, walking together at the end of the trail, the paw prints spilling out behind you. You were side by side, keeping pace with each other, step for step, until you vanished into the sky."

Squirrelflight's eyes stretched wide. "Really? StarClan

showed you that? Then it must mean that Brambleclaw and I are meant to be together!"

"That's right, I think so." Leafpool tried not to sound fearful.

"Oh, wonderful! Thank you so much, Leafpool." Squirrelflight's tail went straight up and she flexed her claws as if she couldn't keep still. "I'm going to tell Brambleclaw. Then he'll know that we don't have to worry about Ashfur. Nothing can stop us being together, nothing!"

She dashed off, passing Brightheart and Whitepaw as she raced past the bramble screen.

"Thanks for the fresh-kill!" Leafpool called after her.

"I just saw Daisy," Brightheart meowed, setting down her bunch of marigold. "She says she's got bellyache."

"She'll need watermint for that," Leafpool replied, slipping inside the cleft to fetch it.

When she returned, Cloudtail had risen to his paws, carefully holding the injured one clear of the ground. "I'll take the watermint to Daisy if you like," he offered.

Leafpool was about to remind him that she had told him to rest, but before she could open her mouth Brightheart snapped, "I don't see you being so keen to help the cats who actually did some fighting." She turned her back on Cloudtail. "Come on, Whitepaw. Let's go and look for juniper."

The apprentice followed her out, casting a bewildered glance back at her father as they went.

Cloudtail stared after them, his jaws sagging open with

amazement. "What did I say?"

Leafpool rolled her eyes. If he didn't know, there was no point in trying to tell him. Besides, she didn't want to get involved in his tangled relationships. She couldn't figure out whether he really wanted to be with Daisy, or whether he still loved Brightheart and was just being a mousebrained tom.

She dropped the watermint in front of Cloudtail. "Okay, you can take this to Daisy," she meowed. "And after that, make sure you get some rest."

She followed the white warrior as far as the bramble screen, and watched him limping across to the nursery. In the center of the clearing, Squirrelflight stood beside Brambleclaw. She was meowing to him urgently, her tail waving in excitement. After a few heartbeats Brambleclaw touched noses with her and twined his tail with hers.

Leafpool suppressed a sigh. The sign of the mingled paw prints couldn't have been clearer. Yet her pelt still prickled with fear when she saw him with her sister.

"Oh, StarClan!" she murmured. "Was I right to tell her?"

CHAPTER 6

The sky above Brambleclaw's head was dark, but the sickly glow of fungus guided his paws along the path. Shadowy ferns brushed his fur with damp, sticky fronds. Every hair on his pelt prickled as he bounded toward the meeting place. The pain from his wounded shoulder had vanished, and he felt stronger and more powerful with every heartbeat.

Soon the path grew wider and opened up into a clearing. Though no moon shone, a pale wash of light revealed Brambleclaw's half brother Hawkfrost crouched beside a rock, where a massive tabby tom was sitting.

As Brambleclaw emerged from the trees Hawkfrost sprang to his paws and raced toward him. "Brambleclaw!" he exclaimed. "Where have you been?"

It was his first really restful night since the badger attack. When he closed his eyes, he had found himself back in the dark forest, as hungry as ever to find out what Tigerstar had to teach him. Brambleclaw tried to ignore the guilt that pricked at him like a stubborn thorn; there was no way he could tell Squirrelflight about walking these paths of dream and meeting Tigerstar. She would never understand that he could be loyal to his Clan and still see his father.

"Badgers attacked our camp," he explained to Hawkfrost as they padded across the clearing side by side.

"Badgers!" Hawkfrost's neck fur bristled. He knew how dangerous they were. "How many?"

"Enough," Brambleclaw replied grimly.

"And you're wounded." Hawkfrost's ice-blue gaze softened into concern as he noticed the long scar on Brambleclaw's shoulder.

"It's nothing." Reaching the rock, Brambleclaw dipped his head to his father. "Greetings, Tigerstar."

"Greetings." Tigerstar's amber gaze pinned Brambleclaw like an eagle's talon. "You have not been here for nearly a quarter moon. If you want power you must commit yourself totally—every hair, every claw, every drop of blood. Anything less is weakness."

"I *am* committed!" Brambleclaw protested. He began to describe the badger attack, though he kept in mind that Hawkfrost was listening; he was not about to reveal to a warrior from a rival Clan exactly how devastating the attack had been, nor how shattered ThunderClan was still. "I've hardly slept since," he finished. "There's been too much to do, repairing the damage."

"You fought with courage," Tigerstar praised him. "I'm proud you were prepared to risk your life to save your Clan."

Brambleclaw twitched his ears uneasily. He hadn't told his father what he had done during the attack, yet Tigerstar seemed to know already. *He must have been watching me all the time.*

That taunt about weakness must have been a test.

"You need to make sure Firestar remembers how bravely you fought and how hard you have worked for your Clan since the attack," Tigerstar went on. "That will serve you well when he comes to choose a deputy."

Brambleclaw stared at his father. He had fought to help his Clanmates, not because it had been one more step toward power! Yet he couldn't help feeling a twinge of satisfaction. Firestar trusted him with important duties; the Clan leader must feel he would be a good choice of deputy.

"I still haven't had an apprentice," he reminded Tigerstar. "And Firestar won't choose another deputy until he's sure Graystripe is dead."

"Then you need to delay his decision for as long as possible, so that you have time to be given an apprentice," Tigerstar meowed. "How are you going to do that? Hawkfrost, what do you think?"

"Encourage him to think Graystripe is alive," Hawkfrost suggested. "It can't be true, of course, but it's what Firestar wants to believe, so it shouldn't be too hard to convince him."

Brambleclaw didn't like the idea of manipulating his Clan leader like that, not when he knew how much Graystripe meant to Firestar. But he couldn't deny the sense of Hawkfrost's advice. The longer Firestar clung to the belief that Graystripe would return, the better Brambleclaw's chances of getting an apprentice before Firestar finally appointed a new deputy.

Tigerstar gave Hawkfrost an approving nod; then his gaze

swiveled once more to Brambleclaw. "What else?"

"Er . . . make sure I take care of the deputy duties," Brambleclaw meowed. "That'll make a good impression on Firestar, and at the same time make him feel it's not urgent to choose a new deputy yet."

"And?"

Brambleclaw cast about wildly in his mind. It was like trying to pin down a piece of prey without the help of sound or scent.

"Make friends with those kits of Daisy's," Hawkfrost mewed, giving Brambleclaw a flick with his tail. "They'll be the next apprentices, won't they? If one of them *asks* for you as his mentor, you're all set."

"Sure," Brambleclaw meowed. "I can do that. They're good kits, even if their mother isn't Clanborn."

I'd like to mentor Berrykit, he decided. He could see the makings of a good warrior in the sturdy, adventurous little tom. But what would Tigerstar think of a kit that wasn't Clanborn?

"Do you think it matters that their mother came from the horseplace?" Brambleclaw ventured. He remembered tales of how Tigerstar had ordered the murder of halfClan cats when he had taken control of RiverClan and ShadowClan. Were the stories not true, or had his father changed his mind since then?

"Their mother should go back where she came from," Tigerstar growled. "She'll never be any use to the Clan. But the kits may do well enough, if they're properly trained."

Hawkfrost's whiskers twitched. "Don't forget that my mother wasn't Clanborn, either. RiverClan won't forget it, that's for sure, but it doesn't make me weak or stupid."

Tigerstar gave his son a curt nod. "Your mother was a rogue, but dedicate yourself to the warrior code, and you will be as good as any of those who despise you. I became leader of a Clan where I did not belong by birth. And Daisy's kits are too young to remember anything but being part of ThunderClan." He paused, then added, "Being Clanborn is important, but we all work with what we're given on the path toward power."

"So even a kittypet like Firestar—" Brambleclaw began.

Tigerstar let out a furious hiss. "Firestar will never lose his filthy kittypet scent!" he snarled. "It only weakens him. Look at the way he let that whining horseplace cat stay. Her kits may grow up more Clan than kittypet, but she will never be any use as a warrior. And now he has welcomed that RiverClan cat who abandoned his Clan, not to mention his mate, who belongs to no Clan and never will."

"Do you mean Stormfur?" Hawkfrost's ears pricked. "Stormfur is back?"

Brambleclaw nodded. "He and Brook turned up just as we drove out the last of the badgers. They stayed to help us recover, but I expect they'll leave for RiverClan soon."

Hawkfrost's eyes narrowed, and Brambleclaw wondered what he was thinking. He wished that Tigerstar hadn't revealed the news about Stormfur's return. He had a sudden impulse to warn Stormfur, yet he couldn't figure out why he felt there might be a threat from Hawkfrost. Besides, he couldn't tell any cat in ThunderClan about these nocturnal meetings.

A powerful blow to his side jerked him back to the shadowy clearing. His paws skidded out from under him and he crashed to the ground. Tigerstar's massive paws held him down and his yellow eyes glared at him furiously.

"*Always* keep watch!" he spat. "An attack can come at any time. How can you protect your Clan if you forget that?"

Still winded, Brambleclaw scrabbled at Tigerstar's belly with his hind paws. He heaved himself upward, dislodging his father's weight. Tigerstar's paw flashed out, aiming for his ear, but Brambleclaw dodged the blow. Scrambling to his feet, he hurled himself at his father, charging into his muscular shoulder. Tigerstar staggered but kept his balance, darting to one side and attacking Brambleclaw again with teeth bared and claws unsheathed. Brambleclaw ducked under the flashing claws and tried to fasten his teeth in Tigerstar's neck. Tigerstar tore free of him and took a pace back.

Brambleclaw gasped for breath. This fight was fiercer than a normal training session, where claws would be sheathed. In the skirmish the wound on his shoulder had torn open again. He could feel blood trickling into his fur, and pain made him hiss through his teeth when he tried to put his paw to the ground.

"You should move faster!" Tigerstar snarled, leaping for him again.

This time Hawkfrost sprang between them, letting out a

screech as he scored his claws down Tigerstar's flank. Tigerstar leaped at him, and the two tomcats rolled over in a furious tangle of legs and thrashing tails. Hawkfrost fought as fiercely as if every badger in the world were attacking him, giving Brambleclaw a chance to recover. When the two cats broke apart at last, even Tigerstar was breathless.

"Enough," he panted. "We will meet again tomorrow night." His amber stare fixed on Brambleclaw. "Before then, speak to those horseplace kits and gain their trust. If you can make one of them want to be your apprentice, your path to becoming deputy will be clearer."

In spite of his wounded shoulder, Brambleclaw bounded back through the forest as though his paws were carried on the wind. Tigerstar had given him nothing but good advice. If he befriended Berrykit and took responsibility for the duties of a Clan deputy, he would still be serving ThunderClan well. His meetings with Tigerstar would make him a better warrior, more loyal to his Clan, with the skills he needed to make him an effective leader.

He woke in the warriors' den to feel a throbbing ache running from his right ear to his belly. Twisting his neck, he saw that the fur on his shoulder was dark and matted with blood. A cold claw seemed to trail down his spine. He had been *dreaming* when he fought with Tigerstar. Why should the wound open up again? And why did he feel so tired, as if he hadn't slept at all?

As Brambleclaw rasped his tongue over the injury,

Squirrelflight, who was curled up beside him, raised her head. His movement and the sharp scent of fresh blood had woken her.

"What have you done?" she gasped, her eyes wide.

"I . . . I'm not sure." Brambleclaw knew he couldn't tell Squirrelflight, of all cats, about his visits to Tigerstar. Especially not now that she trusted him again. "I must have caught it on a branch while I was asleep."

"Careless furball." Squirrelflight gave him a sympathetic flick with her tail. "You'd better see Leafpool and get some cobwebs."

Brambleclaw glanced around. Dawn light was filtering through the branches of the thorn tree, and the other cats were beginning to stir. "Is anyone leading the dawn patrol?"

"I am." Dustpelt spoke through an enormous yawn. He rose to his paws and arched his back in a long stretch. "Cloudtail and Thornclaw are coming with me." He prodded the sleeping Cloudtail with one paw. "Come on, wake up. What do you think you are, a dormouse?"

"It's just as well you're not going, if that shoulder's giving you trouble," Squirrelflight meowed.

"It'll be fine," Brambleclaw replied tensely. "Why don't we go hunting instead?"

Squirrelflight gave him a long look from narrowed green eyes. "Okay," she agreed. "But *after* you've seen Leafpool."

Relieved to escape any more questions, Brambleclaw slid out between the branches and headed for Leafpool's den. His head spun with exhaustion and his paws felt as if they were made of stone. Instead of hunting, what he longed to do was curl up in his nest and go back to sleep.

When he reached her den, the young medicine cat was checking on Birchpaw, who was still curled up behind the bramble screen. As soon as Brambleclaw appeared, she fetched him a pawful of cobwebs to stop his wound from bleeding any more.

"Any cat would think you'd been fighting again," she remarked as she patted them into place.

For one frantic heartbeat Brambleclaw wondered if Leafpool could possibly know about the meetings in the dark forest.

"I don't know how I did it," he mewed evasively. "Is it okay if I go hunting?"

"Well . . ." Leafpool hesitated, then nodded. "Just don't overdo it, and come back if the bleeding starts again."

Promising that he would, Brambleclaw went back into the clearing. Squirrelflight was waiting for him near the warriors' den, along with Stormfur and Brook. Brambleclaw's spirits rose at the thought of hunting with his old friend. If Stormfur was going to leave ThunderClan soon there might not be many more chances to spend time together.

"Hi," Stormfur meowed. "Squirrelflight says you must have been fighting badgers in your sleep."

Brambleclaw winced. Squirrelflight's theory came a bit too close to the truth.

Squirrelflight took the lead as they headed out of the camp. By now the thorn barrier was almost as thick as ever, with a tunnel leading through it into the forest. As Squirrelflight approached, Ashfur appeared in the entrance with a bundle of moss in his jaws.

"Hi there," Squirrelflight mewed.

Ashfur swept a freezing glance over her, ignored Brambleclaw entirely, and stalked away, carrying his moss to the elders.

"I *tried* to explain . . ." Squirrelflight insisted helplessly. "I keep on trying, but he just won't listen. I don't see why we can't be friends."

Brambleclaw doubted that Ashfur would ever be comfortable just being friends with Squirrelflight, but he didn't say so out loud. Gently he touched his nose to her muzzle. "You did your best. Come on, let's hunt."

When they left the camp the forest was damp and misty, full of the sharp scent of new leaves. As the sun rose, the mist thinned to trailing wisps that clung to the lowest branches; above them, the trees cast long shadows, and dew glittered on every cobweb and blade of grass. Some of Brambleclaw's exhaustion vanished as he paused for a moment to let the warmth soak into his fur.

Movement flickered in the corner of his eye. He spun around to see a mouse scuttling across an open space; before it reached the shelter of the bushes Brook sprang after it and killed it with a sharp blow of her paw.

"Great catch!" he exclaimed. "You're getting really good at hunting among trees."

Brook twitched her tail. "It's a bit strange, after the

mountains," she confessed. "But I'm starting to get the hang of it."

In the Tribe of Rushing Water, where Brook had been raised, duties were organized differently: instead of being warriors, cats were either prey-hunters, responsible for gathering fresh-kill—which involved hunting the swift and sharp-clawed birds that swooped above the rocks—or cave-guards, who protected their Tribemates and defended their home behind the waterfall. Brambleclaw knew that Brook was one of the most skillful of all the prey-hunters. She had taught him and Stormfur how to track mice and voles, not as prey, but as a lure for a bigger, winged piece of fresh-kill.

Stormfur padded over to join them. "Good work, Brook," he meowed. "Remember, you won't catch much in the forest by keeping still and waiting. There are too many places for prey to hide. You need to stalk it instead. See—over there?" He twitched his ears toward a spot where a squirrel was scuffling among the roots of a tree. "Watch this."

Keeping low, so that his belly almost brushed the grass, Stormfur crept up on the squirrel, careful to stay downwind. But he was a RiverClan cat, more used to snatching fish out of fast-flowing water, and in the mountains he had pursued his prey over bare rock. He had forgotten how much debris lay on the forest floor. A twig snapped under his paws; alerted, the squirrel sat up. Stormfur let out a hiss of frustration and hurled himself forward, but the squirrel was faster. It scurried nimbly up the tree trunk and sat chittering for a moment on a branch before vanishing into the leaves.

"Mouse dung!" Stormfur exclaimed.

Squirrelflight's tail curled up in amusement. "So, Brook, think of that as a lesson in how *not* to do it."

"Be fair," Brambleclaw meowed. "Any cat can make a mistake. Stormfur and Brook have already brought back loads of prey."

"We were glad to help," mewed Brook.

Brambleclaw froze as he spotted a vole slipping through the curled stems of newly growing fern. He twitched his whiskers. "My turn now."

Setting each paw down carefully—Squirrelflight would never let him forget it if *he* snapped a twig—he glided across the grass and killed his prey with a single swipe.

"Well-done!" meowed Stormfur.

I wish life could always be like this, Brambleclaw thought. Warm sunshine, lots of prey, the company of friends—right now, they meant far more to him than dreams of power. But even as the thought crossed his mind he felt once more the irresistible tug of ambition. He would give anything to be Clan deputy, wouldn't he? And after that, leader, with responsibility for the whole Clan.

What do I really want? he wondered, and for once he couldn't answer.

The sun was high above the trees when the hunting patrol returned to camp, laden with prey. As he emerged from the thorn tunnel, Brambleclaw saw that the dawn patrol had just got back as well. Dustpelt, Cloudtail, and Thornclaw were

standing in the center of the clearing, with several cats clus-
tered around them: Rainwhisker, Daisy and her kits,
Mousefur, and Sandstorm. Firestar was there too, listening to
Dustpelt's report.

Curiosity clawed at Brambleclaw; he deposited his prey on
the fresh-kill pile and padded across to listen.

" . . . a couple more fox traps," Dustpelt was meowing.
"One on the WindClan border and another near the old
Twoleg nest. We sprang them both." He nodded to
Squirrelflight as she bounded up alongside Brambleclaw.
"Your stick idea works well."

"And we heard a buzzing noise from the lake," Thornclaw
put in.

"Buzzing? Was it bees?" asked Rainwhisker.

Cloudtail's whiskers twitched. "No, it was much louder
than bees. It came from some kind of Twoleg monster. The
lake is swarming with them."

Brambleclaw's belly churned. Since the Clans first arrived
at the lake they had seen very little sign of Twolegs; now it
sounded as if their peace was being invaded again. He was
still haunted by the way Twolegs had destroyed the old forest.
Could the same thing happen here?

"What were they doing?" he demanded, shouldering his
way to the front to stand beside Firestar.

"Hurtling across the lake in some kind of water-monster,"
Dustpelt replied. "That's what made the noise. And other
Twolegs were floating in things like upturned leaves, with
white pelts that caught the wind."

"Those are boats," Daisy mewed. "There's a boatplace at the far side of the lake from here. Twolegs go there all the time when the weather is warm."

"What?" Mousefur's neck fur began to bristle. "Does that mean we'll have them bothering us all through greenleaf?"

"Probably." Daisy sounded apologetic. "They like sailing in boats, and swimming in the lake."

"Twolegs swim for fun?" Sandstorm sniffed. "How mouse-brained is that?"

Dustpelt flicked his ears dismissively. "If the boatplace is across the lake, then it's RiverClan's and ShadowClan's problem. With any luck, the Twolegs won't come this far around the shore."

Brambleclaw glanced at Squirrelflight, aware that her green gaze was fixed on him. Did she think he was worrying about Hawkfrost again?

"All the patrols had better keep watch," Firestar meowed. "And we can discuss this with all the other Clans at the next Gathering. Don't forget—a problem for ShadowClan and RiverClan can easily become a problem for us, especially if the other Clans decide it should be."

CHAPTER 7

❧

All day, anxiety had nagged at Leafpool like a thorn snagging her
fur. She couldn't forget how exhausted Brambleclaw had
looked when he came to her for cobwebs to put on his
wound. Had he been walking in dreams with Tigerstar again?

When her duties were done and she settled down in her
den to sleep, she tried to send her dreaming paws along
Tigerstar's dark paths. The shadowy forest, with its pale light
that didn't come from moon or stars, terrified her, but she
owed it to her Clan to discover what Brambleclaw was doing
there. It wasn't just for the sake of her sister; this *must* be part
of her duty as a medicine cat.

She opened her eyes to find that tall, leafless trees loomed
around her. Whispering shadows flickered between their
trunks, and a path lay in front of her, winding between thick
clumps of ferns. Her paws falling as lightly as if she were
stalking a mouse, she began to follow the path.

She had not gone far before she scented more cats ahead.
Cautiously she slid into the shelter of the ferns and crept forward, her pelt prickling with fear that Tigerstar might discover her spying on him.

Heartbeats later she halted, bewildered. Three cats stood on the path, but they were not Tigerstar and his sons. Starshine sparkled at their paws and in their fur. One of them turned her head and Leafpool recognized Bluestar, who had been leader of ThunderClan before Firestar. She had died before Leafpool was born, but the medicine cat had met her sometimes in dreams.

"Come out, Leafpool," she meowed. "We have been waiting for you."

Leafpool padded out of the ferns to stand in front of the blue-gray she-cat.

"You took your time," one of the other StarClan cats rasped; it was Yellowfang, a former ThunderClan medicine cat who had been Cinderpelt's mentor. Her yellow eyes were narrowed in her broad, pale gray face, and she twitched her thick tail with annoyance.

Leafpool didn't recognize the third cat, a magnificent golden tabby. He dipped his head to her and introduced himself. "Greetings, Leafpool. My name is Lionheart. I was with Bluestar when your father first came to the forest."

"I'm honored to meet you," Leafpool replied. "But where am I? Why have you brought me here?" It wasn't anywhere she had visited before in dreams, yet it obviously wasn't the place where Tigerstar walked, because cats from StarClan were here.

None of the cats replied. Bluestar just mewed, "Come," and led the way farther into the forest.

Soon the path reached a clearing lit by a wash of moonlight. Overhead the moon floated in a clear sky. The forest that had seemed so ominous now looked beautiful, the shadowy places beneath the trees filled with mystery instead of danger.

Just above the topmost branches of the trees, Leafpool spotted three tiny stars shining close together. Puzzled, she tried to remember if she had ever seen them before. As she gazed, they seemed to pulse brighter and brighter, until they threatened to rival the moon.

"Bluestar, what's that?" she asked.

Bluestar didn't answer. Instead, she led the way into the center of the clearing and gestured with her tail for Leafpool to sit. The three StarClan warriors gathered around her. Leafpool cast a final glance over her shoulder, but now she couldn't make out the three new stars at all. *I must be imagining things*, she decided.

"Do you have a sign for me?" she asked, giving all her attention to the three StarClan warriors.

"Not exactly," meowed Bluestar. "But we wanted to tell you that the path of your life will twist in ways yet hidden to you."

"Yes." Yellowfang's voice was dry, with an edge to it that made Leafpool almost certain the old medicine cat knew something she wasn't telling. "You will tread a path that few medicine cats have walked before you."

Fear stabbed at Leafpool; she dug her claws into the ground to keep herself steady. "What do you mean?"

"There are cats you have yet to meet," Bluestar told her. "Yet their paws will shape your future."

That's no answer! Leafpool wanted to protest, but her respect for the StarClan cats kept her silent.

Lionheart rested his tail on her shoulder and his scent drifted around her, brave and reassuring. "We have come to give you strength," he meowed.

"Whatever happens, remember that we are always with you," Bluestar promised.

Gazing at the compassion in her blue eyes, Leafpool tried to understand what Bluestar was saying. But it didn't make sense. She *knew* where her life would lead from now on. She was ThunderClan's medicine cat, nothing else, and would be until StarClan called her to walk with them in Silverpelt. She had given up all her dreams of life with Crowfeather.

"I don't understand," she protested. "Can't you tell me more?"

Bluestar shook her head. "Even StarClan can't see everything that will happen. The path ahead of you vanishes into shadow—but we will walk with you every paw step of the way, I promise."

Her words disturbed Leafpool, but they comforted her at the same time. She knew she was not alone. StarClan had not abandoned her, as she had feared when she was struggling with her love for Crowfeather. Perhaps that was why she couldn't walk in Tigerstar's dark forest anymore—by following her heart, she had come back to StarClan.

"Rest," Lionheart purred, bending his head to give her a lick between the ears. "Rest and grow strong for what lies ahead."

"Rest so you can keep that Clan of yours in order," Yellowfang added.

The scent of the three cats wreathed around Leafpool. Her limbs felt heavy, and with a sigh she curled up in the lush grass of the clearing. A faint breeze ruffled her fur. Through the tangle of branches, she could see the three new stars shining even brighter than before. "Thank you," she murmured, and closed her eyes.

Less than a heartbeat later it seemed, Leafpool's eyes opened again. Sunlight was streaming through the cleft in the rock. Outside she could see Birchpaw sitting up in his nest near the mouth of her den.

"I'm starving!" he complained. "Can I go and get some fresh-kill?"

Leafpool got up and checked the apprentice's wounds. The scars on his haunches were healing well, though it would be some time before the fur grew back. The swelling around his eye was almost gone, and the clawmarks there were healing too. There was no sign of infection.

"I think you can go back to the apprentices' den today," she announced.

"Great!" Birchpaw's eyes sparkled and his paws kneaded his mossy nest impatiently. "Can I start training again too? It's *so* boring, sitting around here all day."

Leafpool was relieved that he felt well enough to be bored. "Okay," she told him. "But light duties only. *No* combat training. Anyway, Ashfur was pretty badly hurt. He won't be able to do much for a while yet."

"I'll go and see if there's anything I can do for him," Birchpaw promised, vanishing before Leafpool could change her mind.

"I want to check your injuries every day!" she called after him.

Her dream had comforted and strengthened her, but her worries about Brambleclaw remained. She was sure he was still meeting Hawkfrost and Tigerstar, and she found herself watching him closely for any sign that the dreams were affecting his behavior in the waking world. As the Clan recovered from the badger attack, Brambleclaw seemed nothing less than a loyal and dedicated warrior. But could any cat stay truly loyal under Tigerstar's treacherous influence?

Two nights later, Leafpool returned late to camp with catmint gathered near the abandoned Twoleg nest. The moon was already shining and most cats had withdrawn to their dens. Spiderleg, who was on guard duty near the entrance, nodded to her as she squeezed through the barrier of thorns. Leafpool took the herbs to her den, then slipped over to the fresh-kill pile for something to eat before she slept.

As she crouched to eat a blackbird, she heard a rustling sound from the warriors' den. The branches parted and Brambleclaw's strong tabby body emerged. Without noticing Leafpool, he padded across the clearing, paused for a quick word with Spiderleg, then vanished into the thorn tunnel.

What is he up to? He had left the camp openly, as if he didn't mind who saw him. But why was he going out alone, when all the other warriors were sleeping? Was he going to meet Hawkfrost?

Swiftly gulping down the rest of her blackbird, Leafpool rose to her paws and followed.

"You're working late tonight," Spiderleg remarked as she passed him again.

"Some herbs are best gathered by moonlight," Leafpool replied; it wasn't exactly a lie, but collecting herbs was the last thing on her mind right now.

By the time she emerged from the thorns, Brambleclaw had disappeared, but Leafpool could easily track him by his scent. Her pelt tingled when she realized he was following the same rocky path that she had used when she went to meet Crowfeather on the WindClan border.

But Brambleclaw wasn't heading for WindClan. Leafpool could already hear the faint chuckle of the stream when the tabby warrior's scent trail veered away from the path and into the trees, toward the lake. Leafpool followed, keeping her jaws wide to distinguish his scent from the prey-scents that mingled with it.

Ferns brushed her pelt as she scrambled up to the top of a steep slope and emerged from the trees. Brambleclaw was sitting with his back to her only a couple of tail-lengths away, gazing out over the lake. Leafpool froze, terrified that her clumsy approach had given her away. But Brambleclaw didn't move.

Leafpool retreated a few paw steps into the shelter of a

twisted tree root. Could this be Brambleclaw's meeting place with Hawkfrost? It was a long way for the RiverClan cat to travel.

The moon drifted across the sky while Leafpool waited, watching. But there was no sign of Hawkfrost or any other cat. Brambleclaw sat motionless, his gaze fixed on the star-flecked water. Leafpool wished she knew what was going through his mind.

He and the rest of the Clan, including Firestar, seemed to believe that their troubles were over. It was hard to imagine anything worse than the badger attack; they had survived that, with the help of WindClan, and the scars were healing. But Leafpool couldn't stifle her sense of disquiet, even stronger now that she was alone with Brambleclaw. Bluestar, Lionheart, and Yellowfang had warned her of a dark future beyond their control. What trouble was still to come? And was the dark-furred cat in front of her involved?

As the night wore on, weariness crept over Leafpool. She nodded, jerked awake, then let her eyes close, curling up in a mossy spot between two tree roots. In her dreams she woke again, scrambling up to see that Brambleclaw had vanished. And beyond the place where he had been sitting, the lake was thick and scarlet, as if waves of blood were rolling onto the shore.

Before all is peaceful, blood will spill blood, and the lake will run red.

With a gasp of horror, Leafpool turned to run. She slammed into something solid; her claws scraped against the bark of a tree. She was trapped! Struggling back to wakefulness, she realized that she had stumbled over a tree root and collided with the trunk beside her. Above her, early-morning light was filtering through the branches, dappling the grass.

"Who's there?" demanded a sharp voice.

Before Leafpool could reply, Brambleclaw sprang up onto the root and stood staring down at her. His eyes were dark with anger. "What are you doing here? Are you spying on me?"

"No!" Leafpool retorted indignantly, with a stab of guilt that she had done exactly that. "I was out late last night, gathering herbs. I must have fallen asleep, that's all."

Fear churned in her belly. *He won't hurt me*, she told herself. *He's my Clanmate, for StarClan's sake! Squirrelflight trusts him.* Brambleclaw couldn't possibly be following a path that led to blood and shadow if StarClan had such faith in him and Squirrelflight being together.

But she was still uneasy as Brambleclaw went on glaring at her, not speaking. Clutching at her dignity, she rose and stalked away. Though her paws itched to flee, she forced herself to walk slowly across the open ground, toward the sheltering ferns.

Beyond the trees the lake reflected the pale dawn light. Yet at that moment, the choking scarlet tide that had lapped stickily at the shore seemed far more real to Leafpool than the dove-gray water below her, barely rippled by the breeze.

Before all is peaceful, blood will spill blood, and the lake will run red.

What horror still lay in wait for ThunderClan?

CHAPTER 8

❧

Sighing, Brambleclaw tucked his paws beneath his chest and gazed out over the lake again. Ever since he had returned to Tigerstar's forest in his dreams, his sleep had been uneasy. His restless thrashing had disturbed Squirrelflight and the rest of the warriors, crowded together in what had been salvaged of their den. So he had taken to slipping out at night to keep watch by the lake, to give his Clanmates a bit of peace.

It had been a shock when Leafpool disturbed him. However much the young medicine cat denied it, he was convinced that she had followed him. Did that mean she knew where he went in his dreams? Like her sister, she wouldn't understand that he could visit Tigerstar and still be loyal to his Clan. He tried to tell himself that his meetings with Tigerstar did no harm to any cat, but he was beginning to wonder whether he should go on visiting the shadowy forest. He was afraid of what Leafpool might know and more afraid still that she would tell Squirrelflight. The sisters were so close, it was hard to believe that Leafpool would keep any secrets from her.

Narrowing his eyes, Brambleclaw peered across the lake. In the dawn light he could just make out the Twoleg boats clustered around the half bridge on the opposite side, on the border between RiverClan and ShadowClan. Just as Daisy had said, the Twolegs had stayed there so far, but Brambleclaw couldn't stop worrying that sooner or later they would invade ThunderClan territory.

The growing daylight glimmered on the surface of the water. He remembered what Squirrelflight had told him about Leafpool's vision of their entwined paw prints, and his fur prickled. He wished he had the power of a medicine cat, to read the future in the lake, but to him the reflections of the stars were nothing more than meaningless sparkles on the indigo water: beautiful, but telling him nothing. *Does my future really lie in the paws of StarClan?* he wondered. No starry warriors walked the paths of Tigerstar's forest. Was he turning his back on them by visiting his father? Did they know?

At last he slipped into a doze again and woke to the sound of birdsong. The sun was rising over the hills behind WindClan. Brambleclaw sprang to his paws. He hadn't meant to stay out so long. A cat who wanted to be deputy didn't wander out of the hollow in the night!

He headed back to camp, pausing to hunt on the way so that by the time he approached the thorn barrier his jaws were filled with prey. He was about to enter the tunnel when an eerie wailing rose up from inside the camp, freezing Brambleclaw's paws to the spot. Had the badgers come back?

A heartbeat's thought told him that wasn't possible. The patrols hadn't found any sign of badgers in the territory since the attack, and the thorns in front of him were undamaged.

Then the cry came again, more clearly.

"My kit! Where's my kit?"

Brambleclaw squeezed through the tunnel and into the camp. Daisy was standing outside the nursery, her fur bristling. Cloudtail was with her and two of her kits were peering out of the entrance, their eyes wide with alarm. Leafpool was hurrying across the clearing from her den, with Brightheart hard on her paws. Brambleclaw dropped his fresh-kill on the pile and bounded across.

"I've looked everywhere!" Daisy wailed. "He's not here. Oh, Berrykit, where are you?"

Anxiety stabbed at Brambleclaw. Berrykit had always been the liveliest kit of the litter, and the most likely to get into mischief. It was all too easy to imagine him sneaking out of camp in search of an adventure.

"When did you last see him?" Cloudtail asked Daisy.

"Last night. When I woke up this morning, he had vanished. I've searched and searched, but he isn't anywhere in the camp!"

"Calm down," Brightheart meowed. "Wailing like that won't help, and you'll upset Sorreltail. We'll find Berrykit."

Daisy ignored her. "A badger's eaten him! I know it has."

Brightheart rolled her eyes, and even Leafpool twitched her whiskers impatiently. "Daisy, you know there hasn't been any trace of badgers around here for days. Berrykit has wandered off somewhere, but we'll track him and bring him back."

By now more cats had begun to emerge, drawn from their dens by Daisy's yowling. Firestar leaped down the tumbled rocks from the Highledge, and padded over to Brambleclaw.

"What's going on?"

Brambleclaw explained rapidly.

"We'll send a patrol out," Firestar decided. "Cloudtail, you can lead it. Pick two or three other cats and go at once."

"Oh, no, no!" Daisy wound her tail around Cloudtail's neck. "I need you to stay with me. What if my other kits go missing too?"

Brightheart let out a hiss of annoyance and turned away. Brambleclaw couldn't blame her. Hazelkit and Mousekit looked too scared to set a paw outside the nursery, let alone the camp. He could understand how upset Daisy must feel, but she didn't have to make this amount of fuss. Cloudtail was looking embarrassed, but he didn't try to tell Daisy that no cat countermanded the Clan leader's orders.

"Hazelkit and Mousekit aren't going anywhere," Leafpool mewed calmly. "Cloudtail, take Daisy into the nursery. I'll fetch her some poppy seed to calm her down."

"And I'll lead the patrol," Brambleclaw offered.

Firestar nodded and watched as Cloudtail disengaged himself from Daisy's tail and nudged her back to the nursery. Brambleclaw signaled to Squirrelflight, who was standing a tail-length away with Stormfur and Brook.

"Let's go," he meowed. "I'll skin the little wretch when we find him, upsetting the camp like this."

"No, you won't." Squirrelflight flicked his shoulder with her tail. "You're as worried as the rest of us that he might be frightened or hurt."

Brambleclaw grunted. For all his fierce words, he couldn't deny a sneaking admiration for Berrykit's latest escapade. It took a lot of courage for a kit to venture out alone into the forest, especially after seeing the badger attack. "The sooner he's apprenticed, the better," he muttered, adding silently, *And I'd be more than happy to be his mentor*.

Squirrelflight was the first to pick up the kit's scent a couple of tail-lengths from the end of the tunnel. "He's gone that way," she reported, pointing with her tail in the direction of the ShadowClan border.

"Then we'd better find him fast," Stormfur meowed. "I don't suppose ShadowClan will be too pleased to find a strange kit in their territory."

Berrykit's trail led almost directly toward the border, though occasionally the kit had made a detour to investigate the roots of a tree or a sandy hollow beneath a rock. Brook spotted tiny paw prints in the soft mud beside a pool, as if the kit had stopped to lap the water. A little farther on, there were a few shallow scrapes in the ground.

"The mighty hunter!" Squirrelflight mewed, her tail curling up in amusement. "He must have been pretending to bury his fresh-kill."

"Like that, you mean?" Stormfur pointed with his tail toward a beetle climbing slowly up a frond of fern. If it had been Berrykit's chosen prey, it had survived the experience.

"I don't suppose you were any different when you were a kit," Brook scolded him gently. "At least we know that Berrykit was okay when he got here."

"But the ShadowClan border isn't far away," Squirrelflight pointed out.

Just then Brambleclaw thought he heard something up ahead. He gestured with his tail for the others to be quiet. For a moment he could hear nothing except for the rustle of wind in the trees and the piping of birds. Then the sound came again: a piercing shriek like the sound of prey under a cat's claws.

Squirrelflight turned to him, her eyes wide with alarm. "That could be Berrykit!"

Brambleclaw tasted the air. The kit's scent reached him strongly, along with another that was both familiar and unwelcome.

"ShadowClan!" he exclaimed. "Come on!"

Brambleclaw raced through the trees toward the sound, the other three cats keeping pace with him. That mousebrained kit must have crossed the border and been spotted by a ShadowClan patrol. *If they have laid one claw on him* . . . Brambleclaw thought, fury raising the hair on his neck and shoulders.

He pelted around a bramble thicket and into a clearing near the dead tree on the ShadowClan border. "Berrykit!"

The thin wail of a cat in pain answered him. Brambleclaw saw Berrykit writhing on the ground in the shelter of a clump of ferns. No other cats were near him. At first Brambleclaw thought the kit must be too badly injured to get up. Then he saw a shining silver tendril wrapped around his tail. Berrykit was caught in a fox trap!

Squirrelflight let out a long hiss. Her neck fur bristled as she stared at a spot just across the border. Following her gaze, Brambleclaw made out three ShadowClan cats crouching in the shadow of a hazel bush: Russetfur, the Clan deputy; Oakfur; and Cedarheart. From the look of it, they had been there for some time, watching Berrykit struggle in agony.

"Crow-food eaters!" Squirrelflight spat at them. "Why didn't you help him?"

Russetfur rose to her paws and paused to give her shoulder a couple of slow licks. "Every cat knows that Thunder-Clan ignores borders," she meowed. "But ShadowClan sticks to the warrior code. Besides, that's a kittypet. We have nothing to do with kittypets in *this* Clan."

Squirrelflight let out another hiss; Brambleclaw could see she was too angry to speak. "Forget it," he muttered. "We need to help Berrykit."

Squirrelflight's claws flexed, as if she would like nothing better than to sink them into ShadowClan fur. Instead, she spun around and followed Brambleclaw across the clearing to Berrykit's side.

Stormfur and Brook were already bending over the kit; Brook was giving him a comforting lick around the ears, while Stormfur sniffed at the shining stuff gripping his tail. All around Berrykit the ground was torn up with tiny, desperate scratches as if he'd tried to drag himself free. His wails had sunk to a frightened mewling.

"I'm s-sorry," he whimpered. "I just wanted to hunt some prey and—"

"You frightened your mother and upset the whole Clan,"

Brambleclaw meowed sternly. "Keep still and we'll soon have you out of there."

But when he examined Berrykit's tail, he wasn't sure it was going to be that easy. The kit's haunches were matted with blood, his tail mangled in his struggles to free himself. The shining tendril was pulled tight around it and stretched taut to the stick buried in the ground. Brambleclaw gave it an experimental tug; it didn't move, but Berrykit let out a shriek of pain as the tendril jerked.

"You're hurting him," Squirrelflight gasped. "Let me try biting through it."

She crouched down beside Berrykit, but Brambleclaw could see that the tendril was too deeply embedded in his fur for her to get her teeth to it. Instead, Berrykit let out another wail. "You bit me!"

"Sorry." Squirrelflight stepped back, panting, a smudge of blood on her nose.

Brambleclaw stared down at the trapped kit. Would they have to bite his tail off to free him? He was bracing himself to suggest it when Brook twitched her ears toward the stick that held the tendril.

"If we dig that up, the wire should loosen," she pointed out.

Brambleclaw exchanged a bewildered glance with Squirrelflight.

"The stick's holding the wire," Brook explained. "But it can't hold it tight if it's not stuck in the ground."

"Brook, you're brilliant!" Squirrelflight flung herself at the stick and began scraping furiously. Brook joined her on the other side, tugging the stick to loosen it as Squirrelflight threw up showers of earth. Every time the stick moved Berrykit squeaked in pain. Stormfur crouched over him and licked his ears soothingly, at the same time shielding the kit's face with his body so he couldn't see the state of his tail.

As Squirrelflight dug deeper, Brambleclaw realized the tendril was starting to sag.

"How does that feel?" he asked Berrykit.

"Better," the kit mewed. "Not so tight."

"Keep still," Brambleclaw told him. "It won't be long now."

"Stand back!" Squirrelflight gasped. "I'm nearly there." She fastened her teeth in the stick and tugged hard; her paws shot out from under her as it sprang out of the ground. Berrykit scrambled forward when he felt the trap release him, dragging the stick with his injured tail.

"Stop!" Stormfur meowed. "Let's get this thing off first."

Now that the stick was out of the ground, the tendril was much looser. Delicately Brambleclaw worked one claw under it, then loosened it a little more with his teeth. "Try pulling your tail free," he instructed Berrykit.

Relief flooded over him from ears to tail-tip as the kit managed to draw his tail out of the shining loop. Berrykit tried to get to his paws, staggered, and slumped down on one side, his eyes closed.

"Rest for a moment," Brook mewed. "We'll clean your tail up a bit."

She crouched beside Berrykit and began to lick his

wounded tail. Squirrelflight joined in with swift rasps of her tongue. Brambleclaw winced when he saw Berrykit's torn flesh and the blood that was still trickling out of the wound. He gathered a pawful of leaves and pressed them down over the worst of the bleeding—they wouldn't be as effective as cobwebs, but there wasn't time to look for anything else.

"As soon as we get back to camp, Leafpool will take a look at you," he promised.

Berrykit didn't reply, and his eyes stayed closed; Brambleclaw wondered if the kit had even heard him.

Meanwhile Stormfur had taken a few paces toward the ShadowClan patrol, who were still watching from the shelter of the hazel bush. "Seen enough?" he snarled. "At least you've had a lesson from ThunderClan on how to deal with a fox trap."

"ShadowClan can deal with fox traps, thanks," Russetfur replied with a flick of her tail. "We've seen a couple of them in our territory, but *we* have the sense to stay clear of them."

"More sense than a kit?" Stormfur took another step forward until he stood right on the border. "That must make you so proud. You're really fierce warriors, I can see that."

A growl rose in Oakfur's throat and he sprang to his paws. "Take one step over the border and you'll find out how fierce we are—deserter!"

Stormfur's neck fur bristled. "I was one of the cats who made the journey to the sun-drown-place. I helped the Clans find their new home. And I'll tell you this—I didn't do it so that the four Clans would grow too far apart to even help an injured kit."

"But that's not a Clan kit," Cedarheart sneered, coming over to stand beside Oakfur. "Maybe you've been in the mountains for so long, you've forgotten the warrior code. If you ever knew it in the first place, *halfClan*."

Stormfur unsheathed his claws, and Brambleclaw knew that the insults were on the brink of giving way to a full-blown fight. That was more than he wanted to cope with now, especially when they still had to carry Berrykit back to camp.

He bounded up to Stormfur and nudged him. "We don't want a fight right now," he mewed quietly in his ear. "They're not worth it. Ignore them."

Stormfur's gaze locked with his; his blue eyes were hot with anger. Then he took a deep breath, and the fur on his shoulders began to lie flat. "You're right," he agreed. "But crow-food is still too good for them."

Both cats turned away and padded back to Berrykit. A scornful yowl rose up from the ShadowClan warriors, but neither Brambleclaw nor Stormfur looked back.

When they reached Berrykit, Brambleclaw thought he was still unconscious, but as he bent over to sniff him the kit's eyes flickered open. "Thank you," he whispered. "I'm really sorry."

"That's okay," meowed Squirrelflight.

"Will Firestar still let me be an apprentice?"

Brambleclaw gave Berrykit a comforting lick on the shoulder. "I'll tell you a secret," he meowed. "When Firestar was an apprentice, he got into no end of trouble—isn't that so, Squirrelflight?"

Squirrelflight nodded solemnly. "It's no secret! The whole Clan knows it."

Berrykit blinked. "Firestar? Really?"

"Really," Brambleclaw reassured him. "What you did was wrong, but it was brave too. Firestar will understand that."

Reassured, Berrykit let out a sigh, and his eyes closed again.

"Come on," mewed Brambleclaw, looking up at his companions. "Let's get him back to camp."

Brambleclaw and Stormfur shuffled through the thorn tunnel, carrying Berrykit's limp body between them. His mangled tail was still bleeding. Brambleclaw was sure that the kit was still alive only from the faint rise and fall of his chest. He desperately needed Leafpool's care before they lost him to StarClan.

Squirrelflight followed the two tomcats into the camp and raced off at once to her sister's den. Brook brought up the rear. "I'll tell Daisy," she mewed, heading for the nursery.

As Brambleclaw and Stormfur carried Berrykit across the clearing a shrill wail broke out behind them. Glancing over his shoulder, Brambleclaw saw Daisy shoot out of the nursery entrance; Cloudtail was just behind her, meowing, "Daisy, wait!"

The cream-colored she-cat skidded to a halt in front of Brambleclaw, her eyes wild with terror. "Berrykit! Oh, he's dead, he's dead!"

Brambleclaw, with a mouthful of the kit's fur, couldn't reply.

"He's not dead," Cloudtail panted as he raced up. "Brook said he wasn't, remember? Look, you can see him breathing."

Daisy just stared numbly at Berrykit, as if she couldn't understand what the white warrior was saying. Then she flung herself at her kit and began covering him with desperate licks. Brambleclaw's ears twitched impatiently. Didn't the mousebrained kittypet realize she was in the way? Couldn't she understand that the most important thing was to get her kit to a medicine cat quickly?

"Come on." Cloudtail laid his tail gently on Daisy's shoulder. "Let them take Berrykit to Leafpool. Come and tell Mousekit and Hazelkit that he's going to be okay. They've been worried, too."

Daisy gave him a doubtful look, then let him draw her away, back toward the nursery.

Leafpool rushed out to meet Brambleclaw and Stormfur before they were halfway to her den. "Poor little scrap!" she exclaimed, giving the wounded tail a rapid sniff. "Bring him straight in, please. Brightheart is making a nest for him."

Brambleclaw and Stormfur carried the kit around the bramble screen and laid him in a nest of moss and ferns just outside the entrance to Leafpool's den. He lay on one side, not moving. Brightheart stroked his fur with one paw while Squirrelflight looked on worriedly.

"I'd better tell Firestar," she muttered after a moment, and slipped away.

Leafpool dived through the cleft into her den, and emerged a moment later with a pawful of cobwebs. "We have to stop the bleeding first," she meowed as she bound them around the ragged wounds in Berrykit's tail. The leaves Brambleclaw had used had fallen off during the long trek back through the forest. "Then he can have some marigold to stop infection."

"He's going to be okay, isn't he?" Brambleclaw asked in a low voice.

Leafpool looked up at him, her amber eyes shadowed. "I hope so, but I don't know," she replied honestly. "I'll do the best I can, but he's in the paws of StarClan now."

When he left Leafpool's den, Brambleclaw found Dustpelt and Thornclaw about to go out on patrol. He bounded over to join them, hoping to put his worries about Berrykit out of his mind for a while. But all the way along the stream bordering WindClan, he couldn't forget the kit's limp shape, lying so still. If he died, Daisy would probably take her other kits straight back to the horseplace, as she'd been threatening to do already. And then there would be no more apprentices until Sorreltail's kits were old enough. That was almost six moons away!

Brambleclaw lashed his tail, angry with the way his thoughts were heading. He cared about the bright, disobedient little kit for Berrykit's own sake, not just because Brambleclaw needed an apprentice. But however hard he tried, he couldn't stop thinking about being Clan deputy, and what he needed to do to get there.

Returning to the camp just after sunhigh, he meant to go

and check on Berrykit right away, but paused when he saw Stormfur and Brook crossing the clearing with Firestar and Squirrelflight.

Stormfur waved his tail in greeting and raced ahead of the other cats to meet Brambleclaw. "Hi," he meowed. "We waited for you."

"Why?" Brambleclaw's belly lurched at the shadow of regret in his friend's eyes. What was happening now?

Stormfur touched his nose to Brambleclaw's shoulder. "Brook and I are leaving."

"Now?" Brambleclaw sank his claws into the ground in frustration. It had felt so right, so comfortable, to have Stormfur around again. Though Brambleclaw had known he and Brook would have to leave one day, this seemed much too soon. "I suppose you have to go back to the mountains." He sighed. "But I hoped you would stay longer."

Stormfur hesitated. "No, not to the mountains," he mewed. "To RiverClan. Those ShadowClan cats were right. If we want to stay here, then we have to live by the warrior code, and that means being loyal to RiverClan."

Brambleclaw stared at him. "Is that the only reason you're going? Because of what those mangy crow-food eaters said?"

"No," meowed Brook, padding up to Stormfur's side. Squirrelflight was beside her. "You'll see us again, I promise. We want to stay by the lake for good, and when we get to RiverClan I'm going to train to be a warrior."

Brambleclaw stared at her in astonishment. They were staying for good? That meant they hadn't just come here to make sure the Clans had found their new homes. Why exactly had Stormfur and Brook left the mountains? And why didn't they want to go back? But he couldn't ask; if Stormfur had wanted him to know, he would have told him already. Sharp claws sank into Brambleclaw's heart at the thought that his friend didn't trust him enough to confide in him.

"It's great that you're staying." He forced a purr. "At least we'll get to see each other at Gatherings."

"Yes, we'll expect all the RiverClan gossip," Squirrelflight mewed, pressing her muzzle against Stormfur's and then Brook's. More quietly, she added, "None of us will ever forget our journey. Part of us will walk together always."

Firestar was waiting a couple of tail-lengths away for the friends to say good-bye to one another. "We won't forget what you did after the badger attack," he told the visitors. "You will always have ThunderClan's thanks. We owe you more than we can ever repay."

Stormfur dipped his head. "We're grateful to you too, for letting us stay this long."

With Brook just behind him, he turned and made his way through the thorn tunnel. Brambleclaw and Squirrelflight followed them out and watched, side by side, as the two cats padded into the undergrowth.

"May StarClan light your path!" Brambleclaw called after them.

Stormfur paused to look back, curling his tail in farewell, then both he and Brook vanished among the ferns.

CHAPTER 9

❧

The moon floated above the trees that surrounded the stone hollow, but the nest where Berrykit lay was in deep shadow. Leafpool crouched beside the kit and touched her nose to his. Berrykit's nose felt hot and dry with fever, and he whimpered without opening his eyes. He hadn't regained consciousness since Brambleclaw and the others had brought him back to camp, early the previous morning.

Since then, Leafpool had stayed awake to keep watch over him. After doing her best with cobwebs and a poultice of marigold, she had been forced to admit defeat in her efforts to save the whole of his mangled tail. That afternoon, she had bitten through the last couple of tendons that held the end in place. Berrykit's limbs jerked and he let out a squeal of pain, but he didn't wake up. Patting more cobwebs on the new wound, Leafpool had given the end of his tail to Brightheart to bury outside the camp.

Now she fetched borage leaves from her store, chewed them up, and parted Berrykit's jaws to trickle a little of the juice into his mouth. StarClan willing, that should bring down his fever. She kept watch for a little longer as the moon shadow crept across the clearing, but she was so exhausted that at last her eyes closed, and she slipped into an uneasy sleep.

She found herself standing on the lakeshore with the stars of Silverpelt blazing above her head. A dark shape caught her eye, farther around the lake: a cat, swiftly making his way toward her. As he drew closer she recognized Mudfur, the previous RiverClan medicine cat, who had died in their old home before the Clans made their journey. Now his body was strong and lithe, and his fur was frosted with starlight.

Dipping her head, Leafpool meowed, "Greetings, Mudfur. Do you have a message for me?"

"Yes," the former medicine cat replied. "I need you to take word to Mothwing."

Leafpool tensed. Mothwing, the present RiverClan medicine cat, didn't believe in StarClan, and the spirits of her warrior ancestors couldn't reach her in dreams. Once before, Leafpool had taken a message from Feathertail to Mothwing, warning her of Twoleg poison in RiverClan territory. But she had never felt comfortable about being responsible for this vital part of Mothwing's duties. She was even more reluctant now, after the new commitment she had made to her own Clan.

"A RiverClan elder is suffering from greencough," Mudfur went on. "Mothwing needs catmint to cure him, but she can't find any." His eyes filled with anxiety. "Did I make a mistake when I chose Mothwing to be our medicine cat? The sign of the moth's wing outside my den seemed so clear. . . ." He hesitated, as if he was not sure how to go on. "Leafpool, I beg you to make sure that my Clan doesn't suffer for my poor judgment."

"Do you want me to take her some catmint?" Leafpool asked, remembering the thick clumps that grew near the abandoned Twoleg nest.

"No. There's plenty of catmint just outside her own territory if Mothwing knew where to look," Mudfur meowed. "She must go to the small Thunderpath at the edge of her territory, and follow it away from the lake until she comes to a row of Twoleg nests with gardens. Catmint grows there. Leafpool, will you tell her this?"

He opened his mouth and a thin mewling came out. Leafpool watched in alarm as the old medicine cat faded away, but she could still hear the mewling. Her eyes blinked open and she saw Berrykit thrashing in his nest. "It hurts! My tail hurts!" he wailed.

Leafpool rested a paw on his chest to calm him, and trickled more of the borage juice into his mouth. As she stroked his fur and purred soothingly into his ear, she remembered the anxiety in Mudfur's eyes as he told her about the dreaded greencough.

The moon had vanished, and the first traces of dawn light were appearing in the sky; Leafpool could just make out the dark outlines of trees overhead.

"How *can* I go to RiverClan?" she murmured.

Firestar had given her permission to help RiverClan in the past, but this time she had a sick kit to consider. Berrykit might die if he weren't cared for properly. Besides, not many days ago Leafpool had abandoned ThunderClan to go with Crowfeather—what would her Clanmates think if she disappeared again? Even if she told them she was going to help Mothwing, they wouldn't sympathize with a show of loyalty toward a different Clan.

Mothwing will find the catmint on her own if she looks hard enough. At least tonight is the quarter moon, and I'll be meeting her at the Moonpool. I can pass on Mudfur's message then, without having to leave my Clan.

But as she went on watching over Berrykit, she couldn't push her dream of the old medicine cat out of her mind. Was it part of her duty to carry out his request? She sighed. Why did it suddenly seem so complicated to be a medicine cat? Was her duty to ThunderClan alone, or to StarClan, and therefore all the cats that they watched over?

"I'm not sure I should go," Leafpool meowed anxiously.

The sun was setting, sending bloodred shafts of light into the clearing. Leafpool stood outside her den, gazing down at Berrykit. He was sleeping more peacefully now, curled up in his nest. His fever was waning, but she still wasn't convinced that his injuries were healing properly.

After her vigil Leafpool felt almost too exhausted for the long journey to the Moonpool. Besides, she shrank from the thought of seeing the other medicine cats and telling them that Cinderpelt was dead.

"You have to go," Brightheart told her, flicking her on the shoulder with her tail. "Berrykit will be fine with me. I know what to give him if he wakes up."

Leafpool knew that was true. Brightheart was an efficient helper, and she had all the herbs she would need. And there was Mudfur's message to deliver to Mothwing.

"Okay," she meowed. "I'll go. But I'll be back as soon as I can."

"Don't worry about a thing," Brightheart assured her.

After checking Berrykit one last time, Leafpool padded out into the clearing and headed for the thorn tunnel, saying good night to Thornclaw, who was just settling down on guard duty. It felt strange to be going on this journey without Cinderpelt. She longed to feel Cinderpelt's spirit beside her, but there was no trace of familiar scent, no brush of soft gray fur. Leafpool had never felt so alone.

The sun dipped below the horizon as she headed for the WindClan border and followed the stream up into the hills. The scents of greenleaf wreathed around her as the forest filled with shadows, and the dew was cool on her pads. Her weariness faded away as she thought about crouching down to lap the water of the starry pool and sharing dreams with StarClan. With the other medicine cats around her, and the warriors of StarClan to share tongues with, she wouldn't feel so lonely.

Near the border of WindClan territory, she saw Barkface, the WindClan medicine cat, just ahead of her, and Littlecloud from ShadowClan. They must have scented her, because they stopped and waited while she scrambled up the last slope and fell in beside them.

"Greetings, Leafpool," Barkface rumbled. "It's good to see

you again. I grieve for your loss. It's sad that Cinderpelt had to go so young to join the ranks of StarClan."

"What?" Littlecloud exclaimed, his neck fur rising. "Cinderpelt is dead?"

Leafpool knew that the ShadowClan medicine cat wouldn't have heard the news yet. She nodded. "Badgers attacked our camp. Onestar brought WindClan to help us, but they were too late to save Cinderpelt." *I was too late.*

Littlecloud bowed his head. "She was a great medicine cat. I owed her my life."

Leafpool had heard the story of how Cinderpelt had disobeyed orders many moons ago to help Littlecloud and one of his Clanmates when sickness struck ShadowClan. Littlecloud always said that was what had made him choose to become a medicine cat.

She wondered if she should tell the others what really happened—that Cinderpelt died because Leafpool had turned her back on her Clanmates and all her medicine cat duties. Would they blame her for Cinderpelt's death as much as she blamed herself?

Then she realized that there was nothing but sympathy in Barkface's and Littlecloud's eyes. There was no point in unburdening herself and only adding to their grief.

"You must miss her greatly," Barkface murmured. "But you will be a worthy successor."

"I hope so," Leafpool replied tightly, her throat almost too choked to speak. "I'll never forget her or everything she taught me."

As they climbed farther into the hills, her fellow medicine cats padded one on each side of her, sharing her grief and adding their strength to hers.

Leafpool would have liked to ask Barkface how Crowfeather was, but she knew she couldn't. *You have to stop thinking about him!*

By now night had fallen. Leafpool halted at the top of a swell of moorland and looked back to see the quarter moon shining over the distant lake. There was no sign of Mothwing, and when she tasted the air she could not pick up her friend's scent.

"Did you see Mothwing on the way?" she asked the others.

Barkface shook his head.

"I haven't seen her either, but then she never comes through ShadowClan," Littlecloud meowed. "But don't worry. She's been late before."

Leafpool knew that was true, but she also knew what was going on in RiverClan. She wondered if Mothwing had been unable to come because she couldn't leave the elder who was ill with greencough. Perhaps the sickness had spread further, without a supply of catmint to treat the sick cats.

When Leafpool and the others reached the tumbling stream, there was still no sign of Mothwing. Leafpool bounded up beside the star-filled water and pushed her way through the bushes that surrounded the hollow, half hoping that her friend would already be there.

The waterfall poured down the wall of rock, a moving sheet of silver, churning the pool below so that it seemed full of leaping moonlight. But no familiar golden tabby shape rose to greet Leafpool; no friendly scent reached her. The hollow was empty.

Barkface led the way down the spiral path to the edge of the pool. Leafpool followed, feeling her paws slip into the marks left behind by generations of cats long gone. But this time she didn't feel the peace that always surrounded her in this place. She was too worried about Mothwing and RiverClan, and afraid that if she met Mudfur in her dreams he would blame her for not passing on his message.

She could say nothing about it to the other medicine cats. Instead, she crouched beside them on the edge of the pool and craned her neck to lap from the icy water. The cold seemed to flow into every part of her, gripping her limbs so that she felt like a cat made of ice. Her gaze was transfixed by the churning surface of the water; gradually it stilled, and Leafpool made out the reflections of countless cats, lining the hollow around her.

She looked up. Barkface and Littlecloud, one on each side of her, were motionless, far distant in their own dreams. Around the pool, and lining the sides of the hollow as far as the circle of bushes, were the glimmering shapes of the warriors of StarClan.

A blue-furred cat rose to her paws on a mossy rock jutting out over the water. Leafpool recognized Bluestar.

"Welcome," meowed the former ThunderClan leader. "StarClan welcomes you as the new medicine cat of ThunderClan."

A murmur of greeting rose from the starry ranks around the pool. Leafpool spotted Feathertail sitting beside a beautiful silver-furred she-cat who must be her mother, Silverstream. Closer to the water's edge were Shrewpaw, Larchkit, and Hollykit, Ferncloud's kits who had died in the famine in the old forest. Tallstar, the previous WindClan leader, sat nearby. Leafpool felt herself draw strength from their luminous eyes.

"Thank you," she replied. "I'll do my best to serve my Clan, I promise."

On the opposite side of the pool she could see a group of former medicine cats: her own dear guardian, Spottedleaf, along with Yellowfang and Mudfur. A shadow seemed to hang over them, though above the hollow the moon floated in a cloudless sky. Mudfur's gaze was fixed on his paws; Leafpool's heart lurched as she wondered if he was deliberately avoiding her.

She peered into the shadow, desperate to see Cinderpelt. In spite of what Spottedleaf had said to her, Leafpool was still afraid that her former mentor blamed her for abandoning her Clan.

"Please, Cinderpelt . . ." she whispered. Turning to Bluestar, she asked, "Bluestar, where—?"

But the warriors of StarClan were already fading, the shimmer of their pelts growing dim until Leafpool could see the sides of the hollow through them. For a heartbeat they shone like a thin layer of ice on the rocks; then they were gone, and Leafpool was blinking awake on the edge of the pool.

She rose, stretching to ease her cold, cramped limbs. Beside her, Littlecloud sat up and started to wash his face with one paw, while Barkface gave his rumpled fur a quick grooming. Neither of them spoke of what they had seen in their dreams.

"When I was out yesterday, I found a good clump of watermint, just above the stepping-stones," Barkface told Leafpool as they climbed the path out of the hollow. "You might want to collect some—there's plenty for both of us."

"Thanks," mewed Leafpool. "It's the best herb there is for bellyache."

"I spotted that ginger-and-white cat collecting marigold the other day," Barkface went on, leading the way down the slope. "Brightheart, is it? She looked busy—too busy to notice me."

"Yes, she's been a huge help," Leafpool admitted. "We've needed a lot of marigold to treat wounds after the badger attack."

Littlecloud nodded. "Thank StarClan we haven't seen the badgers in ShadowClan territory," he mewed. "Is ThunderClan recovering? Do you need any help?"

Briefly Leafpool wondered what Blackstar, the ShadowClan leader, would have to say about Littlecloud's offer of help to a rival Clan. It was just as well she could refuse with a clear conscience. "No, thanks, we're fine," she replied. "Our wounds are healing."

Dawn was not yet streaking the sky above the hills, and Leafpool realized she had a chance to take Mudfur's message to Mothwing. But if she was late returning to the hollow, what message would that send to her Clanmates? She had left them once before; they needed to see that now she was completely dedicated to them. Besides, the sooner she returned to check on Berrykit, the better.

Not only that, but to get to RiverClan she would have to travel through WindClan territory, and the risk of running into Crowfeather was too great.

Following the stream down into ThunderClan territory, she refused to even look sideways at WindClan's moorland. That part of her life was over, never to be revisited. She was a medicine cat, with the power to walk among StarClan. There was a good reason why she could never be close to any other cat—she walked a different path and always would. If she could just concentrate hard enough on her duties, her feelings would die away, and Crowfeather would mean nothing more to her than any other warrior.

CHAPTER 10

As *Brambleclaw walked away from the* fresh-kill pile, he spotted Ashfur limping away from Leafpool's den. Fresh cobwebs were plastered on the gash in his foreleg. He was heading for the warriors' den, but before he reached it Birchpaw came bounding over to him.

"Hi, Ashfur!" he meowed. "Brackenfur is taking Whitepaw for a training session. Can we go with them?"

"No." His mentor's voice was an ill-tempered growl. "I fell off a rock and opened this wound again. Leafpool says I can't leave the camp today."

Birchpaw's tail drooped; he turned his head to watch mournfully as Brackenfur and his apprentice, Whitepaw, left through the thorn tunnel.

Brambleclaw strolled over to Ashfur and Birchpaw and flicked the disappointed apprentice with his tail. "Cheer up." To Ashfur he added, "I'm just leaving on patrol. I could take Birchpaw with me, if you like."

Birchpaw's tail shot straight up in the air again and his whiskers quivered with excitement. "Please, Ashfur!" he begged.

Ashfur opened his mouth; Brambleclaw was convinced he was about to refuse. Then a new voice spoke from behind Brambleclaw. "Good idea. Birchpaw missed a lot of training while he was hurt. He shouldn't miss any more."

Brambleclaw turned to see his Clan leader leaping down the rocks from the Highledge. "I thought we'd go up by the ShadowClan border," he meowed. "We'll renew the scent markers and check for fox traps."

Firestar nodded, though Ashfur was staring at Brambleclaw through narrowed eyes. Without saying anything the gray warrior turned away and stalked off to the warriors' den.

"Off you go, then," Firestar meowed to Birchpaw. "Do as Brambleclaw tells you and watch out for those traps. You don't want to lose your tail, like Berrykit."

"I'll be careful," Birchpaw promised.

Brambleclaw stuck his head through the branches of the warriors' den and called Sandstorm and Thornclaw to join the patrol. Ashfur, settling himself among the mossy bedding, ignored him.

The day was overcast, with a damp breeze that promised rain later. Prey-scent was muted, as if all the prey were hiding in their holes, and there was little sound except for the rustle of branches overhead.

Birchpaw was still trembling with excitement; Brambleclaw could see that he was struggling to control himself and pad along quietly beside the rest of the patrol.

"Why don't you run ahead and see if you can spot the

ShadowClan scent markers?" he suggested. "Come back and tell us when you find them."

"Okay, Brambleclaw!" Birchpaw's eyes gleamed, and he bounded off with his tail straight up.

Brambleclaw suppressed a pang of anxiety at the sight of his fuzzy haunches, where the fur was just beginning to grow back. Birchpaw had been lucky to survive the badger attack. But he couldn't be protected by his Clanmates forever. He had to learn the skills he needed to survive, and being out on patrol was a good way to put them into practice. "Be careful of fox traps!" he called after him.

"It's time he ran the itch out of his paws," Sandstorm commented when the apprentice had disappeared. "Between his injuries and Ashfur's, he's hardly been out of camp since the badger attack."

"Maybe Firestar will let you take over his training until Ashfur's fit again," Thornclaw suggested.

"Maybe." Brambleclaw nodded, trying to hide how much the idea pleased him. He was enjoying this taste of mentoring, and his paws tingled with eagerness to have an apprentice of his own.

He still hoped Firestar would choose him to mentor Berrykit. He admired the kit's brave, inquisitive nature, even though it had led to trouble. He was the biggest and strongest of Daisy's litter, too, with the potential to be a fine warrior.

Leaping over the gnarled roots of an oak tree, Brambleclaw spotted Birchpaw standing beside a bramble thicket a few tail-lengths ahead, his jaws open to draw in scent.

"I've found the scent markers, Brambleclaw," he reported.

"What? You can't have." Hadn't Ashfur given Birchpaw any training at all? "We're nowhere near the ShadowClan border."

Birchpaw looked hurt. "But I'm sure . . ." he began.

Sandstorm brushed through the ferns until she reached the spot where Birchpaw had stopped to taste the air. A moment later she came back, her green eyes gleaming with anger. "Birchpaw's right," she meowed. "ShadowClan have set their scent markers just beyond those brambles."

Thornclaw let out a furious hiss. "That's ThunderClan territory!"

Brambleclaw felt a growl rising in his throat. With his patrol behind him, he stalked across the clearing and skirted the brambles. The reek of the ShadowClan scent markers flooded over him after a couple of tail-lengths.

"Those are fresh," he hissed. "If we follow them we should be able to catch up to the patrol and ask them what they think they're playing at." Whirling around, he added, "Birchpaw, run back to camp as fast as you can. Tell Firestar what's going on, and fetch help."

The apprentice took off, racing back along their trail with his belly close to the ground and his tail streaming out behind him.

Brambleclaw checked the scent markers to discover which way the ShadowClan patrol had gone, then bounded off in pursuit, with Sandstorm and Thornclaw a pace behind. The ShadowClan scent became stronger and stronger, until

Brambleclaw reached the top of a gentle slope and spotted the patrol setting more markers in the hollow on the far side.

Bristling with fury, he paused for a couple of heartbeats to size up the enemy patrol. There were four ShadowClan cats: Russetfur, Oakfur, and Cedarheart—the same three who had watched Berrykit struggling in the fox trap—and Rowanclaw. The ThunderClan cats were outnumbered, but Brambleclaw knew there wasn't time to wait for reinforcements to arrive.

"Russetfur!" he called to the ShadowClan deputy. "What are you doing here?"

All four ShadowClan cats whipped around to face the ThunderClan patrol.

"What does it look like?" Russetfur mewed insolently.

"It looks like you're trying to steal our territory," Thornclaw hissed.

"The Clan boundaries were agreed on long ago," Brambleclaw reminded them. "Every cat knows the extent of their territory."

"That was then," meowed Cedarheart.

"ShadowClan needs more space." Russetfur narrowed her eyes at Brambleclaw. "And ThunderClan is too weak to defend it anyway, ever since the badgers attacked your camp."

"What do you know about the badgers?" Sandstorm asked, taking a step forward.

"Enough," Russetfur replied. The tip of her tail twitched. "We know that you are all too badly injured to fight us right now. You're too busy repairing your camp to watch over your borders. *And* you lost your medicine cat."

For a heartbeat Brambleclaw was utterly bewildered. How could ShadowClan have found out about the badger attack? Then he remembered that only three nights earlier Leafpool had paid her half-moon visit to the Moonpool. She must have revealed ThunderClan's weakness to Littlecloud.

His claws sank into the ground; there was no time to think about that now. "Get out of our territory," he snarled at Russetfur. "Or we'll show you the same welcome we gave the badgers."

Russetfur curled her lip. "I don't think so."

Letting out a fearsome screech, Brambleclaw hurled himself down into the hollow. His first rush landed him on top of Russetfur; his claws raked across her shoulder. She tried to fasten her teeth into his throat, but he pushed her off with one paw on her chest. She writhed under his weight, her eyes blazing with anger.

Brambleclaw caught a glimpse of Sandstorm locked in battle with Oakfur, her hind paws battering his belly, while Rowanclaw and Cedarheart had Thornclaw pinned down between them. Brambleclaw aimed one more blow at Russetfur and sprang to help his Clanmate, only to feel Russetfur's claws score his haunches as he bounded away.

Birchpaw, get a move on!

He leaped on top of Cedarheart, gripping the dark gray tom's neck fur in his teeth. Russetfur bit his tail; he lashed out with his hind legs to beat her off. He rolled on the ground in a tangle of fur and mingled scents, hardly knowing which cats were his enemies.

Then he heard a yowling in the distance that rapidly grew louder. Russetfur, her face pushed close to his as she clawed his neck, spat, "Fox dung!" and leaped away from him. Cedarheart wriggled out of his grip. Brambleclaw staggered to his paws to see Firestar and a fresh patrol of ThunderClan warriors racing down into the hollow.

Firestar leaped on Russetfur, caterwauling a challenge, and fastened his teeth in her throat. Russetfur scored her claws across Firestar's shoulder, but she couldn't struggle free. Squirrelflight rushed straight at Cedarheart, carrying him off his paws and pinning him to the ground. Just behind her, Dustpelt leaped on top of Rowanclaw, sinking his claws deep into the ShadowClan warrior's fur. Oakfur let out a screech of terror as he saw Spiderleg and Rainwhisker surging through the bracken toward him; Sandstorm aimed a last blow at his haunches as he scrambled over roots and through brambles, heading for the ShadowClan border.

"Back off!" Russetfur yowled. She managed to stagger to her paws, leaving tufts of fur in Firestar's teeth and claws. She was bleeding from her throat as she retreated.

Firestar flicked his tail, ordering his own warriors to let the ShadowClan cats go. Squirrelflight bit down hard on Cedarheart's ear and sprang away from his flailing paws. Dustpelt rolled away from Rowanclaw and came to his paws snarling. Both ShadowClan warriors turned and fled, but Russetfur stood her ground a few heartbeats longer.

"Don't think you've won, Firestar," she spat, her sides heaving. "ShadowClan *will* set a new border."

"Not here in ThunderClan," Firestar retorted. "Now get back to your own territory."

Her eyes glaring hatred, Russetfur let out a furious hiss before turning to flee after her Clanmates. Spiderleg and Rainwhisker followed hard on her paws, letting out fearsome screeches as they pursued the invaders out of sight.

"Thanks," Brambleclaw gasped as Firestar shook his rumpled fur and padded up beside him. "And you, Birchpaw," he added; the young apprentice, bright-eyed and panting, flanked his Clan leader. "That was well run. You brought help just in time."

Rapidly he explained to Firestar how Birchpaw had found ShadowClan scent marks a long way inside the border, and how he and the rest of the patrol had come across the ShadowClan warriors stealing even more territory. "They thought we'd be too weak to stop them, after the badger attack," he added.

"Are you hurt?" Squirrelflight asked, pushing forward to reach Brambleclaw. Her green eyes were full of concern, and she stood with her pelt brushing his as she examined him for wounds.

Brambleclaw took a moment to check their injuries. To his relief, his wounded shoulder was no worse, though he had lost several pawfuls of fur from his flank, and his tail stung as if Russetfur had done her best to bite it off. Sandstorm had a clawed shoulder, and blood was trickling from a scratch on Thornclaw's throat.

"You'd better all come back to camp and let Leafpool see

to you," Firestar meowed.

"I'm fine," Brambleclaw insisted. "We need to set our scent markers along the proper border, just in case ShadowClan feel like having another try."

"I'm okay too," Sandstorm added. "But Thornclaw, I think you should go back. That throat wound looks as if it could turn nasty."

Thornclaw just nodded; he looked too battered to argue.

"Then I'll come with you," Squirrelflight mewed to Brambleclaw. Her eyes gleamed as she flexed her claws. "And if another ShadowClan cat dares to put one whisker across our border, I'll show them they just made the biggest mistake of their life!"

When Brambleclaw and his patrol returned to camp after renewing the scent markers, his ears pricked at the wails of outrage coming from the stone hollow. He slipped through the thorn tunnel to find Firestar standing on the Highledge, with the rest of the Clan gathered below.

"We should attack their camp!" Mousefur yowled.

Firestar twitched his tail for silence. "We won't attack them," he meowed. "You know as well as I do that we're not back to full strength yet. If we forced a battle and then lost, it would be a disaster."

True enough, Brambleclaw thought. Too many Thunder-Clan cats still bore the marks of the badgers' claws.

"But from now on," Firestar continued, "all patrols should look for signs of ShadowClan warriors on our territory."

Guessing he was about to bring the meeting to a close, Brambleclaw strode forward. "Firestar, there's something I want to say."

Firestar dipped his head, inviting him to speak.

Brambleclaw gazed around until he spotted Leafpool, sitting not far from the entrance to her den. "Leafpool, did you tell Littlecloud about the badger attack?" he demanded.

Leafpool looked confused. "Yes—I told him when we met at the Moonpool."

"And it never occurred to you that he would tell Blackstar? We wouldn't have had this trouble if you had kept your mouth shut."

The medicine cat sprang to her paws, her amber eyes flashing. "I had to tell Littlecloud how Cinderpelt died!" she exclaimed. "Did you think he wouldn't want to know what happened to her?"

Brambleclaw knew he had been too harsh. But the fight against ShadowClan had shaken him; of all cats Leafpool should know when she was putting her Clan at risk!

"Did you tell the other medicine cats *everything*?"

"Barkface already knew," Leafpool replied. "And Mothwing didn't come to the Moonpool." Eyes still gleaming angrily, she added, "Brambleclaw, it's none of your business *what* I say to other medicine cats."

"It is if you need to decide where your loyalties lie," he retorted. "You're a ThunderClan cat as well as a medicine cat."

Leafpool opened her mouth to reply, but said nothing. She

looked stricken, and Brambleclaw realized too late that he shouldn't have accused her so openly of being disloyal.

"How can you say something like that?" Squirrelflight gave him a glare that was fierce enough to scorch his fur. "Of course Leafpool is going to share important news like that with the other medicine cats. Her mentor *died*, for StarClan's sake! That matters to all medicine cats, not just ThunderClan."

"I know, but—" Brambleclaw tried to interrupt, but Squirrelflight swept on.

"It's not Leafpool's fault, or Littlecloud's, that Blackstar and his warriors were mousebrained enough to think they could invade ThunderClan. Besides, we've just shown them how wrong they were."

Brambleclaw couldn't meet her burning gaze. "I'm sorry," he muttered. "Sorry, Leafpool."

"Squirrelflight is right," meowed Firestar from the Highledge. "Blackstar is to blame for allowing his warriors to break the agreement we made. You can be sure of this: I'll take it up with him at the next Gathering." His eyes darkened and he bared his teeth in the beginnings of a snarl. "If he forces a war between our Clans, he'll find ThunderClan is ready and waiting for him."

CHAPTER 11

❧

The full moon floated high in the sky as Brambleclaw leaped off the end of the tree-bridge and onto the island. The mingled scents of many cats surrounded him, and he realized that the ThunderClan warriors were the last to arrive at the Gathering. Firestar was already racing away from the shore, signaling with his tail for his warriors to follow.

Brambleclaw bounded after him, along with Squirrelflight and Dustpelt and the other ThunderClan cats. Flattening himself to the ground, he thrust his way through the thick barrier of bushes and into the moonlit clearing dappled by the spreading branches of the Great Oak.

The tree was in full leaf now; Brambleclaw spotted patches of white fur where Blackstar crouched half hidden on a branch, and the gleam of bright eyes where Leopardstar gazed down on the cats below. Firestar padded up to the roots and nodded to Onestar, before the two remaining leaders clawed their way up the trunk and took their places in the branches.

Almost as soon as he set paw in the clearing, Brambleclaw was aware of a strange tension around him. Cats from other Clans were staring at the ThunderClan warriors as if they were judging them with new eyes; he caught a few murmurs, commenting on the wounds that were still visible on their pelts.

Brambleclaw looked around, hoping to see Stormfur and Brook. He spotted Mistyfoot, the RiverClan deputy, and skirted a group of excited apprentices to sit beside her. "Hi, there," he meowed. "How's the prey running in RiverClan?"

"Fine," Mistyfoot replied. "I hear you had trouble with badgers?"

Brambleclaw nodded, not really wanting to discuss the attack. "How are Stormfur and Brook? Are they here tonight?"

Mistyfoot shook her head. "Leopardstar didn't choose them to come, but they're both okay. It's good to see Stormfur again." Her blue eyes shone; Brambleclaw knew that her brother, Stonefur, had mentored Stormfur, while Mistyfoot had been his sister Feathertail's mentor. "I'm sorry he's only staying for a short time," she added.

Brambleclaw was surprised. Stormfur and Brook had spoken as if they meant to stay in RiverClan for good. They had clearly said something different to the RiverClan cats. Perhaps their welcome hadn't been as warm as Stormfur expected; the fact that they hadn't been chosen to come to the Gathering suggested that too.

"Are they leaving soon?" he asked.

"I don't know exactly when," Mistyfoot mewed. "But I'm sure they'll want to go back to the Tribe eventually, won't they?"

She dipped her head to Brambleclaw and walked away to

take her place on the roots of the tree beside Russetfur and Ashfoot, the ShadowClan and WindClan deputies. Brambleclaw's belly tightened as he looked at the space beside them, yet another reminder that ThunderClan had no deputy to stand with the others.

"Hi."

Brambleclaw jumped. With his eyes fixed hungrily on the three deputies, he hadn't noticed his sister, Tawnypelt, pad over to sit beside him.

"Hi," he mewed. "How are you?"

"I'm fine—but what about you?" The tortoiseshell she-cat sounded sympathetic. "I was really sorry to hear about the trouble you had with badgers."

"I'm perfectly okay, and so is the rest of the Clan." Brambleclaw spoke sharply; although Tawnypelt was his sister, she was a ShadowClan warrior too, and he wanted to make it quite clear that ThunderClan was strong. "We'd be even better if Leafpool hadn't been so quick to tell her medicine cat friends about how much trouble we're in."

Tawnypelt looked puzzled. "Leafpool?"

"She told Littlecloud when they met at the Moonpool."

"But ShadowClan didn't hear the news from him," Tawnypelt meowed. "He never even mentioned it."

"Where did you hear it, then?"

"Hawkfrost told Russetfur and Cedarheart when they saw each other patrolling the RiverClan border," Tawnypelt explained.

Brambleclaw stared at her in surprise. How had

WARRIORS: THE NEW PROPHECY: SUNSET 150

Hawkfrost known about the badger attack, when Mothwing hadn't been at the Moonpool meeting to hear Leafpool's news? Then icy claws gripped him: *he* had told Hawkfrost himself, in the dark forest with Tigerstar. Guilt swept over him. What was worse, he couldn't even apologize to Leafpool for accusing her, because then he'd have to explain what had really happened.

"Hawkfrost said he was just worried," Tawnypelt went on. "He wanted to know if our warriors had seen any ThunderClan cats and if you were badly wounded. He knew the badgers must have done serious damage."

Brambleclaw nodded distractedly. He needed to think this out. Were Hawkfrost's questions really prompted by concern, or could he have some other motive for passing on the news to ShadowClan? He must have known how Blackstar would react. He spotted Hawkfrost sitting with a group of RiverClan warriors, but before he could say good-bye to Tawnypelt and make his way over to him, Firestar yowled from the tree to start the meeting.

Silence spread through the clearing and all the cats turned to face the Great Oak, their eyes glimmering in the moonlight.

"Leopardstar, will you speak first?" Firestar offered.

The RiverClan leader rose to her paws, her dappled fur still half hidden by the leaves. "RiverClan has had an outbreak of greencough," she began. "Our elder Heavystep died, but thank StarClan no other cats were infected."

A murmur of sympathy spread throughout the clearing. Brambleclaw spotted Leafpool sitting beside Squirrelflight, and wondered why the young medicine cat looked so stricken. Surely she had no particular reason to grieve for a RiverClan elder?

"I have better news too," Leopardstar continued when the comments had died away. "Our medicine cat, Mothwing, has taken Willowpaw as an apprentice."

The golden tabby was sitting not far from the tree roots; Brambleclaw guessed that the small gray cat beside her must be the new apprentice. Willowpaw's green eyes shone with excitement, and she dipped her head awkwardly as her Clan called out, "Willowpaw! Willowpaw!"

Leopardstar had stepped back, gesturing with her tail for Onestar to speak next, when Hawkfrost rose to his paws at the foot of the tree. "One moment," he meowed. "Mothwing has some important news."

Leopardstar's eyes narrowed. Brambleclaw could see she hadn't expected this. Then she nodded. "Very well. Mothwing?"

The RiverClan medicine cat rose slowly to her paws. Brambleclaw thought she looked startled, as if she hadn't expected to speak. Curiosity clawed at him. What was Hawkfrost up to now?

"Mothwing?" Leopardstar prompted, when the medicine cat said nothing.

"It's about that sign," Hawkfrost reminded his sister, the tip of his tail twitching.

"Oh, yes . . . the sign." Mothwing sounded confused. "I—I had a dream."

"What's biting her?" Tawnypelt muttered into Brambleclaw's

ear. "She's a medicine cat, isn't she? She must have had loads of dreams before."

"Then tell us what the dream was," Leopardstar mewed frostily. "And explain why you decided to announce it at a Gathering instead of informing your Clan leader first."

"I didn't," Mothwing muttered, sounding more like a mutinous apprentice than a medicine cat. "That was Hawkfrost's idea."

"I think you'll understand when you hear the dream," Hawkfrost put in. "Go on, Mothwing."

"I—I'm not sure this is the right time to say anything," she stammered. "I may have been mistaken."

"Mistaken about what StarClan has told you?" Hawkfrost sounded shocked. "But you're our medicine cat. Only you can interpret the signs our warrior ancestors send to us."

"Yes, go on." Leopardstar sounded interested now. "Let's hear what StarClan told you."

Mothwing shot one more resentful look at her brother before she began to speak. Brambleclaw couldn't understand why she was so reluctant. He noticed Leafpool sitting as if she was carved from stone, staring at Mothwing with dismay in her eyes. Did she know what Mothwing was going to say? He wondered if the medicine cats had received a message from StarClan about something truly dreadful, something they didn't want to share with the rest of the Clans yet.

"I had a dream," Mothwing began, her voice so low that some cat yowled, "Speak up!"

She raised her head and began to speak more clearly,

though Brambleclaw could still see unwillingness in every hair on her pelt.

"I dreamed I was fishing in the stream," she meowed, "and I saw two pebbles that didn't belong there. They were a different color and shape from all the rest. They made the stream ripple and splash so it couldn't flow properly. Then the stream began flowing faster and faster, and—and the current carried the two pebbles away until I couldn't see them anymore. The stream looked just the same as always. . . ." Her voice trailed off and she stared down at her paws.

All around her cats looked puzzled, turning to one another and whispering questions. Brambleclaw couldn't understand why Leafpool looked so upset. He didn't see what was so terrible about the medicine cat's dream. It certainly didn't seem to apply to all four Clans.

"Well?" Leopardstar demanded, when Mothwing's silence had dragged on for several heartbeats. "What does the dream mean? What are StarClan trying to tell us?"

Before Mothwing could reply, Hawkfrost took a pace forward. "The meaning seems clear to me," he meowed. "Obviously there are two things in RiverClan that don't belong. Two things that don't fit in with the other cats. Like the stones, they need to be swept away so the stream can flow as it's meant to."

Urgent whispering broke out again, especially among the cats from RiverClan. All of them looked worried. The young warrior Voletooth spoke louder than the rest. "Does it mean Stormfur and Brook? Are they the two pebbles we have to get rid of?"

WARRIORS: THE NEW PROPHECY: SUNSET   154

Brambleclaw gulped. Did StarClan really believe Stormfur and Brook didn't belong in RiverClan?

Beside him, Tawnypelt dug her claws hard into the ground. She had made the journey to the sun-drown-place with the other cats; Stormfur was her friend, too. "If any cat lays a paw on him, I'll—"

"Keep out of this," Hawkfrost snapped at her. "It's RiverClan business. It sounds to me as if StarClan would be angry if we allowed Stormfur and Brook to stay."

"That's ridiculous!" Mistyfoot sprang up from her place on the oak root. "Stormfur is a RiverClan cat!"

"Stop!" Mothwing begged. "Hawkfrost, I told you I don't know—not exactly—what my dream meant. Please . . ." Her voice quavered. "Please don't read a meaning into it that might not be there. I'll wait for another sign from StarClan . . . next time it might be clearer."

Hawkfrost glared at her through narrowed blue eyes that gleamed like chips of ice. Above them on her branch, Leopardstar looked embarrassed and furious at the same time. Brambleclaw would bet a moon of dawn patrols that she would have stern words for Mothwing about showing such uncertainty in front of the whole Gathering.

"Yes," Leopardstar meowed tersely, "we won't do anything until you know more. And next time, Mothwing, make sure you come to me *first*."

Mothwing bowed her head and sat down again. Leopardstar said nothing more, just beckoned Onestar forward with her tail.

The WindClan leader rose from where he was sitting in the fork of a branch. "WindClan has little to report," he meowed. "Everything is peaceful, and we have plenty of prey." He sat down again, motioning to Firestar to speak next.

Brambleclaw felt a knot of tension in his belly as his Clan leader stepped forward. What would Firestar say about ShadowClan's attempt to steal part of their territory? And how could Blackstar justify his warriors' actions?

Firestar began by telling the story of the badgers' invasion, thanking Onestar for bringing the WindClan warriors to help. "Without you, many more cats would have died," he meowed.

Onestar waved his tail. "It was no more than we owed you."

"It grieves me to report the death of Sootfur," Firestar went on, "and the death of our medicine cat, Cinderpelt. Their Clan honors them."

Most cats seemed to know already that Cinderpelt was dead; murmurs of grief rippled through the clearing like wind through grass. She would be greatly missed, for every cat respected and admired her.

"Leafpool is now ThunderClan's medicine cat," Firestar continued. "She has done an excellent job in caring for our injured warriors, and they are all recovering. We have rebuilt our dens and the entrance barrier to our camp. The badgers have not weakened ThunderClan *in any way*."

He paused for a moment, letting his words sink in, then turned to where Blackstar was sitting among the thickly clustering oak leaves. His voice hardened. "Not long after the badgers attacked us, my warriors found a ShadowClan patrol setting scent markers well inside our territory. Have you anything to say about that, Blackstar?"

Brambleclaw couldn't help glancing at his sister.

"Don't blame me," she hissed under her breath. "I told Russetfur she was a stupid furball even to think of invading ThunderClan, but would she listen?"

Brambleclaw rested the tip of his tail lightly on her shoulder. "It's okay," he murmured. "Every cat knows *you're* an honorable warrior."

Blackstar rose, his huge black paws balancing confidently on the narrow branch. Firestar's accusation didn't seem to bother him. "Since the weather has grown warmer," he began, "Twolegs have brought their boats and water-monsters onto the lake at the edge of our territory. Their kits play in our woods and frighten the prey. Their monsters use the small Thunderpath and leave their reek in the air."

"That's true," Leopardstar put in. "They're in RiverClan territory too, leaving their rubbish everywhere. I've even spotted them here, on this island."

"They lit a fire," Mistyfoot added.

Brambleclaw's fur stood on end, making him shiver. He could just remember the terrible fire that had swept through the old ThunderClan camp when he was a kit. It wasn't hard to imagine hungry scarlet flames devouring the whole of the island, turning the Great Oak to a heap of brittle, charred sticks. What if the Twolegs built fires on the lakeshore, too?

ThunderClan had been safe so far, for no Twolegs had been seen on their side of the lake, but how long would that go on?

"What's that got to do with stealing our territory?" Squirrelflight called out.

"When we set the boundaries of our territories, back in leaf-bare," Blackstar went on, "no cat knew what effect Twolegs would have on us. We never expected to see so many of them. ShadowClan is finding it harder to catch enough prey—"

"And so is RiverClan," Leopardstar mewed.

Blackstar dipped his head to her. "So it seems to me the only solution is to rearrange the boundaries. ThunderClan and WindClan should give up some of their territory to ShadowClan and RiverClan."

As ThunderClan and WindClan broke out into yowls of protest, Onestar leaped to his paws, his neck fur bristling. "Never!"

Firestar waved his tail for silence, but it was some time before the clamor in the clearing died down. Brambleclaw spotted Cloudtail on his paws, hissing defiance at Blackstar, while Dustpelt lashed his tail and Squirrelflight let out an outraged caterwaul. Crowfeather of WindClan stood with his neck fur bristling, his claws digging into the ground; beside him, Webfoot was yowling furiously at Blackstar. Brambleclaw felt hot fury run through his body from ears to tail-tip, but he forced himself to keep silent and wait to hear how his Clan leader would reply.

"We can't agree to that, Blackstar," Firestar meowed as soon as he could make himself heard. "As the boundaries stand now, each Clan has the sort of territory they're used to. You can't expect RiverClan cats to hunt on bare hillside like WindClan."

"We can learn," Hawkfrost insisted. "So much has changed since we came here, surely we can manage new hunting techniques?"

"I'd like to see you try," Crowfeather shot back at him. "It's not as easy as it looks. I know WindClan would find it difficult to hunt in thick woodland like ThunderClan."

"Well, you *would* know about that," Webfoot sneered.

"That's enough," Onestar hissed, glaring down at Webfoot.

Webfoot shot Crowfeather a resentful look, as though it were the dark warrior's fault that he had received a public rebuke from his leader. Brambleclaw realized that some of Crowfeather's Clanmates hadn't forgiven him for being ready to abandon his Clan for the sake of the ThunderClan medicine cat.

"No cat wants trouble among the Clans," Hawkfrost meowed, gazing up at the four leaders. "But ThunderClan and WindClan must be reasonable. What if it was your territory that was being invaded by Twolegs?"

While he spoke, Tawnypelt leaned close to Brambleclaw with a small snort of contempt. "I met Hawkfrost on the border once when I was patrolling with Blackstar and Oakfur," she told her brother. "He was *so* concerned about the Twolegs, saying what a pity it was that the boundaries couldn't be changed. I shouldn't wonder if that was what put the idea into Blackstar's head in the first place."

Brambleclaw stared at her. Surely that couldn't be true? Hawkfrost would never encourage ShadowClan to attack ThunderClan. What he said could only have been a warrior's natural anxiety that his Clan would have enough prey. And Blackstar certainly didn't need any encouragement to attack another Clan.

"Hawkfrost isn't like that," he protested, only to meet a glint of disbelief in Tawnypelt's green eyes.

"Really? And I suppose you're going to tell me that birds don't nest in trees," she responded dryly.

Disturbed, Brambleclaw turned away. He had missed Firestar's response, and now Hawkfrost was speaking again, looking up challengingly at the ThunderClan leader.

"Firestar, are you sure you're not being too stubborn about the Clan boundaries? I've often heard you say that StarClan decreed there should be four Clans in the forest. How can that be, if two of them starve?"

He glanced across at Brambleclaw as if he expected his half brother to support him. Brambleclaw met his gaze, then looked away. Hawkfrost's argument sounded persuasive, but Brambleclaw couldn't believe that ShadowClan and River-Clan were in danger of starving, not in greenleaf when prey was plentiful. At most, they should wait a season or two before they discussed changing the boundaries, to discover exactly what changes the Twoleg invasion made to the territory around the lake.

"You don't look like you're starving to me, Hawkfrost," Firestar meowed.

"RiverClan needs more territory!" Hawkfrost hissed. "If

you don't give it to us, we'll take it anyway."

"Hawkfrost, you don't speak for RiverClan!" Mistyfoot snapped at him.

At the same moment Tornear of WindClan leaped to his paws. "Just try it, if you want a shredded pelt!"

Hawkfrost whirled on him, unsheathing his claws, and his Clanmate Blackclaw shouldered his way through the crowd to join him, his neck fur bristling and his tail fluffed up to twice its size. Three or four WindClan warriors, Crowfeather among them, jumped up to support Tornear.

"Stop!" Mistyfoot ordered, leaping from the root where she sat. "This is a Gathering! Have you forgotten that?"

One or two cats, including Crowfeather, stepped back, but most ignored the RiverClan deputy's order. Brambleclaw spotted Cedarheart and Rowanclaw from ShadowClan on their paws as well, claws extended. Dustpelt and Thornclaw faced them, spitting defiance. As Brambleclaw stared in horror, the ShadowClan cats leaped at his Clanmates; all four rolled on the ground in a shrieking bundle of fur.

"No!" Brambleclaw yowled. "Remember the truce!"

He hurled himself forward, trying to thrust his way between the battling cats, aware that all around him more fights were breaking out. Fastening his teeth into Cedarheart's shoulder, he tried to haul him off Dustpelt, but another cat landed on his back and knocked him off his paws. As Brambleclaw went down in a sea of fighting warriors, he heard Firestar's voice raised in a furious yowl.

"Stop! This is not the will of StarClan!"

CHAPTER 12

Leafpool flattened herself to the ground as fighting surged across the clearing. Horror froze her limbs and made her fur bristle. She couldn't believe that any cat would dare to break StarClan's truce. Then she remembered her dream of sticky scarlet waves washing up on the lakeshore. It was true! There could be no peace until blood had spilled blood.

The clearing was full of spitting, clawing cats. Leafpool tried vainly to spot Crowfeather, terrified that he would be badly injured. She heard her father call out, but his words of command were lost among the screeches of the rival Clans.

"StarClan help us!" she prayed.

As if the spirits of her warrior ancestors had heard her plea, a shadow fell across the clearing and the silver wash of moonlight faded. Looking up, Leafpool saw that a cloud had drifted over the moon, hiding it completely. The shrieks of battle began to fade, or changed to yowls of terror. Some cats stopped fighting and crouched motionless, staring at the threatening sky.

"Look!" It was too dark to see which cat had cried out, but Leafpool recognized the voice of Barkface, the WindClan medicine cat. "StarClan are angry! This must be a sign that the boundaries should stay where they are."

In spite of the authority with which the old medicine cat spoke, several voices were raised in screeches of protest. Firestar's yowl drowned them all out. Leafpool could just make him out in the glitter of starshine, standing on an overhanging branch.

"Barkface is right!" he called. "StarClan have shown their will. The boundaries will stay as they are. The Gathering is over!"

"The next RiverClan cat to raise a paw will answer to me," Leopardstar added, balanced commandingly on her branch. "Every cat go home, *now*."

"That goes for WindClan too," meowed Onestar, raking the clearing with a furious gaze.

Blackstar let out a hiss. "This isn't over," he snarled.

"No, it's not!" another cat called out; peering into the darkness, Leafpool could just make out the massive tabby shape of Hawkfrost. "We'll discuss it again at the next Gathering."

That's not your *decision*, Leafpool thought. Hawkfrost was already behaving as if he were Clan leader, and he wasn't even a deputy. Her mistrust of him made her fur stand on end, even more when she wondered just how much influence he had over his half brother, Brambleclaw.

To her relief, the last of the battle was over. Cats broke apart, licking their wounds and glaring at each other. The leaders leaped down from the Great Oak and began to gather their Clans together.

Leafpool struggled through the shifting mass of cats, all

trying to find their Clanmates for the journey home. She couldn't leave without speaking to Mothwing.

Heavystep was dead! When Leafpool had decided not to take Mudfur's message about the catmint to RiverClan, she had comforted herself with the thought that Mothwing would find it anyway, or that the elder would recover without it. *It's my fault he died.*

And what about the dream Mothwing had reported? The dream of two pebbles in a stream? If she had really started to believe in StarClan and receive signs from them, Mudfur wouldn't have needed Leafpool to take his message. He could have told Mothwing himself. But he hadn't—which meant Mothwing had lied in front of the whole Gathering.

Leafpool couldn't imagine why her friend would do that. What quarrel did she have with Stormfur and Brook, that she would try to drive them out of RiverClan? Leafpool remembered the tension between Mothwing and Hawkfrost, and how keen Hawkfrost had been for his sister to speak out in front of every cat. Could this have been *his* idea? And if Hawkfrost had tried to coerce Mothwing into lying, why would she go along with him? She was a loyal medicine cat, and had refused to tell Leopardstar about any of Leafpool's dreams before now because she hated lying.

Pushing determinedly between a couple of WindClan warriors, Leafpool spotted Mothwing crouching in the shelter of a root of the Great Oak with Willowpaw, as if she had been protecting her apprentice from the battle. But before Leafpool could reach her friend, Hawkfrost appeared; his fur was ruffled but he didn't seem seriously hurt, even though Leafpool had spotted him in the thick of the fighting.

He stalked toward his sister with a look of murderous fury in his eyes. "You mousebrained idiot!" he spat. "You nearly ruined everything."

Mothwing gave Willowpaw a swift glance. "Go and find Mistyfoot," she told her apprentice. "Tell her I'll be along in a moment."

Willowpaw sprang up and scampered off, glancing back nervously at Hawkfrost as she went. Leafpool shrank into the shadows; she hated eavesdropping on her friend, but she had to know what was going on.

"You let me down," Hawkfrost growled. "You promised me you would tell the Gathering about that dream. We would have been able to get rid of those mangy interlopers right away. Now we'll be lucky if any cat believes you next time you open your mouth!"

"Well, why should they?" Mothwing rose and faced her brother, her eyes filled with misery. "We both know it was a lie. I've never had any dreams from StarClan."

Hawkfrost let out a snort of disgust. "But no cat knows that, do they? That's just between you and me. They would have listened to you if you hadn't stood there mewling like a kit. 'I can't be sure . . . I need a clearer sign!'" He mimicked his sister's tones viciously. "I could rip your fur off for this."

"I don't care!" Mothwing retorted. "You made me lie in front of the whole Gathering. That's worse than losing fur."

Leafpool tensed, flexing her claws in case she had to spring to Mothwing's defense. But she could see that Hawkfrost was making a massive effort to control himself. The fur on his shoulders began to lie flat, and his voice was quieter as he continued. "It wasn't really lying. You know it's best if Stormfur leaves. I deserve to be deputy, but if he stays, Mistyfoot will make sure he succeeds her."

"He's a good warrior—"

"Don't tell me that!" Hawkfrost hissed. "He was willing to leave his Clan once, so how do we know he won't leave us again? I've always been loyal to RiverClan, and I deserve to be deputy! You know that, and StarClan know that, so why not make sure the whole Clan knows it too?"

"Because my duty is to my Clan, not to you," Mothwing replied calmly.

Hawkfrost drew his lips back, baring his teeth. "This isn't what we planned!" he snarled. "I didn't help you become a medicine cat for this. What do you think would happen if your precious Clanmates knew the truth about you?"

This time Mothwing did flinch, taking a pace back and turning her head away. Leafpool felt as if she had stepped into an icy torrent, a powerful rush of fear that could sweep her off her paws. How could Hawkfrost have helped Mothwing become a medicine cat? Mudfur had chosen her with the guidance of StarClan. What was "the truth" that could force Mothwing to lie for her brother?

Suddenly Mothwing looked her brother squarely in the eyes. "Do what you want, Hawkfrost," she meowed. "I've tried to be a good medicine cat and to serve my Clan as best

I can, but I can't go on lying. You were made deputy once before, when the Twolegs trapped Mistyfoot, and you'll be made deputy again—if you don't do anything stupid." She paused and added more sharply, "If you tell the truth about me, you won't look so good yourself, will you?"

Hawkfrost raised his forepaw. Leafpool braced herself to rush out and help her friend, but then the tabby warrior spun around and stalked away. He looked exactly like his father, Tigerstar, had in Leafpool's dream.

Mothwing slumped down under the tree as if all her strength had been drained. Leafpool padded up to her and gently touched her shoulder with the tip of her tail. She wasn't sure what to say. She wondered if she should reveal that she had overheard the quarrel. Leafpool was still trying to figure out exactly what she had learned from it. Hawkfrost obviously knew that his sister didn't believe in StarClan. But Leafpool knew it too, and had long since forgiven her. Mothwing tried so hard to be a good medicine cat, even without StarClan to strengthen and guide her.

"Mothwing, it's me," she began falteringly. "I'm so sorry that Heavystep died."

Mothwing looked up, her blue eyes pools of regret. "I searched and searched for catmint, but I couldn't find any," she mewed.

Words of comfort choked in Leafpool's throat. *How can I be responsible for reading the signs for two different Clans?*

"Leafpool?" Mothwing's asked. "Is there something you're not telling me?"

"It's my fault!" Leafpool blurted out. "Mudfur came to me in a dream and told me where you could find catmint. But I was caring for a sick kit, and I didn't have time to come. Anyway, I didn't know if you would believe me," she added.

"Oh, I would," Mothwing replied quietly. "I would never doubt the strength of your faith."

Curiosity nagged at Leafpool, sharp as a thorn in her pad. "Then how do you explain my dreams, if you don't believe they come from StarClan?"

Mothwing paused to think. "Well, you could have known about the catmint anyway. Perhaps Brambleclaw or Squirrelflight spotted it when they first explored around the lake. One of them could have told you, except you've forgotten that's how you know."

Leafpool didn't remember any conversations about catmint; besides, the first exploration of their new territory had taken place in leaf-bare, when not much was growing. "I don't think so," she murmured uncomfortably.

"I'm sure you're not lying," Mothwing assured her. "Just that you remember stuff in dreams that you've forgotten when you're awake. *You* believe in StarClan, so that's how the memory appears to you."

Leafpool shook her head, confused. "Whatever. I'd better tell you where the catmint is, anyway. Go to—"

"Mothwing!" Leopardstar's voice came from the edge of the clearing. "Are you going to sit there gossiping all night?"

"Coming!" Mothwing called, springing to her paws. "I must go. Leopardstar's angry enough with me as it is."

"Follow the Thunderpath away from the lake!" Leafpool called after her friend as she headed toward the RiverClan leader.

But Mothwing gave no sign that she had heard before vanishing into the darkness.

Sighing, Leafpool got up and followed her, scrabbling her way through the ring of bushes until she emerged on the shore of the island. Cats were already making their way across the tree-bridge, slipping and scrambling in the darkness with a desperate need to get away from the disastrous Gathering. Others clustered around the torn-up roots, waiting for their turn to cross.

Padding toward them, Leafpool couldn't stop worrying about Mothwing. She hadn't managed to ask her friend about the pebble dream, or the confrontation with Hawkfrost, or find out why he thought he was responsible for Mothwing becoming a medicine cat. Perhaps it was just as well, she thought. Mothwing might not have wanted to answer.

Leafpool glanced around for her own Clanmates. Clouds still covered the moon, and when she first saw movement in the shadows she couldn't tell which cat it was. Then a familiar scent flooded over her. She stopped dead. *Crowfeather!*

Her paws urged her to flee, but the WindClan warrior had already spotted her. He stepped forward; his lean body was faintly outlined by starlight, his dark gray pelt turning him to another shadow.

"Hi, Crowfeather," Leafpool mewed awkwardly. "How are things in WindClan?"

"Fine." Crowfeather's voice was curt.

Leafpool doubted that was true. During the Gathering it had been obvious that some of his Clanmates still blamed him for leaving WindClan to be with her. "I'm sorry if you're having problems . . ." she began.

"Problems?" Crowfeather shrugged. "I told you, everything's fine."

Being so close to him was making Leafpool's heart pound. She couldn't bear to see him so brittle and tense when she knew how much pain he must be hiding. "I never meant to hurt you," she murmured.

"We chose to be loyal to our own Clans." Crowfeather's voice was quiet and steady, but Leafpool could hear agony in every breath. "It's better if we don't see each other anymore."

Leafpool knew he was right, but pain stabbed her more deeply than a badger's fangs. Couldn't they even be friends?

Crowfeather held her gaze for a heartbeat longer, then walked away, down the shore to the few cats who still waited on this side of the tree-bridge.

"Good-bye," Leafpool whispered, but he didn't look back.

"But look at your poor tail!" Daisy wailed.

Berrykit turned circles in his nest outside Leafpool's den, trying to see the stump of his tail. He didn't seem bothered by it at all. "I'm just like a warrior now!" he boasted. "Every warrior has wounds. It shows how brave they are."

Daisy flinched. "Can't you do something?" she begged Leafpool.

Leafpool suppressed a sigh. "Not even StarClan can grow back a tail," she meowed.

"Oh, I know, and I'm so grateful to you for everything you've done. I thought he would die for sure. I just wish that some cat could make him see that it wasn't a clever thing to do, and he mustn't ever, *ever* do it again."

"You know that already, don't you, Berrykit?" Leafpool prompted.

Berrykit stopped circling and sat up among the bracken, his eyes bright. Leafpool could hardly believe he was the same kit who had lain there wailing from pain and fever, not so many days before.

"Well . . ." he mewed. "I know it was wrong, but camp's so *boring*! I want to go and see the lake."

Daisy let out a squeal of terror. "You'll drown if you go there!"

"You must wait until you're apprenticed," Leafpool told him. "Then your mentor will take you all over the territory."

Berrykit gave an excited wriggle. "Can I be apprenticed *now*? Can Brambleclaw be my mentor?"

Leafpool suppressed a *mrrow* of amusement. It was good to see that Berrykit's terrible experience hadn't dampened his spirit.

"No, you're too young," she replied. "And Firestar decides who your mentor will be."

Berrykit looked disappointed, but soon brightened up again. "Then can I go back to the nursery? I bet Hazelkit and Mousekit can't think of any good games when I'm not there."

Daisy sighed. "You know, he's right," she meowed to Leafpool. "It's been so peaceful, you can't imagine!"

"In another day or two," Leafpool promised the kit. "You need to get a bit stronger first. Rest instead of bouncing around the whole time."

Berrykit immediately curled up among the ferns, managing to wrap his bit of tail over his nose. His eyes still gleamed, watching his mother and Leafpool.

"Thank you so much, Leafpool," Daisy meowed, rising to her paws. "ThunderClan is really lucky to have you as their medicine cat."

Saying good-bye to Leafpool and Berrykit, she left, passing Brightheart, who brushed past the bramble screen with a leafy bunch of catmint in her jaws.

"There!" she exclaimed, after dropping the bundle near the entrance to Leafpool's den. "Don't you just love the smell of catmint?"

Leafpool murmured agreement, even though the scent was making her belly lurch. She thought it would remind her for the rest of her life of the message she had failed to deliver to RiverClan, and the death of Heavystep.

"Leafpool," Brightheart began, "is it okay if I go back to warrior duties now? Only Ashfur still needs his wounds checked every day. There's really not much for me to do here."

Leafpool looked at her in surprise. She had grown used to having the ginger-and-white she-cat's help this past moon. It was hard to remember how much she had resented her when

Cinderpelt was alive, and she realized that she wasn't looking forward to being medicine cat all alone. But Brightheart was right—there was no reason to keep her from her regular duties anymore.

"Sure," she replied. "I'm really grateful for everything you've done."

Brightheart dipped her head, looking slightly embarrassed. "I've enjoyed it," she meowed. "I've learned a lot—from you as well as Cinderpelt. I'll come back to help anytime you need me."

"Thanks, Brightheart."

Leafpool watched her friend vanish around the brambles, then turned and picked up the catmint to take it into her den. Her supplies of herbs and berries were looking untidy; she began to sort through them, making sure everything was in its proper place.

She noticed that some of her juniper berries were shriveled and started to examine them to pick out those that could still be used. A pang of grief shook her as she remembered Cinderpelt doing the same, showing Leafpool which berries were too old and could be discarded. Now she couldn't even pick up Cinderpelt's scent in her den; the air was too thick with the scents of herbs, moss, and stone. It was as though her mentor had never been, as though individual medicine cats didn't matter, only the skills that were passed down the generations.

If that's true, then what I feel doesn't matter either, Leafpool told herself firmly. *I will serve my Clan as best I can.*

It might be time to think about training an apprentice of her own; perhaps one of Sorreltail's kits, when they were old enough. She hoped she would find a cat as good as RiverClan's Willowpaw. Leafpool remembered how helpful the new apprentice had been when many RiverClan cats got sick from the Twoleg poison. *Are StarClan pleased with Mothwing's choice of apprentice?* Leafpool wondered. Surely they must be. But how could Mothwing teach Willowpaw to be a proper medicine cat, when she didn't believe in StarClan? How could she show her apprentice how to interpret signs and dreams from StarClan, when she never received any herself?

Thinking of Mothwing reminded Leafpool of the golden cat's bitter quarrel with her brother at the end of the Gathering the night before. What was going on between them?

Just then, she heard an excited squeal behind her. She turned to see Hazelkit and Mousekit frisking around outside the den, and opened her mouth to warn them not to disturb Berrykit, who was sleeping quietly now. Before she could speak, a butterfly fluttered into the den, high above her head, and the two kits came leaping after it. They scrambled past Leafpool, scattering the carefully sorted juniper berries, and letting out little joyful mews as the butterfly flew just out of reach of their paws.

"Hey!" Leafpool exclaimed. "Watch where you're going."

The two kits took no notice, chasing the butterfly out into the open air again. Sighing, Leafpool padded after them, checked that they hadn't disturbed Berrykit, then poked her head out from behind the brambles to make sure that they weren't getting into more trouble. She was just in time to spot Hazelkit and Mousekit pursuing their prey behind some thornbushes that grew close to the rock wall.

"Kits!" she muttered. They were likely to get stuck in there, or even try climbing the wall. She set off after them, hearing a yowl of triumph as she whisked around the bristling thorn branches.

Inside the thicket, the two kits were looking down at the butterfly, lying dead on the ground with one bright speckled wing torn off.

Hazelkit looked up as Leafpool appeared. "I got it," she boasted. "I'm going to be the best hunter ever!"

Leafpool felt her pelt prickle as she gazed down at the butterfly's torn wing. Somehow the sight was familiar, though she couldn't recall ever looking closely at a dead butterfly before.

Before she found an answer, Mousekit interrupted her thoughts. "The tortoiseshell cat showed the butterfly to us. She told us we could chase it."

Leafpool was puzzled. "Do you mean Sorreltail?" Her friend was the only tortoiseshell cat in the Clan just now, and she was still in the nursery with her kits.

"No, another tortoiseshell cat." Hazelkit sounded a bit scornful, as if she thought Leafpool was being mousebrained. "She called us out of the nursery. I've never seen her before, but she smelled like ThunderClan."

"And she knew our names," Mousekit added.

The prickling in Leafpool's pelt swept over her again, much stronger than before. "Where is she now?" she asked carefully.

Mousekit shrugged. "I dunno. Gone."

Losing interest, the two kits scampered back into the clearing. Leafpool stayed where she was, staring down at the torn butterfly. There was only one tortoiseshell cat who could have visited the kits like that and vanished with no other cat seeing her. She must have sent them after the butterfly for a reason, but what was it? *Spottedleaf, what are you trying to tell me?* Leafpool patted the remains with one paw, snagging her claw on the torn wing. A butterfly's wing . . . a moth's wing . . . Mothwing!

Standing frozen with her eyes wide open, Leafpool saw a scene unfold in her mind: Hawkfrost with a moth's wing pierced on one claw, slipping through the shadows in the old RiverClan camp and carefully laying it outside Mudfur's den. Leafpool shivered. RiverClan had accepted the old medicine cat's choice of Mothwing to be his apprentice because he found a moth's wing at the entrance to his den. He had taken it to be a sign that StarClan approved his choice . . . but had Hawkfrost *put it there on purpose?*

Leafpool was sure Mothwing hadn't known the sign was false until much later; she could still remember the wonder in her friend's eyes when she first spoke about the moth's wing. She must have been devastated when Hawkfrost told her, but her commitment to serving her Clan as a medicine cat would have forced her to keep the secret.

Leafpool shook the butterfly's wing from her claw. She wanted to believe that she was wrong, that no cat would do such a dreadful thing, not even Hawkfrost. But she couldn't deny what Spottedleaf seemed to be telling her; it explained too much that had been hidden in shadows until now.

At the Gathering, Hawkfrost had threatened Mothwing with revealing a secret, and he had said that he helped her become her Clan's medicine cat. He was obviously holding the secret over her, forcing her to invent messages from StarClan to help him gain power in RiverClan.

Leafpool had always doubted whether Hawkfrost was trustworthy, but there was no room for doubt now. Her claws scored the ground in front of her; she wished she could sink them into Hawkfrost's fur. But fighting him would solve nothing. Leafpool considered challenging him at a Gathering, but that wouldn't work either. After all, she had no proof. And accusing him would mean denouncing Mothwing, too. If RiverClan knew the moth's wing sign had been false all along, would they let her continue as their medicine cat?

Spottedleaf, show me what to do. You must have told me this for a reason.

Then she remembered Willowpaw. The young apprentice must believe in StarClan, like all Clanborn cats. Perhaps she would be able to take over those parts of Mothwing's duties that involved StarClan. If Mothwing knew that, it might give her courage to stand up to her cruel brother. Willowpaw couldn't solve the problem altogether, but she might help.

But how can I show her? Leafpool asked herself. *She's Mothwing's apprentice, not mine. How can Willowpaw learn about StarClan when her mentor doesn't believe in them?*

CHAPTER 13

Ferns brushed Brambleclaw's pelt as he raced through the forest of shadows toward his meeting with Tigerstar. Strength flowed through him now that his shoulder was fully healed, and his paws itched to show off his fighting skills to his father and Hawkfrost. He was sure Tigerstar would be pleased by what he had to tell.

Reaching the clearing, he came to an abrupt halt in the shadow of a thorn tree. His father was sitting on the rock in the center, his head bent to speak to a slender tortoiseshell warrior.

Tawnypelt! What's she doing here?

Curiosity sank its claws into his heart. With his belly fur brushing the ground, he crept around the clearing until he could get closer to the rock in the shelter of a clump of long grass. With his ears pricked, he could just make out the other cats' voices.

"I've told you before," Tawnypelt snapped. "I don't want any part of your ambitions. I have my own plans."

Brambleclaw tensed. No cat spoke like that to Tigerstar!

But the massive tabby didn't seem angry. His tone was

pleased as he replied, "You have my spirit, Tawnypelt, and you're a brave warrior. But there are times when spirit becomes foolishness. Don't throw away what I can offer you. I can make you a leader."

"Fox dung!" Tawnypelt snarled. "I'm a loyal ShadowClan cat. If I'm ever made deputy or leader it will be because I have earned it myself—and because my Clanmates and StarClan wish it. You're twisting the warrior code to get what you want, just like you did when you were alive."

A growl rumbled in Tigerstar's throat. Brambleclaw caught the gleam of unsheathed claws and his heart pounded in fear for his sister.

But Tawnypelt held her head high. "You don't frighten me," she meowed calmly. "And I don't want anything you can give me."

Spinning around, she stalked across the clearing and straight into the clump where Brambleclaw crouched in hiding.

She let out a hiss of surprise. "What are you doing here?"

"I could ask you the same thing," Brambleclaw retorted, peering through the grass stems to make sure Tigerstar hadn't spotted him. To his relief, the huge tabby had turned away.

Tawnypelt's eyes were cold as she gazed at her brother. "You've been here before, haven't you?" she meowed. "You think he can give you power. Have you got thistledown for brains? You know what he did when he was alive."

"That was then." Brambleclaw twitched his ears uncomfortably. "Now he's just helping us to become good warriors—me and Hawkfrost. We train together. Tigerstar teaches us stuff."

"I bet he does!" Tawnypelt let out a snort of contempt. "Brambleclaw, *think*, will you? You're an amazing cat already; you're brave and loyal and you have tremendous warrior skills. Why do you need Tigerstar?" Without giving her brother a chance to reply, she swept on. "We've spent a long time trying to break free of our father's legacy. When we were kits in ThunderClan, most cats didn't trust us. Our Clan *leader* didn't trust us, for StarClan's sake! That's why I left to join ShadowClan. Tigerstar welcomed me, but then I saw what his leadership was like, and I was *glad* when Scourge killed him! I don't want any part of his blood. I've survived just fine without him, and so have you."

"Maybe," Brambleclaw mewed defensively. "But he died before I had a chance to know him. Maybe this is my chance now."

His sister's eyes narrowed. "That's not what's happening here and you know it." She let out a sigh, part weariness, part exasperation. "Brambleclaw, I think you'd make a fantastic leader. But only if you go about it the right way." She touched her nose to his ear in farewell. Her voice was more affectionate as she added, "Think about it, mousebrain."

Brambleclaw watched her stalk away. He wondered if Tigerstar had summoned his other daughter Mothwing to meet him here. He doubted it; Mothwing was a medicine cat, and all her dreams would be spent with StarClan. Besides, medicine cats couldn't lead their Clans; their paws were set on another path.

Part of Brambleclaw wanted to listen to Tawnypelt. He knew Squirrelflight would say the same thing, if she knew about these meetings. But there was nothing wrong with accepting his father's help, he argued with himself; every warrior thought about leading their Clan one day. And if StarClan approved of his relationship with Squirrelflight, surely that meant they knew about his ambitions as well? He crushed down the small voice of his conscience and stepped out into the clearing to greet Tigerstar.

Brambleclaw woke with a start at the sound of a piercing cry from outside the warriors' den. He sprang to his paws, his neck fur bristling.

"Keep your fur on," Spiderleg mewed from his mossy nest. "It's only Ferncloud. She was in here just now, looking for that horseplace cat."

"Daisy? Is she missing?"

"Well, Ferncloud says she wasn't in the nursery," Spiderleg explained. "But she must be around here somewhere. She'd be the last cat to go wandering off. She's hardly left the hollow since the badger attack."

That was true, which made it all the more unsettling. Brambleclaw pushed his way out through the thorns to see Ferncloud standing in the middle of the clearing, with Cloudtail beside her.

The white tomcat was awkwardly stroking her shoulder with his tail, trying to calm her down. "She can't be far away," he comforted her. "Remember how scared she was when Berrykit wandered off."

"But the kits have gone too," Ferncloud pointed out fretfully. "She must have taken them away deliberately."

As Brambleclaw padded toward her, another yowl rose from behind him. He turned to see Sorreltail bounding over from the apprentices' den.

"Whitepaw and Birchpaw haven't seen them either," she panted. "I don't think they're in the camp."

Brambleclaw stood for a moment, thinking. The sun had barely risen above the tops of the trees. If Daisy had left the camp she must have done so as dawn was breaking. What could have been important enough to draw her out into the forest, when she was so frightened of what she believed was lurking there?

"What happened?" he asked Ferncloud.

The gray she-cat's eyes were wide with distress. "I went into the nursery with some fresh-kill for Daisy and Sorreltail," she explained. "The nest was still warm, but Daisy and the kits were gone."

"We've searched the whole camp," Sorreltail added, lashing her tail. "We'll have to send out patrols to look for them."

"Well, *you* won't be going," Ferncloud told her, brushing her muzzle against Sorreltail's shoulder. "You need to stay with your kits."

"Brackenfur's with them," the young tortoiseshell queen mewed. "I want to help look for Daisy."

"Yes, but—"

Ferncloud broke off as a flash of flame-colored fur

announced the appearance of Firestar from his den on the Highledge. The Clan leader ran down the rocks and across the clearing toward them.

"What's going on?"

Ferncloud explained; before she had finished speaking, Brambleclaw spotted Dustpelt emerging from the thorn tunnel, at the head of the returning dawn patrol. Squirrelflight, Sandstorm, and Brightheart were with him.

Brambleclaw beckoned them over with his tail. "Did any of you see Daisy while you were out?"

"Yes, she slipped out of camp just behind us," Dustpelt replied, looking puzzled. "Why—is there a problem?"

"She's gone!" Ferncloud pushed her way through the cats to his side. "Why didn't you stop her?"

"For StarClan's sake!" Dustpelt hissed. "I thought she was going to make her dirt. Why would I want to stop her?"

"Were the kits with her?" Cloudtail asked.

"I didn't notice them," Dustpelt replied.

"I did," meowed Sandstorm. "They followed her out."

"Berrykit was complaining about something," Squirrelflight added, "but we didn't stop to listen."

"It's obvious what's happened." Firestar spoke with deep concern, and every other cat turned to look at him. "Daisy has been talking about taking her kits back to the horseplace to live. Berrykit's being caught in that trap must have made up her mind. As soon as he was fit to travel, she left."

"No!" Cloudtail sounded outraged. "After the badger attack, I *promised* that the Clan would look after her."

"And then her kit lost half his tail in a fox trap," Firestar pointed out. "I'm sorry, Cloudtail. I know you did your best." His green eyes looked regretful. "For a while, I really thought it was going to work. Her kits were settling in well." He twitched his ears. "I'd better tell the Clan."

He bounded off toward the rocks beneath the Highledge. Cloudtail and Brambleclaw exchanged a glance; Cloudtail's blue eyes were sparking with anger.

"Is that it?" he meowed. "Isn't Firestar going to do anything to find Daisy?"

Firestar's yowl sounded before Brambleclaw could reply. "Let all cats old enough to catch their own prey join here beneath the Highledge for a Clan meeting."

Brambleclaw waited, his claws flexing in and out, while the rest of the Clan emerged from their dens. Leafpool came out from behind her screen of brambles. Brightheart darted across to her and began mewing quietly, obviously telling her what had happened. Mousefur and Goldenflower appeared from beneath the hazel bush, one on each side of Longtail. Mousefur's eyes were sharp with curiosity as the cats found a place to sit near the rockfall.

At the sound of Firestar's yowl, Brackenfur poked his head out of the nursery, then bounded across to Sorreltail. "What are you *doing*?" he demanded, covering her ears with anxious licks. "Look at you, you're shaking with exhaustion! You shouldn't be wearing yourself out like this."

Sorreltail leaned against his shoulder. Brambleclaw could see that she was quivering, though whether it was from tiredness or distress at losing Daisy, he couldn't tell.

"I thought I'd be able to find her," she mewed softly. "But she must have gone back to the horseplace."

"Then there's nothing else you can do," Brackenfur told her. "Come back to the nursery. The kits are all wailing their heads off. They're hungry, and I can't feed them!"

"Why didn't you *say* so?" Sorreltail whisked around and headed for the nursery, her tail high as if her weariness was forgotten.

Squirrelflight slipped past Sandstorm and Dustpelt to join Brambleclaw. "If only I'd stopped to talk to Daisy this morning, I might have persuaded her to stay."

"It's not your fault," Brambleclaw murmured, fighting down his own disappointment. He had always doubted that Daisy had the makings of a true Clan cat, but the loss of her kits was disastrous. *What about my apprentice?* He guessed from what Squirrelflight said that Berrykit hadn't wanted to go. That just proved the kit's spirit; thanks to Daisy, a fine warrior had been lost to the Clan.

"Daisy must have decided that she and her kits belong in the horseplace," Firestar was explaining. "We'll all miss her and her kits, but we have to respect her wish to leave."

"That's mousebrained!" Cloudtail burst out.

Firestar gazed down at him, the tip of his tail twitching, but Cloudtail didn't seem bothered about showing disrespect toward his Clan leader.

"Daisy is no safer in the horseplace than she is out here," he protested. "She came here in the first place because she was worried the Twolegs would take her kits away. Besides, there hasn't been a sniff of a badger in the territory since the attack. I think we should go and bring her back."

Squirrelflight let out a soft hiss. "Look at Brightheart," she murmured, flicking her tail in the direction of the scarred she-cat. "I bet she doesn't want Daisy to come back."

Brambleclaw took a swift glance. Squirrelflight was right. Brightheart's expression was a mixture of anger and distress.

"Cloudtail," Firestar began, "we can't force Daisy to do anything. She—"

"We should at least go and talk to her," Cloudtail interrupted. "Then we could make sure she got back safely."

"I agree," Brambleclaw meowed, taking a pace forward to stand beside the white warrior. He knew he might regret it for the rest of his life if he didn't make an effort to retrieve Berrykit. "If it's okay with you, Firestar, I'll go with Cloudtail."

Squirrelflight twitched her whiskers in surprise. "I seem to remember some cat making rude remarks about kittypets joining the Clan."

A wave of embarrassment flooded over Brambleclaw. "Yeah, well, I'm sorry about that," he replied. "But ThunderClan needs more kits, and Daisy's would have made good warriors."

"Very well," Firestar meowed. "You can go, but if Daisy says she wants to stay where she is, come straight back and leave her in peace. Best wait until sunset," he added. "There won't be so many Twolegs around."

"Great!" Cloudtail's tail shot up in delight.

Brambleclaw glanced across at Brightheart again, in time to see her vanish behind the bramble screen into Leafpool's den.

The sun was going down over the lake, turning the water scarlet, as Brambleclaw and Cloudtail padded down to the shore. The pine forest in ShadowClan's territory was a black outline against a sky the color of blood. Brambleclaw hoped that wasn't a bad omen for their journey to the horseplace.

They crossed WindClan territory swiftly, staying within two tail-lengths of the water's edge. Brambleclaw scented a patrol, but as the sun slipped below the trees the moorland slopes were shadowed, and they saw no sign of any cats.

Darkness was gathering by the time they arrived outside the horseplace, and clouds had filled the sky, covering the moon. Cloudtail halted, tasting the air, while Brambleclaw peered through the Twoleg fence. At the far side of the field was the Twoleg nest, a dark mass with one yellow light gleaming. Brambleclaw hoped they wouldn't have to go near it.

Much closer was another, smaller building with no lights showing. Brambleclaw remembered passing it in daylight, and thinking it looked a bit like the barn where Barley and Ravenpaw lived.

"Over there, maybe?" he suggested, gesturing with his tail.

"Yes, Daisy said they lived in a barn," Cloudtail replied. "Let's go."

He flattened himself to the ground and crept under the

fence. Brambleclaw followed, feeling his pelt prickle as he entered this strange Twoleg territory. He padded after the blur of Cloudtail's white pelt in the gathering darkness, then froze as he heard the high-pitched cry of a horse. A heartbeat later the ground shook with the thudding of hooves.

Fighting panic, Brambleclaw whipped his head back and forth, trying to see where the noise was coming from. Then two horses burst out of the night almost on top of him, a whirl of glossy pelts and gleaming hooves. Their eyes were rolling back; something had spooked them into flight.

Cloudtail took off with a yowl of terror. Brambleclaw dashed after him. "No! This way! Keep together!"

He wasn't sure where the barn was anymore. The horses had disappeared into the darkness again but he could still hear the thunder of their hooves. He and Cloudtail might run straight into them and be pounded into the grass.

Then he spotted a pale shape dashing across the field. It was Smoky, the horseplace tomcat who had fathered Daisy's kits.

"Follow me!" Smoky gasped, skidding to a halt and spinning around to run back the way he had come. "Quick!"

Brambleclaw and Cloudtail raced in his paw steps. Brambleclaw caught another glimpse of the horses, storming past with manes flying. Then they were gone, and Smoky was slowing down, leading them up to the wall of the barn.

"In here," he meowed.

The barn was built of piled-up stone, with a door made of strips of wood. There was a narrow gap at the bottom; Smoky slipped inside, followed by Cloudtail, and Brambleclaw squeezed after them, finding it hard to fit his shoulders through the small space. He stood panting, trying to catch his breath and letting his fur lie flat again.

Inside, the barn was almost completely dark. It was smaller than Ravenpaw's home, but Brambleclaw could just make out familiar stacks of hay and straw. Their scent filled the air, along with the smell of mice and cats. Relief swept over Brambleclaw as he distinguished the well-known scents of Daisy and all three kits; at least they had made it back safely.

"Well, I never expected to see you here," Smoky mewed.

"What do you want?" Another cat had come up beside Smoky, gazing at the two forest cats with curious eyes. Her pelt was gray and white like Daisy's; Brambleclaw wondered whether they might be littermates.

"This is Floss," Smoky told them.

"I'm Cloudtail and this is Brambleclaw." The white warrior flicked his tail at his Clanmate. "We've come to see Daisy."

He broke off at the sound of heavy footsteps outside the door of the barn. Brambleclaw's heart started to pound again as it opened. *Twolegs!* He and Cloudtail flashed a glance at each other, and dived for the cover of the straw bales.

As he pulled the end of his tail into a tiny space hardly big enough to contain him, Brambleclaw heard an amused *mrrow* coming from Smoky. "There's no need to hide. It's only the Nofurs."

Brambleclaw managed to wriggle around in his cramped

hiding place so that he could peer out. At first he could hardly see anything because a bright yellow light was shining straight in his eyes. Then the beam shifted, and he realized the dark shape behind it was carrying the light in its paw. In the other forepaw it held a bowl like the ones Brambleclaw had seen in a Twoleg nest on his journey to the sun-drown-place. The Twoleg shook it and something rattled inside. He heard Floss meow, "Dinner! And about time, too."

The Twoleg put the bowl down in front of the two horse-place cats and went out again, taking the glaring light with it.

Once the door had closed, Brambleclaw crept out, feeling slightly embarrassed. Smoky turned toward them, while Floss plunged her face into the food bowl.

"You've come to see Daisy?" He sounded surprised. "I didn't think you'd want to see her again, once she left."

"We like Daisy a lot," Cloudtail mewed.

"Yes, we wanted to make sure she and the kits are okay," Brambleclaw added.

Before he had finished speaking, shrieks of delight erupted from the far corner of the barn. Daisy's three kits dashed out, wild with excitement, and hurled themselves at Brambleclaw and Cloudtail.

"You came, you came!" Berrykit squealed. "I said you would." He crouched down in front of Brambleclaw, his fur fluffed up and his teeth bared in a pretend growl. "I chased a mouse on the way here," he boasted.

"Did you catch it?" Brambleclaw asked.

Berrykit looked downcast. "No."

"Never mind, you will next time."

The young kit brightened up, waving the stump of his tail. "I'm going to catch all the mice in this barn!"

"Leave some for us!" Hazelkit protested. She had charged into Cloudtail, knocking him off his paws, and now she was scrambling over him. "We want to catch mice too. We want to be apprentices like Birchpaw and Whitepaw."

"Are they warriors yet?" Mousekit asked.

"Warriors!" Cloudtail let out a *mrrow* of laughter. "Come on! You've only been away for a day."

"It feels like moons!" Berrykit wailed. "It's *boring* here."

"But it's safe." Brambleclaw looked up at the sound of Daisy's voice. The she-cat padded over to join them, sweeping her tail around to flick Hazelkit on the shoulder. "Get off at once! Is that any way to show respect for a warrior?"

Hazelkit bounced to the floor, allowing Cloudtail to get up and shake scraps of straw from his pelt. "Hi, Daisy," he meowed.

Daisy halted a couple of tail-lengths away and steadily held his gaze. "I know why you're here. Please don't ask me to come back to the forest. I've made up my mind."

"But every cat misses you, and your kits," Cloudtail mewed. "ThunderClan needs new warriors. And you know we'll do everything we can to make you feel at home."

"*We* want to go back," Berrykit added, nudging his mother. Mousekit and Hazelkit squeaked their agreement.

Daisy shook her head. "No, you don't. You're too young to understand."

"I don't think that's true," Brambleclaw put in. "When you brought them into the forest they were so young that they won't be able to remember much about this place. Living in our camp is all they know. They're almost Clanborn, like the other warriors. Of course they want to go back."

Daisy let out a long sigh. "It can't possibly work. I've always lived close to Nofurs. I'm used to regular feeding times and a roof over my head. You warriors *despise* that way of life."

"We don't despise you, Daisy," Cloudtail promised quietly.

"But everything in the forest is so strange!" Daisy protested. "I don't understand half of what's in that warrior code of yours. I don't feel like I could ever belong."

Her eyes, fixed on Cloudtail, were huge with sorrow. Understanding struck Brambleclaw like a flash of lightning. She was in love with the white warrior! And she must know that there would never be any cat for him but Brightheart. He let out a purr of sympathy. Perhaps Daisy was right to leave. It must hurt to see Cloudtail every day and know he would never be more than her friend.

Cloudtail didn't seem to realize the strength of Daisy's feelings. "I still think you should come," he argued. "There'll always be a place for you. And every cat misses you. I know Brightheart does."

Daisy winced. Brambleclaw thought Cloudtail was being a little optimistic in mentioning Brightheart. "But I'm so useless out there," she meowed. "I feel like every cat in the Clan is fed up with looking after me."

"That's not true." Brambleclaw tried to reassure her.

"You've helped Sorreltail with her kits, haven't you?"

"Don't worry, I'll look after you. I'll protect you from the badgers. And I'll teach you the warrior code," Berrykit promised his mother, the stump of his tail quivering. "When I'm an apprentice, I'll tell you everything my mentor teaches me."

"So will we," Hazelkit added. "*Please* take us back! We want to be warriors and catch our own prey. We don't like that yucky Twoleg food."

Mousekit flexed tiny claws. "We want to learn to fight."

Smoky, who had listened in silence until now, padded up to Daisy and brushed his muzzle against hers. "Maybe you should go," he mewed.

Daisy turned toward him, her eyes questioning and a little hurt. "I thought you missed me."

"I did. I missed all of you. But it's obvious that our kits aren't going to settle here. They've done nothing but talk about the forest ever since they set paw in the barn." The gray-and-white tomcat blinked affectionately at her. "You could always come back yourself once they're fully grown."

"Or you could come to the forest too," Cloudtail suggested to him, making Brambleclaw flinch.

"Me!" Smoky's eyes opened wide with astonishment. "Live in the open in the pouring rain and have to catch every mouthful of food? No thanks! Besides," he added, "it sounds way too crowded. I'd never remember all your names." He glanced back at the other she-cat, who had finished eating and was washing her face with one paw. "And I couldn't leave Floss all by herself, could I?"

Berrykit nudged Daisy again. "Can we go back? Can we?"

Daisy looked at her kits. "You really want to go live in the cold and wet with no proper food in a forest full of badgers and traps?"

"Yes!" All three kits bounced up and down, eyes blazing with excitement. "Yes! Yes!"

"Well, I suppose . . ."

Berrykit let out a high-pitched yowl of triumph. He and his littermates scurried around in a circle, their tails held high. "We're going back to the forest! We're going back to the forest!"

"That's great!" Cloudtail looked nearly as pleased as the kits. "These three are just what ThunderClan needs. They'll be fine warriors one day."

Brambleclaw spotted a flash of pain in Daisy's eyes. Cloudtail seemed more pleased that the kits were coming back than that their mother was coming with them.

He touched her shoulder with his tail. "Ferncloud and Sorreltail will be really glad to see you," he mewed. "They were both terribly upset when they found you'd gone."

Daisy blinked at him, a faint glow in the depths of her eyes. "They're good friends," she murmured.

"When can we go?" Berrykit demanded, halting in front of his mother. "Now?"

"No, not now." Cloudtail stepped forward before Daisy could answer. "It's dark out there. We'll go in the morning."

"You're welcome to spend the night here," Smoky offered. He swept his tail toward the food bowl. "Help yourselves."

"Okay, thanks." Cloudtail padded over to the bowl and plunged his muzzle into it.

Brambleclaw remembered hearing about how the white warrior used to sneak off to eat food the Twolegs gave him, until they made him a prisoner and shut him up in their nest. He had come back to the Clan when Firestar helped him to escape, but he obviously still had a fondness for kittypet food.

"Not for me, thanks," he meowed to Smoky with a polite dip of his head. "I'll catch my own."

"Show us how," Berrykit pleaded, at the same time Mousekit asked, "Can we watch?"

"You don't learn how to hunt until you're apprenticed," Brambleclaw told them. "But you can watch if you like."

The three kits crouched down together, gazing at him with huge eyes as he tasted the air. Now that they were quiet, the whole barn seemed to be filled with the scuffling and squeak-ing of mice. Brambleclaw soon spotted a plump one, nibbling on a seed at the foot of a pile of straw bales. Very cautiously, not letting his claws scrape on the stone floor of the barn, he crept toward it. *This is one mouse I can't afford to miss*, he thought as he pounced and swiftly bit it on the back of the neck.

All three kits let out a squeal of excitement as he turned back with his limp prey in his jaws. Berrykit dropped into the hunter's crouch, waggling his haunches just as Brambleclaw had done. He almost had the position exactly right. *He'll be a great hunter*, Brambleclaw thought.

"Here," he meowed, after dropping the mouse in front of the three kits. "You can share that one, if your mother says it's okay. I'll catch another."

Daisy gave her permission, shaking her head slightly as she watched her kits eat the fresh-kill. A moment later she turned away and joined Cloudtail at the food bowl.

Brambleclaw soon caught himself a second mouse. By the time he had finished eating, Daisy had gathered her kits together and vanished with them into the straw. Cloudtail clawed at the stiff stems until he had pulled enough out of the bale to make a nest. "I'll be glad to be back in camp," he mewed. "This stuff isn't nearly as comfortable as moss."

As Brambleclaw made a nest for himself, he had to agree. The straw poked into him, and a chill seeped up from the stone floor underneath. He curled up and tucked his nose into his tail, missing the warriors' den, its air warmed by the breath of his Clanmates. Most of all he missed Squirrelflight, her sweet scent and the soft touch of her fur. Sleep was a long time in coming, but out here in the horseplace, far from his Clan, no dreams disturbed it.

CHAPTER 14

Leafpool curled up in her nest of moss and bracken, but she shifted around for a long time before she slept, feeling as though ants were crawling through her pelt. How could she get in touch with Willowpaw to tell her about StarClan?

When at last she drifted into unconsciousness, she opened her eyes and found herself at the top of a slope overlooking the lake, not far from the place where Brambleclaw had sat, staring across the water. There was no sign of the tabby warrior tonight. Instead, as she brushed through the long grasses, each blade outlined in silver, there was a different cat waiting for her by the lake. The frosty glimmer of StarClan shone in its fur as it gazed out over the water.

Spottedleaf? Leafpool quickened her pace until she was racing through the undergrowth to the water's edge. But when she reached the shore and saw the StarClan cat more clearly, she realized it was Feathertail, Stormfur's sister, who had died in the mountains on the way back from the sun-drown-place.

The beautiful silver-furred tabby let out a welcoming purr. "I hoped you would come, Leafpool," she mewed. "We have a task tonight, you and I."

"What's that?" Leafpool asked, her pelt prickling with excitement.

"StarClan want me to help you visit Willowpaw in her dreams," Feathertail explained.

Leafpool stared in astonishment at the StarClan warrior. Each medicine cat dreamed his or her own dreams of StarClan—they never appeared in each other's. She had assumed that the only way she could meet Willowpaw was in the waking world. "Can that be done?"

"Yes, but very rarely, and only in times of greatest need. Follow me."

Rising, she brushed her muzzle lightly against Leafpool's, then bounded away along the lakeshore. Leafpool raced after her. Moonlight shone all around her and she felt as though her paws were lighter than the wind. She skimmed across the stream that marked the WindClan border without even feeling the water touch her paws. Was this what it felt like to be a warrior of StarClan, she wondered—as though she could run forever, leap into the sky, and toss the moon like a shining leaf?

The whole journey might have lasted for several seasons, or no more than a heartbeat. The horseplace flickered past, and Feathertail slowed down as the two cats drew closer to the RiverClan camp. They crossed the stream and padded silently up the bank on the other side; Leafpool set her paws down as delicately as if she were stalking a mouse, even though she knew this was only a dream and she couldn't wake the sleeping RiverClan warriors.

Mothwing's den was in a cave hollowed out by the stream on the far side of the camp. As Feathertail led the way toward it, Leafpool spotted the small gray shape of Willowpaw curled up in a nest of moss just outside.

Feathertail flicked her ear gently with the tip of her tail. "Willowpaw," she breathed. "Willowpaw, we need to speak to you."

The small gray cat's ears twitched and she curled up more tightly. Feathertail nudged her with one paw, softly repeating her name. This time Willowpaw blinked and looked up.

"Do you mind?" she mewed crossly. "I was chasing this huge fat mouse and I was just going to sink my claws in it when—" She broke off, gazing from Leafpool to Feathertail and back again. "I'm still dreaming, aren't I?" Her eyes stretched very wide. "You're Leafpool from ThunderClan, and you must be a warrior from StarClan." Looking dismayed, she slapped the tip of her tail over her mouth. "I'm so sorry I snapped at you," she mumbled through her fur.

Feathertail's blue eyes glimmered with amusement. "Don't worry, dear one. You'll soon get used to visits in your dreams, now that you're a medicine cat apprentice."

Willowpaw scrambled to her paws. "Welcome to RiverClan," she meowed formally. A puzzled look crept over her face. "You have RiverClan scent," she mewed to Feathertail, "but I don't know you."

"My name is Feathertail," the silvery she-cat replied. "You weren't even born when I left on the journey to the sun-drown-place."

Willowpaw's eyes filled with awe. "And you never came back," she whispered. "You gave your life to save your friends and the Tribe in the mountains. I've heard the story. RiverClan will never forget you."

Feathertail blinked affectionately and let her tail rest for a moment on Willowpaw's shoulder. "Enough of that, dear one," she mewed. "Tonight we're here to show you something."

"Me?" Willowpaw exclaimed. "Are you sure? Do you want me to fetch Mothwing?"

Leafpool and Feathertail exchanged a glance. Leafpool wasn't sure how much Willowpaw understood. Did she realize that her mentor had no contact with StarClan?

"No, this sign is for you," Feathertail assured her. "You can tell Mothwing about it when you wake up. Now you must come with us."

The young apprentice's paws danced in the grass. "Are we going a long way?" she asked. "As far as the sun-drown-place?"

"Not this time," Leafpool told her. "Just to the edge of your territory."

Remembering what Mudfur had told her about where to find the catmint, she took the lead, crossing the stream and heading across RiverClan territory to the small Thunderpath. Drawing closer to it, she could pick up the reek of Twoleg monsters and more smells from the Twolegs who came to sail their boats on the lake, almost drowning the scent markers of both Clans. Even in a dream, she was cautious as she emerged from the undergrowth on the edge of the Thunderpath, but everything was dark and silent. All the Twolegs must have gone back to their nests when darkness fell.

With Willowpaw right behind her and Feathertail bringing up the rear, Leafpool padded along the Thunderpath, away from the lake. When she crossed the border scent markers she still hadn't found the Twoleg nests Mudfur had told her about, but as she followed the Thunderpath around a wide curve, she spotted a light in a hollow not far ahead: a reddish light that didn't come from moon or stars.

Her pelt prickled as she thought of fire, but she could not feel any heat or hear the crackle of burning. There was no scent of smoke either, but as she drew in air, she tasted the faintest possible trace of catmint.

"Down there," she murmured over her shoulder.

She padded on more cautiously, and realized a few moments later that the light came from a hole in the side of a Twoleg nest. It was shining behind a pelt that gave it a reddish color. Looming up ahead of her was the dark shape of a Twoleg fence. Gathering herself, she leaped up and balanced herself on the top. Willowpaw scrambled up beside her, while Feathertail remained below.

The smell of catmint was stronger now. Willowpaw had picked it up too, and her eyes glinted in triumph. "Catmint!"

"That's right," Leafpool mewed. "A very useful herb for medicine cats, and quite hard to find, unless there are Twolegs to grow it for us."

Willowpaw nodded. "Yes, it cures greencough. I wish we'd had some when Heavystep was ill. Mothwing and the patrols looked all over the territory."

Leafpool swallowed another pang of guilt. "Tomorrow she can fetch some from here," she told Willowpaw. "But be sure to warn her to wait until after dark, when there aren't so many Twolegs around."

Still balanced on top of the fence, she tasted the air again for any likely dangers. "No kittypets or dogs," she meowed with relief. "Willowpaw, do you know what dogs smell like?"

The apprentice shuddered. "Yes, some of the Twolegs who come to the lake bring their dogs with them. They smell yucky."

"Well, I don't think there are any here, but tell Mothwing to check again when she comes for the catmint. And now we'd better be getting back," she added.

Leaping down, they rejoined Feathertail and made their way back through RiverClan territory to the camp.

"Sleep deeply now," Feathertail told Willowpaw as she settled in her nest again. "See if that fat mouse is still waiting."

Willowpaw looked up at the two cats. "I'm so glad you came," she mewed. "It's great being a medicine cat. I can't wait to tell Mothwing!"

Leafpool and Feathertail left her curled up again and set off around the lake to ThunderClan territory. This time they padded along more slowly.

"Thank you, Leafpool," Feathertail meowed. "You've done well tonight." She paused beside the stream that formed

ThunderClan's border with WindClan. Her gaze locked with Leafpool's. "I spoke with Spottedleaf," she mewed. "She told me about the butterfly sign."

Leafpool felt a shiver run through every hair on her pelt.

"You understand, don't you?" the StarClan cat continued. "You know what that means for Mothwing?"

"I guessed that Hawkfrost must have put the moth's wing outside Mudfur's den," Leafpool confessed, the words threatening to choke her. "I don't know how I'm going to face Mothwing now. What can I say to her?"

"Say nothing." Feathertail's voice was quiet, but filled with certainty. "Mothwing must learn to live with it."

"Then . . . then does this mean Mothwing can't be a medicine cat anymore?" Leafpool stammered. "She cares so much—"

"I know," Feathertail interrupted with a soothing purr. "The whole of StarClan knows. Mothwing has proved her skills and her loyalty many times over. It is StarClan's will for her to stay where she is and teach Willowpaw all she knows."

"But she *doesn't* know about StarClan," Leafpool protested. "How can Willowpaw learn to understand signs if Mothwing can't tell her?"

"That will be your task." Feathertail touched Leafpool's shoulder with the tip of her tail. "You have no apprentice yet—and no need for one," she added. "You will be here to serve your Clan for many seasons more. So will you sometimes visit Willowpaw in RiverClan and speak to her at the Moonpool? You can teach her everything she needs to know, without having to walk in her dreams again."

"Yes, of course." Leafpool felt her paws tremble with relief. StarClan wanted Mothwing to stay as RiverClan's medicine cat. That meant she was safe from her brother's threats to reveal the truth. All of Willowpaw's medicine cat training would be taken care of: Mothwing would pass on her healing skills, while Leafpool could teach her to interpret the signs from StarClan.

"But what about Hawkfrost?" she asked.

"His fate is in the paws of StarClan too," Feathertail replied. "Spottedleaf led the kits to the butterfly because she felt it was time for you to know the truth. She believed she could trust you to use your knowledge wisely and accept the responsibility of helping Willowpaw."

Leafpool bowed her head. "I'll try."

Feathertail led her through the forest toward the stone hollow. The moon still rode high, washing every fern and blade of grass with silver. The trees rustled in a faint breeze, setting light and shadow dancing around Leafpool's paws. She had no idea how much time had passed, though she guessed that in the waking world the sky would be paling toward dawn.

Outside the thorn tunnel, Feathertail stopped. "I must leave you here," she murmured, touching noses with Leafpool. "Dear friend, there are great changes ahead, but you can trust me to be with you always."

"Great changes?" Leafpool echoed in dismay. "What do you mean?"

But Feathertail had already slipped away. For a heartbeat

her pelt gleamed silver in the shadows, and then she was gone.

Uneasy once again, Leafpool gazed up through the trees to the frosty glitter of Silverpelt, as though her faraway warrior ancestors could give her an answer. No words came to her, but through the branches overhead she spotted the three stars she had seen in her earlier dream. Tiny though they were, they glowed more strongly than any other star in Silverpelt, throbbing with pure white light. Leafpool still didn't know what they meant, but somehow she knew they were shining directly on her, and she felt safe again, sure that whatever happened, StarClan were watching over her.

Leafpool woke with a start to feel tiny paws pummeling her fur. Her eyes flew open to meet Berrykit's excited gaze, no more than a mouse-length away.

"We're back!" he announced. "Cloudtail and Brambleclaw came to fetch us."

Leafpool scrambled up from the nest of bracken. She had overslept; already the sun was climbing toward sunhigh. Warm yellow rays poured down into the hollow, soaking into her fur.

"I'm so glad to see you," she meowed. "Did you have a good journey back? Is your mother okay?"

"She's fine," Berrykit told her. "Hazelkit and Mousekit and I looked after her all the way, so she wasn't scared."

"She must be tired, though," Leafpool commented, "going all that way twice in two days." The kits ought to be tired too, though Berrykit looked as if he was bursting with energy. "I'll bring her something to help her get her strength back."

Slipping inside her den, she snagged a couple of juniper berries on her claws, then rejoined Berrykit, who immediately dashed out into the main clearing. Leafpool followed just in time to see Daisy and the other two kits disappearing into the nursery. Berrykit pelted across to join them, while Leafpool followed more slowly.

She had almost reached the entrance to the nursery when she heard Brightheart exclaim, "No! Cinderkit, come back here!"

A heartbeat later the fluffy gray kit tottered out into the open, blinking blue eyes in the sunlight. Brightheart emerged after her, swooped down, and seized her gently by the scruff. She carried the adventurous kit back into the nursery without noticing Leafpool.

The medicine cat's pelt pricked. It was bad luck that Brightheart had chosen to visit Sorreltail at the very moment that Daisy returned. It couldn't be easy for the ginger-and-white she-cat to encounter the cat she thought of as her rival, especially when she might have been hoping that Daisy had gone for good.

Leafpool hovered at the entrance to the nursery, wondering whether to go straight in, or come back another time. Before she could decide, she heard Daisy's voice just inside the thicket of brambles.

"Brightheart, I'm glad you're here. There's something I wanted to say to you."

"What?" Brightheart sounded wary.

"The reason I left . . . well, it was only partly because of the danger out here. I've been worried about the kits since the badger attack, but I'm their mother—I'd worry about them wherever we were. Mostly it was because I—I don't have any cat in the Clan that I'm close to. Not like you and Cloudtail."

There was a heartbeat's tense silence. Leafpool started to back away, and Brightheart's reply, when it came, was too low and indistinct for her to hear it.

"No," Daisy responded more clearly. "Cloudtail is very kind to me, but he would be kind to any cat in trouble. He's a good warrior and he loves you very much."

Another pause, until at last Brightheart mewed softly, "I know." Her voice shook as she added, "Thank you, Daisy. I'm really glad you decided to come back. ThunderClan needs more young cats, and your three will make excellent warriors."

Daisy replied something in a low voice and a moment later Brightheart left the nursery, passing Leafpool with a nod. Leafpool tried to look as if she had only just arrived. She couldn't miss the joyful look in Brightheart's good eye, and prayed to StarClan that she and Cloudtail would become as close as they had once been, and that Daisy would turn out to be a friend to them both.

When Leafpool left the nursery after giving Daisy the juniper berries, Brightheart was crouched beside the fresh-kill pile, nibbling a vole. Cloudtail was in the center of the clearing, calling Thornclaw and Rainwhisker for a hunting patrol.

Leafpool beckoned him with her tail. When he padded across to her, she suggested, "Why don't you ask Brightheart to go with you? You haven't hunted together for a long time."

Cloudtail looked puzzled.

Mousebrain! Leafpool thought. "You remember Brightheart?" she prompted him. "Your mate? Whitepaw's mother?"

The white warrior's expression cleared. "Oh, I see what you mean! Right, I'll do that," he meowed. "Good idea, Leafpool."

He swung around and bounded toward his mate. Leafpool saw him speak to Brightheart; then the she-cat rose to her paws and their tails twined together. Pelts brushing, they headed for the thorn tunnel, leaving Thornclaw and Rainwhisker to dash after them.

"I think some cat interfered." An amused voice spoke behind Leafpool.

Leafpool whirled around to see her sister watching her. "Squirrelflight, you frightened me out of my fur! What do you mean 'interfered'?"

Squirrelflight rested her tail on her sister's shoulder. "In a good way, I mean. It's about time some cat opened Cloudtail's eyes to what Brightheart needs from him." She glanced around the clearing, where some cats were dozing in the warm sunlight, while others put the finishing touches to the newly repaired dens. "Life's good," she mewed with satisfaction. "Maybe now we can have a bit of peace."

Right now, it did look as if ThunderClan's troubles were over. Remembering her sense of security as she gazed at the three tiny stars in her dream, Leafpool opened her mouth to agree when a strange darkness clouded her sight. The reek of blood rose around her and she felt sticky scarlet waves wash over her paws. An unfamiliar voice rasped the words of the prophecy in her ear, low and sinister and insistent:

Before all is peaceful, blood will spill blood, and the lake will run red. . . .

CHAPTER 15

❦

On the day after Daisy's return, Brambleclaw emerged from the warriors' den to see Berrykit wrestling with his brother and sister outside the nursery. He padded across to watch; Berrykit cuffed Mousekit over the head and sent the smaller kit sprawling in the dust.

"Well-done," Brambleclaw mewed approvingly. "But if Mousekit were your enemy, would you stand there staring at him? Mousekit, what are you going to do?"

"Attack him!" Mousekit sprang up, shook rumpled fur, and lunged at his brother.

"Dodge!" Brambleclaw directed Berrykit. "Trip him as you go by."

Berrykit flashed out a paw, but Mousekit sidestepped and landed a blow on his ear. Berrykit crouched, snarling, and pounced on Mousekit's tail.

"Well-done, both of you," Brambleclaw meowed. "You'll both make good fighters one day."

Leaving the kits to scuffle, Brambleclaw turned away and saw Firestar in the center of the clearing, listening to a report from the dawn patrol. A moment later the patrol separated in search of rest and fresh-kill, and Firestar beckoned with his tail for Brambleclaw to join him.

"Dustpelt reports Twolegs on our border," he began.

Brambleclaw felt his neck fur begin to rise. "They're not building another Thunderpath, are they?"

"No, nothing like that," Firestar replied. "Dustpelt says there are some green pelt-things propped up on sticks, like little dens, in the clearing between us and ShadowClan. Twolegs have been sleeping in them."

Brambleclaw's eyes widened. "That's mousebrained! Why would Twolegs come and sleep here when they have perfectly good nests of their own?"

Firestar shrugged. "Why do Twolegs do anything? I'm not too worried about the green pelt-things," he went on. "They don't sound permanent. What bothers me is how ShadowClan are going to react. We all know they're looking for an excuse to take some of our territory."

Brambleclaw flexed his claws. "I'd like to see them try."

"I'd rather settle this peacefully if we can," Firestar told him. "Listen, I want you to see exactly what's happening in the clearing, then go around the lake and find out what the Twolegs are up to on the border between RiverClan and ShadowClan. I want to know how serious the disturbance is, and how likely it is that Blackstar and Leopardstar will demand more territory at the next Gathering."

Brambleclaw knew that made sense. As the weather grew warmer, more and more Twolegs had appeared, roaring across the lake in their water-monsters or bobbing around in the boats with white pelts. The air was filled with buzzing, and when the wind was in the right direction the cats could hear the yelps and yowls of Twolegs even in the stone hollow.

"Do you think the Twolegs will come here next?" he asked Firestar.

"They might," Firestar replied seriously. "But I think the forest comes too close to the water's edge in our territory for them to land their water-monsters. That might keep them away—but that's part of what I want you to find out. Have a good sniff around, and *don't* get caught. I don't want ShadowClan or RiverClan to know you've set paw on their territory."

"They won't," Brambleclaw promised, and set off with a wave of his tail. He felt his head swim with pride as he brushed through the thorn tunnel. Firestar must trust him a lot to have chosen him for such an important mission! Tigerstar was right: he could achieve great things by following the warrior code and being loyal to his Clan.

He cut through ThunderClan territory until he came to the clearing. The stream bordered it on one side, then veered away into ShadowClan territory. The tabby tom crouched at the water's edge, screened by a clump of bluebells, and peered across.

The green pelts Firestar had mentioned were dotted all across the clearing. Since at this point the stream marked the border, they were actually in ShadowClan territory.

"ShadowClan is welcome to them," he muttered. But he wasn't so sure; Blackstar might see the Twoleg invasion as another reason to extend his territory.

Dustpelt seemed to be right that the Twolegs were sleep-ing under the pelts. At least, as Brambleclaw watched, several Twolegs crawled in and out, and Twoleg kits were playing between the little dens, tossing something brightly colored from one to another, and yowling in delight when they caught it.

A shiver went through Brambleclaw when he spotted flame spurting up from the opposite side of the clearing. Were the Twolegs really mousebrained enough to light a fire among the trees? Then he noticed that the fire was encased in some shiny Twoleg thing that seemed to stop it from spreading. He could smell the strange, acrid scent of Twoleg food drifting across, mixed with the tang of charred wood.

Brambleclaw watched the scene for a while longer, but nothing else seemed to be happening. At last he eased back from the water's edge, being careful to tread silently and stay out of sight until he was well away from the clearing. He had learned all he could from these Twolegs; now it was time for the more dangerous part of his mission.

A mouse scuttled across open ground just in front of him; Brambleclaw flashed out a paw and pinned it down, killing it and devouring it quickly. He was about to leave his own ter-ritory, and he wouldn't risk stealing prey from a rival Clan.

He followed the stream down toward the lake, tasting the air for the scent of ShadowClan patrols. The border markers were strong and fresh here, but the scent of cats was fading; he guessed that a patrol had been that way at dawn.

When he reached the edge of the trees, there were no ShadowClan cats visible along the lakeshore. Brambleclaw waded cautiously across the stream, his pelt prickling. Blackstar had agreed only grudgingly to allow cats from other Clans to cross his territory; besides, Firestar had ordered Brambleclaw not to let ShadowClan know about this mission.

Though he kept well within two tail-lengths of the water's edge, he felt as though every one of the dark pine trees concealed the piercing gaze of a ShadowClan warrior, waiting to leap out and challenge him. He crept along with his belly fur brushing the pebbles, taking advantage of every rock and hollow to hide and pausing every few paw steps to taste the air.

One Twoleg boat was already out on the lake, floating along quietly with a huge white pelt spread above it. Brambleclaw could see a couple of Twolegs inside it, leaning over to trail their forepaws in the water. As he drew closer to the border with RiverClan another Twoleg thing—more like a monster than the boat with its pelt—roared away from the half bridge, leaving a scar of bubbling white foam on the surface of the lake. Brambleclaw sprang onto a rock to keep his paws dry as waves slopped up onto the shore.

The reek of Twoleg monsters was stronger here, drowning any scent of cats. Brambleclaw's gaze flickered uneasily along the line of trees, alert for any movement, but he saw nothing. Perhaps ShadowClan had withdrawn deeper into the forest to stay clear of the Twolegs. Or perhaps unseen eyes were watching him; he braced himself in case a patrol appeared.

Not far from the border Brambleclaw had to head for the trees to avoid a litter of Twoleg kits who were standing at the water's edge, yowling and throwing stones into the water. *They're making enough noise to warn any cat in the territory*, he thought. It was clear Blackstar was just using the Twolegs as an excuse. There was plenty of prey, and the Twolegs weren't posing a serious threat. No cat could imagine that ShadowClan really needed more space to hunt.

Cutting diagonally across the shore, Brambleclaw streaked along close to the ground until he reached the wide area near the half bridge, covered with hard black stuff like the Thunderpath. Twoleg monsters were crouched side by side, almost filling the space. Brambleclaw crept along its edge, his legs beginning to tremble with tension and the effort of staying alert for danger.

Two or three tail-lengths from the Thunderpath that marked the border between ShadowClan and RiverClan, he reached the shelter of a tall Twoleg thing made of shiny stuff like the tendrils of the fox traps, woven into a mesh like a cobweb. It was stuffed full of Twoleg rubbish; Brambleclaw twitched his whiskers at the reek of crow-food, but at least it would disguise his own scent.

Cautiously he looked out from behind the Twoleg thing. Several monsters loomed in front of him, but they were all silent and he guessed they were asleep. As he watched, another monster appeared, veered off the Thunderpath, and stopped, its roar cutting off abruptly. Two Twolegs and a couple of kits got out of its belly. The kits let out a screech and dashed off to the half bridge, their hind paws pounding on its wooden strips.

Brambleclaw stiffened as a dog leaped out of the monster after them with a flurry of excited yelps. One of the Twolegs grabbed it and fastened a long tendril of some brightly colored stuff to its collar. Brambleclaw guessed the dog had scented him, but couldn't get at him, because the Twoleg kept tight hold of the tendril.

It's no better than a kittypet, Brambleclaw sneered. *I'd like to see any Twoleg try to put a collar on me.*

While he waited to see what the Twolegs would do next, Brambleclaw was distracted by a movement on the opposite side of the Thunderpath, in RiverClan territory. A clump of bracken waved wildly a heartbeat before a squirrel shot out and crossed the Thunderpath. A slender gray-brown cat darted after it; shock thumped into Brambleclaw as he recognized Brook.

At almost the same moment Stormfur emerged from the bracken and stood at the edge of the Thunderpath. "Brook! No!" he yowled. "Come back!"

Brook was already leaping for the squirrel, hardly a tail-length into ShadowClan territory. She brought it down with two rapid blows from her forepaws and bit down into its neck.

"Come back now!" Stormfur repeated urgently.

Brook spun around, the squirrel dangling from her jaws. Just as she launched herself back across the Thunderpath, a monster appeared; Brambleclaw dug his claws into the ground and squeezed his eyes shut, picturing the young she-cat crushed under its round black paws.

"No!" he heard Stormfur yowl.

Brambleclaw opened his eyes again to see the monster swerve, screeching, and barely miss Brook's tail as she plunged back into RiverClan territory. Stormfur ran up to her, pressing his muzzle against hers.

"What do you think you're doing?" A new voice spoke, harsh and angry. Brambleclaw looked up to see Hawkfrost shouldering his way through a clump of ferns at the top of the bank above the Thunderpath. His ice-blue eyes blazed with fury. He paced down to confront Stormfur and Brook. "You stole that prey from ShadowClan!" he hissed at the young she-cat.

Brook dropped the squirrel and turned to Stormfur. "What's he talking about?"

"She didn't steal it," Stormfur started to explain. "It's a RiverClan squirrel. It ran across the Thunderpath, and Brook just—"

Hawkfrost ignored the gray warrior. "Don't you know the most basic rules of the warrior code?" he demanded, thrusting his muzzle forward until it was less than a mouse-length from Brook's. "You *don't* steal prey."

"That's what I'm trying to tell you," Stormfur meowed. "She *didn't* steal it. It's one of ours."

Hawkfrost rounded on him, his eyes still sparking with fury. "She shouldn't have followed it across the border. Doesn't she even know not to trespass on another Clan's territory?"

"I'm sorry," Brook mewed, still sounding confused. "I barely set paw on the other side—just enough to catch the squirrel."

Hawkfrost let out a snort of exasperation. "You obviously have no idea how to behave. What if a ShadowClan patrol had spotted you?"

"Well, they didn't, so . . ." Stormfur was obviously trying to smooth his Clanmate's ruffled fur.

"No thanks to her," Hawkfrost interrupted.

"I'm sorry," Brook repeated. "When I lived with the Tribe, we didn't have to worry about boundaries. I'll remember next time."

"If there is a next time," Hawkfrost retorted.

"What do you mean?" Brambleclaw saw Stormfur's neck fur bristle. "Why shouldn't there be? Brook's training really hard to be a RiverClan warrior."

The big tabby tom's lips drew back in a sneer. "She'll *never* be a RiverClan warrior!" he hissed.

Brambleclaw swallowed nervously. His half brother sounded exactly like Tigerstar!

"And who are you to say that?" Stormfur challenged. "You're not in charge of us."

For a heartbeat Brambleclaw thought that Hawkfrost would lash out and rake his claws across Stormfur's face. "Just wait and see what happens when I report this to Leopardstar," he growled. He twitched his tail in the direction of the RiverClan camp. "Come on back to camp. *Now.*"

Stormfur and Brook glanced at each other. Stormfur was

obviously wondering whether to obey, when his Clanmate had no right to give him orders. Then he shrugged.

"Come on." He sighed. "We might as well get this straightened out."

Hawkfrost stalked off up the bank; Stormfur followed close behind him. Brook picked up her squirrel again and brought up the rear.

Once they had disappeared into the ferns at the top of the bank, Brambleclaw cautiously crossed the Thunderpath and padded after them. He wanted to know what was going to happen to his friends. Keeping well back so none of the RiverClan cats would spot him, he followed their tracks. Fortunately the breeze was blowing toward him, so they were unlikely to pick up his scent, and he kept his ears pricked and his mouth half-open in case any other warriors from RiverClan were close by.

Hawkfrost led the way directly to the RiverClan camp, and leaped the stream close to a hollowed-out place under the bank where Mothwing was sitting with her apprentice, Willowpaw. As he passed the medicine cat, Hawkfrost jerked his head savagely. "Come on, you're wanted," he ordered.

Brambleclaw's ears twitched in surprise that Hawkfrost would talk like that to his sister. He waited, hidden in a clump of reeds, until Mothwing and the others had gone, and Willowpaw was busy sorting through a pile of herbs. He wasn't sure what to do. He would certainly be spotted if he tried to follow the others right into the RiverClan camp, but he couldn't just leave his friends in trouble and go home.

The RiverClan warriors had made their camp on a wedge-shaped patch of ground between two streams. Mothwing's den was beside the narrower stream, not far from where they joined. Brambleclaw padded along the bank until he passed the thorn barrier that marked the edge of the camp. Cautiously he tasted the air, but he could make out nothing except for the powerful scent of cats from the camp itself.

A sudden yowl from inside the camp made him decide. He was too worried about what would happen to Stormfur and Brook if he left. Hawkfrost was right about the warrior code not allowing a cat to catch prey in another Clan's territory, but surely Leopardstar would make allowances for the Tribe cat who was unfamiliar with Clan ways?

Brambleclaw leaped from the bank to a rock in midstream, water bubbling around his paws. A second leap brought him to the far bank, where he clawed up a beech tree whose branches overhung the thorn barrier. By creeping among the rustling leaves, his claws sunk into the bark to hold him steady, Brambleclaw could look down into the camp.

Reeds and bushes grew thickly along the banks of both streams, but there was a clear space in the center of the camp. Leopardstar, the Clan leader, stood there, with her deputy Mistyfoot beside her and several other cats in a ragged circle around them. They were staring at Stormfur and Brook, who stood close together, shifting their paws uneasily. At first Brambleclaw couldn't see Mothwing.

Hawkfrost stood in front of his leader. He was in the middle of reporting what had happened. "So this mousebrained excuse for a cat," he meowed, flicking his tail at Brook, "chased the squirrel across the border into ShadowClan and killed it. And was almost flattened by a monster on the way back. It's a pity it missed, is all I can say."

Brambleclaw was too far away to hear Stormfur's snarl, but he saw the fur on his neck and shoulders begin to bristle.

"There's no need to say things like that." Leopardstar's voice was calm. "Brook, is what Hawkfrost says true?"

Brook dipped her head awkwardly. "Yes, Leopardstar, it's true. But I didn't realize that what I did was wrong. It won't happen again."

"It shouldn't have happened even *once*." Brambleclaw's heart sank as he saw Blackclaw thrusting his way to the front of the crowd. He was one of the most aggressive RiverClan warriors. "Even a kit knows that you don't cross Clan boundaries."

"Did any ShadowClan cats see this?" Leopardstar asked.

It was Stormfur who replied. "I don't think so. I didn't spot any, and you can't scent anything down there except for Twolegs and their monsters, so they'll never know we were there."

Leopardstar nodded, but before she could speak, Hawkfrost broke in. "It doesn't matter whether ShadowClan saw her or not. It's still against the warrior code. No cat has a place here if they don't know that."

A murmur rose from the listening cats; Brambleclaw sank his claws deeper into the tree branch when he realized most of them sounded as if they agreed with Hawkfrost.

"We should send her back where she came from," Blackclaw declared.

Stormfur whipped around to face him. "If she goes, I go."

Blackclaw didn't reply, just opened his jaws in an insolent yawn. Stormfur unsheathed his claws, only to freeze at a sharp command from Mistyfoot.

"Stormfur, no!" The deputy stepped forward until she stood facing the gray warrior. Her blue eyes were regretful as she continued, "Think carefully, Stormfur. How long do you and Brook plan on staying here, anyway? We are all glad to see you again, but perhaps it's time you went back to your Tribe."

"Yes, get rid of *her*," some cat meowed from the back of the crowd. "Stormfur can stay if he likes, but what use is she?"

"She can't even fight," Blackclaw added. "My apprentice could rip her fur off."

Stormfur's eyes gleamed with fury. "Where Brook comes from, the cave-guards fight, and the prey-hunters feed the Tribe. Brook was a prey-hunter. She never had to fight until she came here."

"I'm doing my best to learn," Brook added.

"You're doing fine." Stormfur touched her shoulder with the tip of his tail. "You'll fight as well as any cat soon."

"If she gets the chance," Blackclaw mewed. "Can't you see the Clan doesn't want her here?"

"Yes, what about Mothwing's dream?" another voice asked. "StarClan told us there are two things that don't belong in the Clan."

Brambleclaw's belly clenched as he remembered the dream Mothwing had described at the Gathering, of two stones in the stream that looked different from all the others, interrupting the smooth flow of the current. The stream had flowed properly again only after the stones had been washed away. Did that really mean Stormfur and Brook had no place in RiverClan?

"Mothwing?" Hawkfrost glanced around. "Mothwing, where are you?"

The golden tabby rose to her paws. She had been sitting at the back of the cats, and her paws dragged as she padded forward to stand beside her brother.

"Have StarClan sent you a clearer sign?" Hawkfrost demanded.

Mothwing hesitated, her head bowed.

"Well, Mothwing?" Leopardstar prompted, her voice edged with impatience.

The medicine cat looked up, meeting her brother's gaze. Her voice was steady as she replied, "No. StarClan have told me nothing. I said at the Gathering that we shouldn't be too quick to assume we know what the dream meant—if it meant anything. Sometimes a dream is just a dream."

Yowls of protest rose from the Clan. "Have you forgotten what I said to you at the Gathering?" Hawkfrost snarled.

"No, but—" Mothwing began, breaking off as Leopardstar interrupted her.

"Mothwing, you are the medicine cat. You need to tell us what to do."

"I'm sorry." Mothwing's head dropped again.

"The dream seems clear enough to *me*," Blackclaw snarled. "Nothing will be right in RiverClan unless we get rid of these two."

Murmurs of agreement filled the clearing. Leopardstar glanced at Mistyfoot and said something to her deputy, too quietly for Brambleclaw to hear. Meanwhile Hawkfrost padded across to Stormfur until the two cats stood nose to nose. "You obviously have no respect for the warrior code, either of you," he rasped. "Go back to the Tribe, where you belong."

Stormfur let out a yowl of pure fury. Leaping at Hawkfrost, he bowled the huge tabby over and battered at his belly with his powerful hind paws, clawing out tufts of fur. Hawkfrost retaliated by sinking his claws into Stormfur's shoulders and trying to bite his throat.

"No!" Brook screeched, trying to thrust herself between the two battling warriors. "Stormfur, stop!"

Brambleclaw raked his claws along the branch. Every hair on his pelt was telling him to hurl himself out of the tree and join in the fight on Stormfur's side, but he had to stay where he was. It would just cause even more trouble, and Firestar would be furious if one of his warriors launched an attack in another Clan's camp.

Below, Stormfur was holding his own, ignoring Brook's pleas to stop as he slashed his claws along Hawkfrost's side. The tabby warrior flailed under Stormfur's weight, doing little more than shielding his face with his paws. Brambleclaw's eyes narrowed; surely Hawkfrost could fight better than this? Their training sessions with Tigerstar had made him stronger and more skillful than any cat in the forest, except perhaps Brambleclaw himself. Now, instead of throwing himself into the fight, he was trying to dodge Stormfur's attack, and his few blows were feeble and badly aimed.

Brambleclaw knew exactly what he was doing.

Hawkfrost didn't want to beat Stormfur in a fight; he wanted him gone for good. He must have been turning his Clanmates against the visitors for a long time. At the Gathering he had been the one to insist that Mothwing tell her dream, and he had interpreted it for her. Brook's mistake with the squirrel had given him the excuse he needed, and now he had provoked Stormfur into attacking him so the others would drive him out.

Part of Brambleclaw admired his half brother's cunning and the force of his ambition. Tigerstar would be proud of him. But Brambleclaw knew he would never have the courage to make such a blatant bid for power himself. Could this really be part of the warrior code?

"Enough!" Leopardstar snapped. "Mistyfoot, Blackclaw, pull them apart."

The RiverClan deputy leaped onto Hawkfrost's shoulders and wrenched his head back. Blackclaw pushed Brook aside and raked his claws across Stormfur's nose; the gray warrior reared back, losing his grip on Hawkfrost. Both cats scrambled to their paws and stood panting, glaring at each other. Blood was oozing from Hawkfrost's belly and his side.

Stormfur had no obvious wounds, except for blood spattering his muzzle from Blackclaw's blow.

"Stormfur, you attacked your Clanmate!" Leopardstar sounded deeply shocked. "It's obvious you have forgotten the warrior code, or else it doesn't mean anything to you anymore."

Stormfur opened his mouth to speak, but Leopardstar swept on. There was genuine regret in her voice as she meowed, "You will have to leave RiverClan. There is no place for you here. Your path lies with the Tribe now."

Stormfur and Brook exchanged an appalled glance, and Brambleclaw wondered what was so terrible about having to return to Brook's mountain home.

For a heartbeat he thought Stormfur would protest. Then the gray warrior lifted his head proudly. "Very well." His voice was cold. "We'll go. But it's RiverClan's loss, not ours. This isn't the same Clan I once belonged to."

He swept his tail around to draw Brook close to him. Without looking back, the two cats padded out of the clearing and vanished into the undergrowth.

Hawkfrost watched them go, triumph glittering in his ice-blue eyes.

Anxious not to be discovered, Brambleclaw climbed down the tree, crossed the stream again, and slipped into the undergrowth, heading for the lake. The scene he had just witnessed had pushed his mission from Firestar to the back of his mind. All he wanted to do now was speak with Stormfur.

Halfway to the waterside he stopped to taste the air, pick-

ing up the mingled scents of Stormfur and Brook, so strong
and fresh that he knew they were nearby. Scrambling up a low
hill, he spotted them farther down the other side. They were
heading for the lake, their heads hanging low and their tails
twined together.

Brambleclaw didn't dare call out to them this close to the
RiverClan camp. Alert for any sounds of pursuit, he followed
them, flitting from one clump of ferns or hazel bush to the
next. He caught up to them on the shore not far from the
tree-bridge that led to the Gathering island.

"Stormfur!" he hissed. "Wait!"

Brook jumped, while Stormfur whipped around to face
Brambleclaw, his claws unsheathed and his neck fur bristling.

"Brambleclaw!" he exclaimed. "I thought you were that
mangy, crow-food-eating—"

He broke off when Brook touched his shoulder with her
tail. "Don't," she murmured. "That won't help."

Stormfur let out a sigh, allowing the fur on his neck and
shoulders to lie flat again. "What are you doing in RiverClan
territory?" he asked Brambleclaw.

"It doesn't matter," Brambleclaw replied. He retreated farther from the water's edge, beckoning with his tail for
Stormfur and Brook to follow until they reached the shelter
of a twisted thornbush where they could talk without being
seen. "I saw what happened," he meowed. "And I'm really
sorry. You didn't deserve that."

"Hawkfrost has been out to cause trouble ever since I
came back to RiverClan," Stormfur snarled. "He's afraid that

if I stayed, Mistyfoot would choose me for deputy once she becomes leader."

Brambleclaw wasn't surprised; Hawkfrost had been deputy once before, while Mistyfoot was trapped by Twolegs, but at that time Stormfur had been on the journey to the sun-drown-place. Once he had settled into his Clan again, he would have been a formidable rival.

"Will you go back to the mountains?" he asked.

"That's not possible right now," Stormfur replied. He sounded awkward, not meeting Brambleclaw's eyes.

Brambleclaw didn't press him. He suspected something was wrong and wanted to know more, but he knew Stormfur wouldn't tell him until he was ready. "Why don't you come back to ThunderClan with me?" he suggested. "Firestar will be glad to give you food and shelter for tonight at least."

Stormfur's whiskers twitched. "We can't do that," he meowed. "It would only cause trouble for you with RiverClan."

"Firestar doesn't ask other Clans to approve what he does," Brambleclaw pointed out. If Stormfur and Brook couldn't go back to the Tribe, their only other choice might be to become loners, and live outside the protection of any Clan. It was a hard and difficult life, especially for cats who were used to living among others. "Come on," he urged. "It's too late to go far before nightfall anyway, especially when you don't know the territory well."

Stormfur turned to Brook. "What do you think?"

"You decide," she murmured, pressing her muzzle into

Stormfur's shoulder. "You know I'll come with you wherever you go."

Stormfur closed his eyes for a moment as if he were bracing himself. "All right," he meowed to Brambleclaw, opening his eyes again. "We'll go back with you. Come on, Brook."

Brambleclaw led the way down to the lakeshore and headed back toward ThunderClan territory, taking the route through WindClan this time. As they padded along, heavy-footed with shock and exhaustion, he thought about what he had seen and overheard in the RiverClan camp.

"You know," he mewed to Stormfur as they were passing the horseplace, "Hawkfrost had a point. You shouldn't have attacked him."

"I know, I know." Stormfur lashed his tail. "But he goaded me into it. He *meant* for me to attack him, and you know that as well as I do."

Brambleclaw didn't know how to respond. In his heart he knew Stormfur was right, but he also knew why Hawkfrost had done it.

Before he could speak, Stormfur halted and faced him. "Brambleclaw, be careful," he warned quietly. "The path you walk can only lead to trouble."

Brambleclaw stared at him, a hot flush of guilt soaking through his pelt. There was no way Stormfur could know about Brambleclaw's meetings with Hawkfrost in dreams, or their training sessions with Tigerstar. Did he realize Brambleclaw was closer to his half brother than some cats might think?

Stormfur twitched his ears as if he were flicking away a fly. Without saying anything else he turned away and plodded on around the lake.

Brambleclaw stared after him. He felt bad for his friend and Brook, cruelly driven out of their Clan. Yet he couldn't believe Hawkfrost was entirely wrong. If this was the best way for him to achieve power, didn't that make his actions right, in some way at least?

CHAPTER 16

❧

The sun had set by the time Brambleclaw led Stormfur and Brook through the thorn tunnel into the ThunderClan camp. Shadows lay thickly in the stone hollow, and only one or two cats still lingered by the fresh-kill pile. Rainwhisker, on guard by the entrance, jumped in surprise at the appearance of Stormfur and Brook, but seeing that Brambleclaw was with them he just gave them a nod of greeting and said nothing.

"Let's go and see Firestar," Brambleclaw suggested, bounding across the clearing to the rockfall.

When he reached his leader's den, with Stormfur and Brook scrambling up behind him, he found Firestar already curled in his mossy nest at the back of the cave. He raised his head as Brambleclaw paused in the opening.

"Good, you're back," he meowed, sitting up and shaking scraps of moss from his pelt. "What did you—" He broke off when he realized that Brambleclaw was not alone. "Is that Stormfur and Brook?" he mewed in surprise.

"That's right." Brambleclaw stepped inside and dipped his head to his Clan leader. "I'm sorry, Firestar. Something happened."

Firestar beckoned Stormfur and Brook into the den with a sweep of his tail. "Is there a problem in RiverClan?"

"You could put it that way," Brambleclaw replied. Rapidly he told Firestar everything, from the moment when he spotted Brook chasing the squirrel, to when he invited the banished cats to come back with him to ThunderClan.

"You did the right thing," Firestar meowed when he had finished. "You couldn't have left Stormfur and Brook with nowhere to spend the night." Turning to Stormfur, he added, "You're both welcome to stay for as long as you want."

Stormfur's ears twitched. "We thought just for tonight—" he began.

"That's up to you," Firestar told him. "But you deserve some time to decide what you want to do. ThunderClan owes you that, at least, after all the help you gave us when the badgers attacked."

"Thank you," mewed Stormfur, and Brook added, "You don't know how much this means to us."

It was obvious to Brambleclaw that Firestar would be quite happy to welcome Stormfur and Brook into ThunderClan permanently. Much as he liked Stormfur and his Tribe mate, he wasn't sure that was the right decision. What about the rest of the Clan? And how would RiverClan react when they found out?

"Brambleclaw, take them to get something to eat, and then find them sleeping places," Firestar directed. "We'll talk more in the morning."

Brambleclaw led the way out of the den and down into the

clearing. He realized just how hungry he was; he hadn't eaten since that morning, when he caught the mouse near the Twoleg pelts. There wasn't much left on the fresh-kill pile— hunting patrols would need to go out first thing—but Brambleclaw chose a magpie for himself, while Stormfur and Brook shared a rabbit.

By the time they had finished eating, it was completely dark, and Silverpelt glittered above their heads as Brambleclaw led the way to the warriors' den. The thorn tree's new growth hadn't covered all traces of the damage from the badgers, and the warriors were curled closely together in their mossy nests. Most of them were asleep or drowsily sharing tongues, and at first no cat took much notice of the new arrivals.

"Are you sure there's room for us?" Stormfur asked as they slipped between the outer branches.

"Plenty," Brambleclaw assured them.

He headed for some spare space closer to the rock wall, accidentally treading on Dustpelt's tail as he padded past. The brown tabby tom lifted his head. "What's going on?" he mewed irritably.

"Sorry," Brambleclaw muttered. "It's only Stormfur and Brook. They're staying for a while."

Dustpelt grunted. "Does Firestar know about this?"

"Of course." Brambleclaw bristled at the suggestion that he would bring strange cats into the den without asking the Clan leader.

Dustpelt just twitched his whiskers and curled up again,

pointedly drawing his tail close to his side. Brambleclaw managed to escort his friends to an empty space without disturbing any other cat. To his relief Squirrelflight was nearby; she looked up as Brambleclaw approached. Her voice was friendly as she meowed, "Hi, Stormfur, Brook. What are *you* doing here?"

"I'll tell you in a moment," Brambleclaw replied. "Let's get Stormfur and Brook settled in first."

"Sure." Squirrelflight moved over to make more space. Cloudtail was asleep next to her; she poked one paw hard into his side. "Move over, will you? You're taking up more room than a badger."

"Badger? Where?" Cloudtail looked up, blue eyes wide with alarm.

"Nowhere, mousebrain," Squirrelflight snapped as several more cats stirred, heads popping up all over the den. "Go back to sleep."

Brambleclaw helped Stormfur and Brook make nests for themselves in the moss, and finally settled down beside Squirrelflight. His jaws parted in a huge yawn; he could hardly stay awake to tell the story yet again.

"I wish I'd been there," Squirrelflight mewed when he had finished. "I'd have shredded Hawkfrost's ears."

"No, you wouldn't," Brambleclaw responded. "Not in the middle of the RiverClan camp."

Squirrelflight flexed her claws. "He'd better stay out of my way, that's all. Do you think they'll stay?" she added, angling her ears toward Stormfur and Brook, who were already asleep, curled closely together among the moss and bracken.

"I hope so." His jaws gaped in another yawn; his voice was blurred as he added, "ThunderClan needs good warriors."

"RiverClan's loss is our gain," Squirrelflight agreed.

She rasped her tongue over Brambleclaw's ears; the warm, rhythmic strokes were the last thing he felt as he slid into sleep.

Gray dawn light was filtering through the branches of the thorn tree when Brambleclaw awoke. Outside he could hear Sandstorm beginning to sort out the patrols. Hurriedly he sprang up and pushed his way out into the clearing.

"Why don't you take Stormfur and Brook on the dawn patrol?" he suggested to the ginger she-cat. "It would be a good way for them to start learning the territory."

Sandstorm twitched her ears, then nodded. "Okay. Good idea."

"What do you mean, learn the territory?" Brambleclaw jumped as Dustpelt came up behind him. The tabby tom still sounded cranky after being disturbed the night before. "I thought they were only staying overnight."

"Nothing's been decided yet," Brambleclaw replied, wishing that he'd been more tactful, or that Dustpelt hadn't overheard.

"Well, it doesn't matter," Sandstorm meowed. "They're here now, so they may as well make themselves useful."

She poked her head through the branches of the den to call Stormfur and Brook. When they emerged, the four cats headed out together; Dustpelt didn't say anything, though Brambleclaw saw the tip of his tail twitching as he vanished into the thorn tunnel.

Brambleclaw joined Squirrelflight, Cloudtail, and Brightheart on a hunting patrol. When they returned, loaded with fresh-kill, he noticed more cats than usual standing about in the clearing, as if they were waiting for something. Uneasiness prickled his fur.

"What's going on?" Squirrelflight asked, dropping three mice and a vole on the pile. "Hey, Brackenfur!" She waved her tail at the ginger warrior as he padded past. "What's happening?"

"Mousefur just called a Clan meeting," Brackenfur explained.

"*Mousefur* called a meeting?" Brambleclaw echoed. "Can she do that?"

Brackenfur shrugged. "She's done it."

"Oh, *good*," Cloudtail meowed sarcastically. "More trouble. Just what we need."

"I'm going to see if Leafpool knows anything." Brightheart bounded off toward the medicine cat's den, and with a disgusted lash of his tail Cloudtail followed her.

Brambleclaw's uneasiness increased. Across the clearing, he could see the wiry brown elder standing beneath the Highledge. Dustpelt was with her; both cats looked angry.

"See that?" Brambleclaw nudged Squirrelflight.

Squirrelflight nodded. "I don't know what all this is about," she mewed, "but I bet I can guess."

"So can I." Brambleclaw looked around until he spotted

Stormfur and Brook, sitting close together by the thorn barrier. He wondered whether they were reluctant to join in a meeting of a Clan where they didn't belong, or if they wanted to be sure they could escape if things turned ugly.

He padded over to them, Squirrelflight at his shoulder.

"Are you okay?" he asked. "Has any cat said anything to you?"

Brook shook her head. "We're fine," she murmured, but her eyes gave away her distress.

"We had a great patrol this morning," Stormfur meowed. "Sandstorm was friendly, and Dustpelt—well, Dustpelt is rude to every cat, so you tend not to notice. But when we got back we could see cats glaring at us, and hardly any cat wanted to talk to us. I think Dustpelt went to see the elders, and then Mousefur called this meeting."

He broke off at the sound of Mousefur's yowl from across the clearing. "Firestar! Firestar!"

A moment passed before Firestar appeared on the Highledge. A ray of sunlight turned his pelt to flame and traced his ears in gold. "What is it?" he asked.

"The Clan needs to talk with you," Mousefur replied.

As Brambleclaw padded closer, beckoning with his tail for his friends to follow, Firestar leaped down the rocks and joined the rest of his Clan in the clearing. Brambleclaw thrust his way to the front so that he could hear everything and join in if he had to.

"Well, Mousefur?" Firestar faced the elder, his green gaze level. "What's this all about? I thought it was the Clan leader's duty to call meetings."

It was Dustpelt who replied. He kept his anger under control and spoke with deep seriousness. "We're not trying to undermine you, Firestar," he began. "But we're worried about the way ThunderClan is becoming . . . well, *mixed*. First it was Daisy and her kits. Now Stormfur and Brook. If it goes on, we won't be ThunderClan anymore, just a collection of loners and kittypets."

"Mousebrain!" Squirrelflight hissed into Brambleclaw's ear. "Has he forgotten where Firestar came from?"

Brambleclaw didn't reply, because Mousefur had started to speak.

"Dustpelt is right," she declared. "You're taking in too many strange cats. This is not the warrior code as I was taught it." More sharply, she added, "You can punish me if you like, Firestar. I tell it as I see it."

Firestar touched her shoulder with the tip of his tail. "I wouldn't dream of punishing you, Mousefur. Every cat has a voice in what affects the Clan. But in this case I think you're wrong."

Mousefur's neck fur bristled. "Why?"

"Because ThunderClan needs more cats. Until Daisy came, we had only two apprentices and no kits at all. Now we have plenty of kits, but we need strong warriors to defend our borders and protect our Clan. You know what Blackstar and Leopardstar said at the last Gathering. They want more territory. We've already had to fight ShadowClan when they tried to move the border."

"Not to mention the foxes and badgers in the forest," Sandstorm added.

Firestar flicked an ear to acknowledge her support. "Stormfur and Brook would be helpful for training young warriors, too," he went on. "Brook knows hunting techniques that we've never learned."

"That might be useful if we had a mountain in our territory," Dustpelt pointed out drily.

"We don't know when it might be useful," Firestar retorted. "And we'll need mentors for the kits who are in the nursery now—more, if more kits are born."

Murmurs of disagreement echoed around the hollow. Rainwhisker's voice rose above them. "But there are ThunderClan cats who've never had apprentices."

"Stormfur is half ThunderClan," Brambleclaw meowed, pushing forward to stand beside Firestar. "You could argue he has a right to be here."

"True." Firestar gave him a grateful glance. "He grew up in RiverClan, but every cat knows he had a ThunderClan father."

"And *that* explains a lot." The mutter came from just beside Brambleclaw. "Firestar would do anything to get Graystripe's kin into the Clan."

Brambleclaw's head whipped around and he found himself staring into Longtail's blind gaze. He would have liked to claw the tabby warrior's fur off, but he contented himself with a faint hiss. Had Firestar heard the remark? he wondered. *And is it true?* Stormfur looked very much like his father,

Graystripe, and he shared Graystripe's courage and fierce loyalty to friends and Clan. It wouldn't be surprising if Firestar felt drawn to Stormfur, when he was missing his old friend so much.

"Graystripe and Firestar have been friends for seasons," Thornclaw meowed to Longtail. "Of course he feels he owes something to Graystripe's kin." His tone was quiet, and Brambleclaw couldn't tell whether he agreed with Firestar's decision or not.

"As for Brook," Firestar continued, "what matters is not where a cat was born or who their kin may be."

Argue with that, Brambleclaw thought. *Our Clan leader was a kittypet, and he's one of the greatest cats the forest has ever seen.*

"Loyalty is what matters," Firestar declared, "and that exists *now*, not in the past. Loyalty has to be proved every day, in every piece of fresh-kill brought back for the Clan, every claw mark on our enemies, every patrol, every training session."

"But what if ThunderClan ever has to fight with RiverClan?" Dustpelt asked. "What would Stormfur do then?"

"Are you saying he would be a traitor?" Brambleclaw snarled. He glanced at his friend, but Stormfur was studying his paws, as if none of this applied to him.

"I'm saying he'd be torn between Clans," Dustpelt retorted. "Would you wish that on any cat?"

Brambleclaw had to admit that the tabby warrior was right. Stormfur had felt that pain already, when he decided to abandon RiverClan and stay with Brook in the mountains. He must be feeling it again now, as he was driven out of the Clan where he had grown up. But what other choice did he have?

"Stormfur's our friend." Squirrelflight's voice broke into the argument. "He made the journey to the sun-drown-place. Brook's Tribe took us in when we traveled through the mountains. And they both helped us after the badger attack. How many of you would even be *alive* without them? Is this how you want to repay her?"

"That was different!" Rainwhisker called out. "We never meant to stay with the Tribe for good."

"Besides, that's not the problem now," Mousefur added. "We have to think of the future of ThunderClan."

"Enough!" Firestar lashed his tail. "I've listened to you, but I'm not going to change my mind. If Stormfur and Brook decide to leave, then we'll give them what help we can. If they want to stay, then we *will* make them welcome. This meeting is over." He turned and stalked back toward the rocks leading up to his den.

For a few heartbeats, shock kept the Clan silent. Firestar never snapped out orders like that; he never got angry with warriors who disagreed with him. Brambleclaw guessed that this meant more to him because of his kittypet background, and because offering help to Graystripe's son was one last thing he could do for his absent friend.

As Firestar vanished into his den, the rest of the Clan broke up into groups, murmuring quietly to one another.

Some cats shot hostile glances at Stormfur and Brook; Brambleclaw could see that it wasn't just Dustpelt and Mousefur who were unhappy with Firestar's decision.

With Squirrelflight beside him, Brambleclaw padded over to his friends. Stormfur looked up as they approached, his blue eyes full of pain.

"We'll go," he meowed. "We can't disrupt the Clan like this."

"You're not going anywhere," Brambleclaw argued. "I'm not going to let a few hostile Clanmates drive you out." *Not like RiverClan*, he added silently. "I'll go and talk to Firestar. We'll figure something out."

Without waiting for Stormfur to agree, he headed for the Highledge. Behind him he heard Squirrelflight meow, "How about a hunt? I found a great place for prey the other day, just crawling with mice."

When Brambleclaw poked his head into Firestar's den, the Clan leader was sitting in his nest, his gaze fixed on the rock wall. He jumped when Brambleclaw appeared.

"Oh, it's you," he mewed. "Come in." Still with the distant look in his eyes, he added, "I was just remembering when Stormfur was born. Graystripe took him and Feathertail to RiverClan because he thought they would be safe and wanted there."

Brambleclaw let out a murmur of sympathy. He couldn't remember that far back, when he had been a tiny kit in the nursery with his sister, Tawnypelt. She had left too, to become a warrior of ShadowClan. For a heartbeat, loneliness clawed at his throat and he felt Firestar's pain as if it were his own.

"Firestar, I have to talk to you," he began reluctantly.

"What is it?" Some of the old fire returned to Firestar's eyes. "I thought you wanted Stormfur and Brook to stay?"

"I do. I think you're right that the Clan needs new warriors. But . . ." His claws scratched on the hard stone floor of the den. "I'm not sure you're going about it the right way."

He half expected a cuff over the ear for being rude, but Firestar just held him with a piercing green gaze.

"Go on."

"Every cat in ThunderClan is loyal. They would all die for ThunderClan if they had to. But Dustpelt and Mousefur feel—every cat feels—that they have to make a stand for the sake of the Clan. They're worried about the Clan looking weak."

"So what do you suggest?" Firestar growled. "Give in to them? Drive out two great warriors just because the Clan doesn't like where they came from?"

"No. But you have to show them that ThunderClan has strong leadership. That there's nothing to worry about, that we are strong, and that whatever happens the Clan will stick together."

Firestar narrowed his eyes. "And how do you suggest I do that?"

Brambleclaw swallowed. He knew what he had to say, though the words stuck in his throat like a stubborn piece of fresh-kill. Somewhere in the back of his mind, in the place

where dreams are born, he seemed to hear Tigerstar screeching at him in uncontrollable rage. But none of that mattered.
His loyalty to his Clan had to come first.

"You need to appoint a new deputy."

Firestar stared at him, and in that searching gaze
Brambleclaw could see that Firestar knew exactly what he
was asking.

But his leader's only response was, "Why?"

"Because a united leadership—two loyal cats in charge—
would do more than anything else to convince the Clan that
we're strong again in spite of the badger attack. Don't you
know that warriors like Blackstar sneer at us and call us
weak?"

The hair on Firestar's neck and shoulders bristled, and his
voice was a soft growl. "Weak? I wish Blackstar dared say that
to my face."

"Weak," Brambleclaw repeated. He took a deep breath.
"The Clan is vulnerable when there's no deputy, because if
other Clans see it as a weakness, they're more likely to attack
us. ShadowClan have already made one attempt to set their
scent markers on our territory. It's *dangerous* to leave things as
they are. Firestar, every cat knows how much you grieve for
Graystripe. But you *must* appoint a new deputy."

Firestar's green gaze was fixed on the wall of the den, as if
he could see past the stone to some scene Brambleclaw could
not begin to guess at. "Do you remember," he began softly,
"how I had to leave the Clan for a while when you were a new
warrior? Graystripe promised me then that he would keep

the Clan safe. 'I'll wait for you,' he said to me. 'I'll wait for you as long as it takes.' Do you think I shouldn't do the same for him?"

"No, Firestar." Brambleclaw felt desperately sad to hear the anguish in Firestar's voice as he recalled his old friend's unswerving loyalty. "But if you had died on your quest, even Graystripe would have had to accept it, sooner or later."

Firestar's tail lashed once. "Graystripe is *not* dead! I'll never give up hope until I have some kind of sign from StarClan telling me he isn't still alive."

"StarClan can't see everywhere."

Firestar froze as a new voice spoke. Brambleclaw glanced over his shoulder to see Sandstorm standing at the entrance to the den. She was right. In the mountains, the Tribe of Endless Hunting prowled the skies. Those paths were unknown to StarClan. If Graystripe still lived, perhaps he too walked under different skies, and StarClan did not know his fate.

Sandstorm slipped inside the den and went up to Firestar, pressing her muzzle against his. "I know it's hard," she meowed. "Graystripe was my friend too. But it might be time to accept that he isn't coming back."

Firestar's gaze rested on her for a moment, then shifted to Brambleclaw. There was a world of hurt and betrayal in his eyes. "How can you both doubt me? Would you be so quick to give up hope for me, too?"

Sandstorm sat beside him, a flick of her tail indicating that Brambleclaw should leave. Brambleclaw dipped his head and backed away. Part of him respected Sandstorm's wisdom, and hoped she could persuade the cat who was her mate as well as her leader to accept that his closest friend was never coming back. Partly he was filled with frustration that Firestar could be so blind. It was obvious to every other cat that ThunderClan needed a deputy. If Firestar went on refusing to admit that, Brambleclaw thought grimly, he might find himself challenged by more than an unexpected Clan meeting.

CHAPTER 17

❧

When the meeting was over, Leafpool retreated to her den and busied herself making a poultice of yarrow for Goldenflower, who was complaining of cracked pads. Uneasiness wreathed her like fog. Firestar had never faced a challenge to his leadership like this. What had happened to ThunderClan's trust in him that had brought them through their long journey to their new home? Had they really forgotten everything Firestar had done for them?

She had other worries, too, suspicions that troubled her even more deeply. She remembered Feathertail's warning, and how Bluestar had told her in a dream that her path would twist in ways she could not foresee. *It can't be true*, she told herself. *If it is, what will I do?*

Pushing the troubling thoughts firmly out of her mind, Leafpool scooped up the poultice on a leaf, ready to take to the elders' den. Suddenly she heard paw steps just beyond the bramble screen. Expecting a sick or injured cat, she popped her head out of her den and found herself face-to-face with her father.

"Firestar!" she exclaimed. "Are you sick?" He looked ill, his green eyes dull and his tail drooping.

Firestar shook his head. "I'm fine," he mewed unconvincingly. "Your mother said I should come and talk to you. I need a medicine cat's advice."

Leafpool motioned to him to sit in the bracken outside the entrance to her den. It was warm here in the sun, but they were hidden from the rest of the camp by the screen of brambles. Sitting beside him, she curled her tail neatly over her paws and murmured, "I'm here if you need me. I'll do anything I can to help."

Firestar heaved a sigh. "Brambleclaw spoke to me. He thinks Graystripe is dead, and I should appoint a new deputy. Sandstorm agrees with him. Do you think they're right?"

Leafpool's pelt prickled. However much she tried to ignore her personal feelings, she still found it hard to trust Brambleclaw after she had seen him in the dark forest with Hawkfrost and Tigerstar. But how could she tell that to Firestar? What could Firestar do about it, when in the waking world Brambleclaw was a loyal and energetic Thunder-Clan warrior? Besides, what true medicine cat would walk beyond StarClan? How could it be part of her duties to pass on what she had seen in the forest of shadows?

She wondered whether Brambleclaw had brought this up because he hoped Firestar would choose him as the new deputy. She had seen ambition gleaming in his amber eyes, and she knew he wanted power. But she reminded herself that Brambleclaw couldn't be made deputy because he had never had an apprentice. He must have put his own ambition aside for the good of the Clan; perhaps she was being unfair when she looked for the darkness in him.

Firestar was waiting for an answer, his green gaze fixed patiently on her. "Is there no hope for Graystripe?" he prompted. "Hasn't StarClan shown you any sort of sign about him?"

Leafpool shook her head. But she knew she trusted her own inner voice this time. "I think you should accept that Graystripe is gone," she told her father, her voice shaking as she saw the pain in his eyes.

"We've lost so many cats," he murmured. "Graystripe and Cinderpelt were my closest friends."

"The whole Clan will grieve for him," Leafpool told him. "Stormfur, too."

As if her words had called him up, she caught a glimpse of the gray warrior padding across the clearing with Brook and Squirrelflight, bringing prey for the fresh-kill pile.

"Wait here," she told her father, and bounded out to meet him.

She caught up to Stormfur as he deposited his fresh-kill on the pile. "I want you to come and talk to Firestar," she meowed. "I think he needs you. He . . . he is trying to decide whether he should appoint a new deputy or keep waiting for Graystripe to come back."

Stormfur hesitated, confusion clouding his eyes for a moment. Then he nodded. "Will you be okay?" he asked Brook.

The Tribe cat nodded. "Don't worry, I'll be fine."

"Sure she will," Squirrelflight added. "We'll go to the clearing and practice some fighting moves."

Stormfur waited until the two she-cats were heading out of camp again, then fell in beside Leafpool as she padded back to her den. Firestar was still sitting in the bracken, his eyes unfocused.

"Graystripe was the first Clan cat I ever met," he meowed absently. "He jumped on me when I strayed out of my housefolk's garden. I'd heard tales of the wild cats that lived in the forest, but I'd never seen one. No cat ever had a better friend."

"Or a better father." With a glance at Leafpool to show he understood exactly what was going on, Stormfur went to sit beside Firestar. "If he were still alive, not even StarClan could stop him from coming to find us."

"Not if Twolegs have kept him shut up somewhere," Firestar argued. "I *won't* believe that I'll never see him again."

Stormfur rested the tip of his tail on Firestar's shoulder. "I know it's hard. I want Graystripe to be alive as much as any cat, but life has to go on."

For a long moment Firestar was silent. Then he turned his head to look directly at Stormfur. "Do you think I should appoint another deputy?"

Stormfur met his gaze. "You must do whatever you think best," he began. "But I know one thing. Nothing meant more to Graystripe than your friendship and his Clan. Even when he was in RiverClan, he longed to go home. He would want to see ThunderClan as strong as it could possibly be, even if that meant accepting that he's not coming back."

Leafpool thought her heart would break. It was so, so hard to imagine that Graystripe was dead.

Firestar let out a long sigh. "You're just like him, you know," he told Stormfur.

Pride glowed in Stormfur's eyes. "I wish I could believe it. But I'll never be half the warrior my father was." Then he twitched his ears and sat straighter, as if dismissing his dark thoughts. "I'm sorry, Firestar," he meowed. "Brook and I have made things difficult for you. We never intended to stay in ThunderClan forever."

"I know," Firestar responded, "but you're welcome to stay as long as you want. I know you have loyalties elsewhere, but until the time is right for you to return to the Tribe, this is your Clan."

Stormfur bowed his head. "Thank you."

Firestar rose to his paws. For a heartbeat, he rested his muzzle on Stormfur's head, as if he were appointing a new warrior. Then he arched his back in a long stretch and padded out into the clearing.

"Let all cats old enough to catch their own prey join here beneath the Highledge for a Clan meeting!"

Firestar's yowl rang out confidently but Leafpool knew how much this must be hurting him. She and Stormfur followed him out past the screen of brambles. The sun was going down, filling the stone hollow with bloodred light. Firestar stood in the center, his pelt blazing, waiting for his Clan to gather. He had come down from the Highledge to face their challenge; he stayed with them now to share their grief at what he had to say.

Leafpool watched the cats gather from around the clearing. Brambleclaw was first to emerge from the warriors' den, followed closely by Dustpelt, Cloudtail, and Brightheart. Ashfur got up from the fresh-kill pile and stood at the back. Brackenfur and Ferncloud both appeared from the nursery, while Daisy remained in the entrance with her kits. The two apprentices joined their mentors. The elders padded out of their den beneath the hazel bush; Goldenflower was limping as she guided Longtail, and Leafpool guiltily remembered the poultice she had yet to deliver.

Last of all, Squirrelflight and Brook shot in through the thorn tunnel and raced across to Leafpool and Stormfur.

"We heard Firestar call from the clearing," Squirrelflight panted. "What's going on?"

"Listen," was all Leafpool could reply, too sick at heart to explain.

Firestar waited until the whole Clan was gathered around him. "Cats of ThunderClan," he began, "the day has come that I never wanted to see. You all know that Graystripe was lost to us when Twolegs trapped him in the old forest. Since then I've tried to believe that he was still alive, and that he'd come back to us one day. But now . . ."

His voice faltered, and he stood a moment with his head bowed before going on. Then he straightened up again and his voice was steadier.

"I have to face the fact that ThunderClan can't go on any

longer without a deputy." He looked up at the darkening sky, where a single warrior of StarClan had appeared, right above the hollow. "Graystripe is dead."

For a heartbeat the Clan was silent; Leafpool could hear nothing but the faint rustling of the trees. The ThunderClan warriors looked at one another, eyes stunned with grief. Then a soft murmur rose, of compassion and acceptance. Leafpool saw several cats, including Mousefur, nodding with sad approval. They believed Firestar was right. He had their support again, but Leafpool knew what the cost had been to him.

"Tonight we will sit vigil for Graystripe," Firestar went on. "And before moonhigh I will appoint the new deputy."

The last of the daylight rippled on the cats' fur as they moved into the center of the clearing and crouched down. Leafpool almost felt as if she could see Graystripe's powerful gray body lying in the midst of them.

"He was my mentor," Brackenfur meowed. "I learned more from him than from any cat."

"We trained together," Dustpelt added. "We fought and hunted together, and StarClan knows we fell out at times, but I always knew I could trust him."

"He never gave up, and he always fought to keep his Clan safe," mewed Sandstorm.

Firestar had not moved from where he stood beneath the Highledge, but he added his voice to the rest. "He was loyal through and through. He was the truest friend a cat ever had. StarClan will receive him with honor." His voice shook again and this time he made no attempt to steady it as he added,

"Farewell, Graystripe. May StarClan light your path."

He bowed his head and padded slowly to the rockfall, to climb up to his den and grieve alone.

Leafpool crouched with the rest of her Clan in the whispering silence, while the night grew darker and StarClan gathered overhead. Were they greeting a new warrior? The last time she had met with StarClan at the Moonpool, there had been no sign of Graystripe. Perhaps Graystripe wasn't lost under different skies; perhaps he wasn't dead at all.

She stirred uneasily and her gaze went to the crack in the rock wall that led to Firestar's den. Even if that were true, Leafpool was as certain as ever that ThunderClan needed a new deputy. Whether Graystripe was alive or not, he wasn't here to carry out his duties and give his strength to the Clan.

She raised her eyes to the glitter of Silverpelt above her head. "Please, send me a sign," she murmured. Then she closed her eyes and waited for the dream from StarClan.

She found herself in the forest on a bright day in newleaf, with sunshine dancing golden on moss and fern. She thought she was near the hollow, but when she padded along the path that should have led her to the entrance, she found herself confronted by a thick wall of bramble.

The air was filled with the scent of ThunderClan cats, and from the middle of the bramble thicket she thought she could hear the happy squealing of kits at play. Curious, she leaped into the nearest tree, scrambling up until she could see what lay on the other side of the brambles.

She was looking down into the ThunderClan camp. She

could see the familiar dens, a well-stocked fresh-kill pile, and her Clanmates padding back and forth or sprawled lazily in the sunlight. But instead of high stone walls, the clearing was surrounded by tall barriers of bramble.

Suddenly Leafpool felt herself swooping down from the branch until she was hovering above the topmost tendrils, as if she were a bird. From here she could gaze right into the wall of thickly intertwining stems. Every branch bristled with thorns and, as Leafpool looked closer, she saw that they weren't thorns at all, but cats' claws, strong and curved and pointing outward to keep out ThunderClan's enemies.

Bramble claws! Brambleclaw was keeping the Clan safe.

The understanding jerked her awake. Around her the Clan cats still kept their vigil for Graystripe. Silverpelt blazed overhead, and the moon skimmed the branches of the trees, shedding its pale light into the clearing. Moonhigh had almost come, and soon Firestar would name his new deputy.

Shivering, Leafpool sat up and drew a paw over her face. She had prayed to StarClan for a sign, and they had answered her prayer as clearly as any cat could wish for: Brambleclaw was the cat they wanted to protect ThunderClan. Even though he had never had an apprentice, even though the starry warriors must know about his meetings with Hawkfrost and Tigerstar, he was still the cat they had chosen.

Quietly, so as not to disturb her grieving Clanmates, Leafpool got up and extended her forepaws in a long stretch. Then she headed for her father's den.

When she reached it, she found Firestar crouched in his

nest with his paws tucked under him. She was thankful to see
that the stunned look of grief had faded from his eyes; he was
deep in thought and started as she spoke his name.

"Leafpool, is that you? What can I do for you?"

"I have to talk to you, Firestar. StarClan have sent me a
sign." Rapidly, aware of the moon steadily rising above the
camp, Leafpool told him her dream.

"Brambleclaw?" Firestar echoed when she had finished.
"Yes, he's a good warrior. He would make an excellent
deputy." He shifted among the moss and ferns. "I'd almost
decided to appoint Brackenfur," he went on. "He would be a
good deputy too, and he is a loyal warrior. But I have to
remember that I'm not only choosing a deputy, I'm choosing
the cat who might be the next leader of ThunderClan. And
somehow . . . I'm not sure Brackenfur is that cat."

"Brambleclaw could be," Leafpool mewed. "I know he
hasn't had an apprentice yet, but I don't think StarClan
would have sent me that sign if it mattered to them. These
are unusual times—ThunderClan has never had so few
apprentices. I . . . I truly believe that Brambleclaw is the right
choice." In spite of all her misgivings, she couldn't ignore the
tabby tom's courage and warrior skills, and the determination
that had led his companion cats to the sun-drown-place and
brought them home with the prophecy that had saved the
Clans. He had been chosen by StarClan then; this could be
the next paw step they wanted him to take.

Firestar nodded thoughtfully. "Thank you, Leafpool." He
rose and gave himself a quick grooming. "Come on. It's time."

He padded out of the den and onto the Highledge. Leafpool followed and stood at his shoulder, looking down into the clearing. The Clan were already gathering below, aware that moonhigh was only moments away. Their eyes gleamed pale in the moonlight as they stared up at the ledge.

"The time has come to name ThunderClan's new deputy," Firestar announced. "I say these words before StarClan, that the spirits of our ancestors, and Graystripe's spirit, wherever it may be, may hear and approve my choice."

He paused, as if even now he was reluctant to let go of the last hope that Graystripe would come back. But his voice was stronger as he continued.

"Brambleclaw will be the new deputy of ThunderClan."

Gasps of surprise came from the cats below. "What, that bossy furball?" Spiderleg exclaimed, then looked embarrassed that he'd spoken aloud.

Leafpool could see astonishment reflected on the faces of every cat, though none was more astonished than Brambleclaw himself. His amber eyes stretched wide with shock. "But I've never had an apprentice!" he blurted out.

"That's against the warrior code," Dustpelt pointed out sharply.

"Firestar, do you think you can do anything you like?" Mousefur's wiry body was taut with anger. "We want a deputy to make the Clan strong, not an inexperienced young cat we can't trust."

"Who says we can't trust him?" Squirrelflight demanded.

"Silence!" Firestar lashed his tail. "Brambleclaw has

experience that few cats in the forest share. As for his lack of an apprentice, that will be put right soon. Daisy's kits are almost ready for mentors, and as soon as that day comes, Brambleclaw will mentor Berrykit."

In spite of the tension around her, Leafpool had to suppress a *mrrow* of amusement when she heard the squeal that went up from the direction of the nursery. Craning her neck to peer through the branches, she spotted Berrykit madly chasing his tail in excitement.

"But those weren't my only reasons for choosing Brambleclaw," Firestar continued. "Leafpool, tell the Clan about your dream, please."

Leafpool stepped forward to the edge of the Highledge and described the sign that StarClan had sent her, of the circle of brambles keeping the Clan safe. When she finished, she saw Dustpelt dip his head.

"I can't quarrel with StarClan," he meowed.

"Well, I can!" To Leafpool's surprise, the challenge came from Ashfur. He marched forward until he stood directly beneath the Highledge, the moonlight turning his gray pelt to silver. Instead of addressing his leader, he turned to face the Clan. "Doesn't any cat think it's odd that Squirrelflight is Brambleclaw's mate, and our medicine cat is Squirrelflight's sister? It's very convenient that she had a sign about Brambleclaw just now, isn't it?"

Leafpool felt her neck fur bristling. How *dared* Ashfur suggest that she would invent a sign to help her sister's mate become deputy! Even if he was bitter at losing Squirrelflight to Brambleclaw, he should know that a medicine cat would never lie.

"Ashfur, you—" she began.

Her words were drowned in a furious yowl from Squirrelflight. "Say that to my face, fox dung!"

The ginger warrior lunged at Ashfur, but Brambleclaw thrust her to one side and wrapped his tail around her neck. He was saying something to her, speaking fast and urgently, too low for Leafpool to hear.

"Do any other cats agree with Ashfur?" Firestar demanded calmly.

Leafpool saw Spiderleg glance uneasily from side to side; he opened his jaws to speak and then obviously thought better of it.

"None of us agree," Brackenfur called out. "Leafpool is an honest cat. If StarClan chose Brambleclaw, that's enough for us. I think he'll make a great deputy."

Brambleclaw stepped away from Squirrelflight with a last warning glance. He dipped his head to Brackenfur and then, more deeply still, to Firestar. "Thank you," he meowed. "I know I can never fill Graystripe's place, but I'll do my best to be a good deputy for ThunderClan."

The tension within Leafpool faded as the Clan crowded around Brambleclaw to congratulate him, pressing up against him and calling out his name. Stormfur and Brook were among the first, and even Mousefur was among them. The only cat to hold back was Ashfur, who stalked off alone to the warriors' den.

As the cats began to leave the clearing, some to their dens, some to continue the vigil for Graystripe, Leafpool thought she saw another cat twining itself around Brambleclaw. A muscular tomcat, broader in the shoulders, but with the same dark tabby fur. The shape was gone almost at once, but not before Leafpool had seen its powerful, curved claws and the gleam of triumph in its amber eyes.

Tigerstar still haunted the paw steps of his son, and had been beside him when Firestar made him deputy.

CHAPTER 18

Brambleclaw raced through the dark forest. He felt as though every limb, every hair on his pelt, was bursting with energy. He couldn't wait to tell his father and Hawkfrost the news. Clan deputy! When Firestar made the announcement, he hadn't been able to believe it. But it was true. Not only Firestar, but StarClan themselves had chosen him. Now he had the chance to show the whole of ThunderClan what he could do.

He pelted into the clearing where Tigerstar waited on his rock with Hawkfrost sitting on the ground below. "Tigerstar!" he panted. "Great news!"

Tigerstar fixed him with an amber gaze that brimmed with pride and satisfaction, and Brambleclaw realized that he already knew. "ThunderClan deputy," he meowed. "You have done well."

"Deputy!" Hawkfrost exclaimed. Brambleclaw caught the glitter of jealousy in his ice-blue eyes. "Without an apprentice?"

"I was StarClan's choice," Brambleclaw explained. "They sent Leafpool a sign."

Tigerstar spoke sharply. "Do not speak of StarClan here.

261

You have gained your position through your own skills and through everything you have learned from me. And yet when power was within your paws you almost threw it away." His gaze darkened, so that Brambleclaw had to brace himself not to flinch. "Why did you remind Firestar that you hadn't had an apprentice?"

"I'm sorry," Brambleclaw meowed. "I was so shocked I couldn't believe what he was saying."

To his relief, Tigerstar nodded. "Perhaps it was not so foolish after all," he decided. "Now none of your Clan can accuse you of seeking power unfairly." He swiped his tongue around his jaws and turned to Hawkfrost. "As for you, your time will come."

Hawkfrost's lip curled, showing his sharp teeth. "I doubt it. It sometimes seems like Leopardstar and Mistyfoot will live forever."

Tigerstar lashed his tail. "No son of mine admits defeat. Leopardstar is the oldest of the Clan leaders, and when she goes to join StarClan, who else could Mistyfoot appoint as deputy? Don't forget that you have already been deputy once."

Hawkfrost nodded and seemed to make an effort to shrug off his ill temper. "Congratulations," he mewed to Brambleclaw.

"Thanks," Brambleclaw replied. "I'm sure you won't have to wait long for your turn."

"Enough of this," Tigerstar meowed with a flick of his tail. "There are more plans for us to make. The two of you are destined to rule the whole forest, and every cat will do as you command. Not one bite of prey will be eaten by any cat unless you say so."

Hawkfrost's eyes gleamed, but Brambleclaw took a pace back. What was Tigerstar talking about? It was a huge step from being Clan deputy to ruling the entire forest.

"What do you mean?" he asked. "How can—?"

Tigerstar silenced him with a snarl. "Once you are both leaders, Hawkfrost will take over ShadowClan as well as RiverClan. They will welcome him because I was their leader once, and he is my son. And you, Brambleclaw, will lead WindClan alongside ThunderClan."

"But Onestar leads WindClan!" Brambleclaw pointed out. "And they've been ThunderClan allies for many seasons."

Tigerstar's tail-tip twitched. "Which is why taking control of their Clan won't be a problem. Those weak fools in WindClan are so used to taking orders from ThunderClan that they'll hardly notice the difference."

Brambleclaw stared up at his father, daunted by the blaze of certainty in his amber eyes. "But there have always been four Clans," he objected, knowing how feeble his words must sound.

"There used to be, in the forest." Tigerstar flicked his ears, dismissing the Clans' former home. "But now that everything else has changed, perhaps it's time for that to change too. It *will* change, if you have the strength."

For a few heartbeats, Brambleclaw let himself get swept up in his father's vision of the future. It was tempting to imagine himself controlling a vast swath of land, with two Clans of strong, powerful warriors at his command. He could lead them well, he knew. StarClan had chosen him to be ThunderClan's deputy; perhaps this was just the first tiny paw step on his way to a glorious destiny.

"Of course we have the strength," Hawkfrost meowed. "At the next Gathering we should start making friends in our future Clans, so that we'll have their support when we take over."

Tigerstar nodded, but Hawkfrost's words disturbed Brambleclaw. He already *had* friends in WindClan. They wouldn't support him if he tried to take over; they would think he had betrayed them. He glanced at Hawkfrost, who was obviously waiting for him to respond, and gave a non-committal murmur. He wasn't going to agree to anything until he'd had time to think this through.

"A Gathering would be the perfect opportunity to take power," Hawkfrost went on, his eyes gleaming. "Brambleclaw, when you and I are leaders of our Clans, we could choose our strongest cats to come with us to the Gathering—"

"Cats who will carry out your orders without question," Tigerstar put in, dipping his head to Hawkfrost as if he already guessed his son's plan and approved of it.

"Of course. And then we simply kill the other two leaders and take over their Clans while they're all trapped on the island."

"What?" Brambleclaw felt his neck fur rising. He couldn't believe what he had heard. "At a *Gathering*?"

"Yes—that's the clever part of it," Hawkfrost explained. "No cat will be expecting trouble."

"And two strong warriors will be all you need to guard the end of the tree-bridge," Tigerclaw added. "No cat will be able to escape."

Brambleclaw took a step back. "How can you suggest killing at a Gathering? StarClan would never forgive us if we broke their truce."

Hawkfrost shrugged. "StarClan were angry when the fight broke out at the last Gathering—or so Barkface said. But I didn't see any cat being hurt because of it."

"Everything is possible." Tigerstar's voice growled deep in his chest; his amber eyes were fixed on Brambleclaw with a baleful glare. "You will never be a powerful leader if you keep cringing to StarClan. Or if you're afraid to get blood on your paws."

"I'm not afraid of anything," Brambleclaw retorted. "But I won't kill at a Gathering."

Hawkfrost padded over to him and swept his tail across Brambleclaw's shoulder. "Keep your fur on," he mewed. "It was only an idea. If you don't like it, there are other ways."

"There'd better be." Brambleclaw wasn't sure he wanted to go on with this at all, but he found it hard to talk freely—or even think—under Tigerstar's ominous amber gaze.

"We need to talk properly about this." Brambleclaw jumped as his half brother seemed to echo his thoughts. "Why don't we meet when we're awake?"

There can't be any harm in that, Brambleclaw decided. Perhaps if he could discuss things with his half brother without their father listening to every word, he could get things straight in his own mind. He might even be able to convince Hawkfrost that leading their own Clans would be enough, without trying to take over the others.

"Okay," he mewed. "Where?"

"Your territory, I think," Hawkfrost replied. "I'll find it easier to get away than you will, now that you're deputy."

Brambleclaw nodded; that made sense. "By the lake, then. Just beyond the ShadowClan border the woodland stretches right down to the water's edge. Let's meet there." That way, he added to himself, Hawkfrost could stay within the agreed two tail-lengths from the shore. No cat could accuse them of doing anything wrong.

"Fine," Hawkfrost agreed. "Let's meet in two days, at sunrise. You'll need all of tomorrow to get used to your new duties," he added with a friendly flick of his tail.

"Excellent." Tigerstar's voice rumbled in his throat, the nearest the fierce cat ever came to a purr. "Go now. We will meet again soon and discuss the plans you have made."

Brambleclaw turned to go, only to glance back as Hawkfrost called his name. His half brother's ice-blue gaze was fixed on him with glittering intensity.

"You won't forget our meeting?" Hawkfrost meowed.

"No, of course not."

"Remember, the way to power is hard, and paved with difficult choices," Tigerstar warned.

He held Brambleclaw with an unwavering stare. For a heartbeat Brambleclaw felt like a piece of prey, trapped and unsure of which way to run.

"I'm not afraid," he meowed, trying to sound confident. "I'll be there, don't worry."

"Hey, wake up!" A paw prodded Brambleclaw sharply in the side. "Are you planning to sleep until leaf-bare? It's time to appoint the patrols."

Brambleclaw blinked his eyes open to see Squirrelflight standing over him. "You're deputy now," she informed him. "Or had you forgotten?"

Brambleclaw scrambled up, shaking himself to scatter scraps of moss and fern from his pelt. To cover his confusion, he gave his chest fur a few quick licks. Since the Clan had been in their new home, the senior warriors had divided the deputy's duties among themselves; now they would all fall on his shoulders.

I can handle it, he told himself.

A misty light was already filling the warriors' den; the dawn patrol would have to leave right away.

"Okay," Brambleclaw meowed. "I'll lead the dawn patrol. Squirrelflight, will you come with me? Cloudtail, we'll take you as well, and Rainwhisker."

Cloudtail stretched his jaws in a huge yawn, mumbled, "Right with you," and woke the younger warrior by tickling his nose with the tip of his tail. Rainwhisker sat bolt upright, staring around as if he wasn't sure what had disturbed him.

"Sandstorm," Brambleclaw went on, feeling awkward to be giving orders to a senior warrior, "would you choose a hunting patrol, please?"

The ginger she-cat dipped her head in agreement. "Two

would be a good idea, don't you think?" she suggested. "Which cat would you like to lead the other?"

"Er . . . Dustpelt?" Brambleclaw would have been quite prepared for the tabby tom to react with annoyance at being ordered around by a younger cat, but all he did was stretch and mutter, "Okay."

"You know, Brambleclaw," Sandstorm meowed, a trace of amusement in her voice, "you don't need to worry about giving us orders. You're deputy, and that's that."

"Thank you," Brambleclaw replied. Trying to sound convincing, he added, "I'll be loyal to my Clan as long as I have breath enough to fight."

He repeated the words in his mind as he led his patrol out through the thorn barrier and up the slope toward the ShadowClan border. It was true. Nothing mattered to him more than the well-being of ThunderClan. He would show every cat in the forest what a great deputy he could be. Regretfully he realized that there was still more than a half moon to wait before the next Gathering, when Firestar would announce his deputyship to the other Clans, and he would be able to sit on the oak roots with Mistyfoot, Ashfoot, and Russetfur.

When they reached the border he half hoped that they might meet a ShadowClan patrol, so that he could mention his new position to them, but everything was quiet. The scents of ShadowClan cats were fading, suggesting that their dawn patrol had passed by earlier. Brambleclaw's pelt prickled with impatience. He was desperate to tell his news to some other cat; he almost felt that if a mouse crossed his path he would stop to inform it that it was about to be eaten by the ThunderClan deputy.

By the time the dawn patrol returned, the hunting patrols were bringing in their first catches. Brambleclaw dispatched Birchpaw and Whitepaw to take prey to the elders, and to Firestar and Leafpool. Then he called the remaining cats around him and started assigning patrols for the following day. He didn't want to be flustered again as he had been this morning; besides, he wanted to be sure he was free for his meeting with Hawkfrost.

While Brambleclaw was speaking, Berrykit scurried out of the nursery and skidded to a halt in front of him. "I want to go on patrol," he announced. "Can I?"

"No," Brambleclaw told him firmly. "Not till you're an apprentice."

"You'll take me then, won't you?"

"Yes, of course."

Berrykit's eyes shone. "I'm going to be the *deputy's* apprentice," he announced to every cat within earshot.

Brambleclaw gave him a friendly nudge with one paw, and went on giving out the duties.

"Hey, bossypaws." Squirrelflight's voice held a *mrrow* of laughter as she flicked his ear with her tail-tip. "You've already assigned Ferncloud to a hunting patrol. She can't do the dawn patrol as well."

"Sorry," Brambleclaw muttered to a confused Ferncloud. "You go hunting with Dustpelt. I'll find another cat for the dawn patrol."

"Later will do," Squirrelflight told him. "First you can

come and eat." She led the way over to the fresh-kill pile, glancing over her shoulder to add, "Deputies do eat, I suppose? They don't have to do their duties *all* the time?"

Brambleclaw relaxed; in spite of her teasing words, there was a warm gleam of affection in Squirrelflight's green eyes. But would Squirrelflight still want to be near him, would her eyes still glow as she gazed at him, if she knew that he had arranged to meet Hawkfrost tomorrow?

He knew what the answer was. He would lose Squirrelflight forever if she found out. What else might he lose as well? Tigerstar had been stripped of his deputyship and sent into exile when Firestar uncovered his plot to kill Bluestar. Would the same thing happen to Brambleclaw if his meetings with Hawkfrost and Tigerstar were revealed?

Brambleclaw tried to tell himself that no cat could ever uncover his secret, but he shivered in the warm sunlight of greenleaf. *I'm not planning to kill any cat*, he told himself. All he wanted was to make ThunderClan strong again. His Clanmates had been without a deputy for too long; now they had one, and Brambleclaw knew he would do anything to justify StarClan's faith in him.

CHAPTER 19

As Leafpool set out for her meeting at the Moonpool, her pelt still prickled with uneasiness. Brambleclaw's first day as deputy had gone well; he gave orders with quiet authority and he worked harder than any cat on his own patrols. But she couldn't forget her vision of Tigerstar shadowing him as Firestar announced that he would be deputy. Somehow, she knew, Brambleclaw was still in contact with his murderous father. And that meant the whole Clan could be in danger.

Hoping for a sign when she shared tongues with StarClan at the Moonpool, she padded through the forest and emerged from the trees near the stream where it gurgled around the stepping-stones. Barkface and Mothwing were waiting for her, and in the twilight Leafpool could just make out the shape of another, smaller cat—Willowpaw! Leafpool had forgotten that this was the night when the young gray she-cat would be officially received by StarClan as Mothwing's apprentice.

"Hi," she meowed, bounding up to them. "Willowpaw, it's great to see you."

Willowpaw ducked her head shyly. Her eyes shone; she

looked almost too excited to speak. "Hi, Leafpool," she mewed. "It's great to be here."

To Leafpool's relief the apprentice didn't mention the dream they had shared about finding the catmint. Barkface might overhear, and he would think it very strange that another Clan's medicine cat had to guide Mothwing's apprentice.

"Where's Littlecloud?" Leafpool asked. "He isn't usually late."

Barkface shrugged. "No idea. He may have gone ahead."

"We'd better get on. The moon will be up soon," Mothwing added.

Leafpool could see tension in every hair of her friend's pelt. She could understand why. Mothwing was about to present her apprentice to StarClan when she herself didn't believe in them. She must be terrified of what would happen. Perhaps StarClan wouldn't even accept Willowpaw when her mentor couldn't reach them.

No, Leafpool comforted herself. *Feathertail came to Willowpaw in my dream, and promised her she would have lots more dreams of StarClan.*

She wished she could comfort Mothwing, but in front of Barkface she couldn't even admit that the problem existed.

The four cats had just crossed the ThunderClan border when a yowl sounded behind them and Littlecloud raced up to them.

"Sorry," he panted. "Cedarheart turned up with a thorn in his paw just as I was about to leave. Welcome," he added, dipping his head to Willowpaw. "Don't be nervous about tonight. You'll be fine; you've got a great mentor."

Mothwing said nothing, but Leafpool didn't miss the flash of panic in her eyes.

The moon floated high in the sky by the time the medicine cats pushed their way through the barrier of bushes and stood at the top of the hollow. Willowpaw stared in delight at the silver stream pouring down the rock in front of her, and the bubbling Moonpool that seemed to be full of starlight.

"It's so beautiful!" she whispered.

Barkface took the lead down the dimpled path to the waterside. Mothwing followed with Willowpaw just behind her, while Leafpool and Littlecloud went last.

Beside the pool, Mothwing turned and faced her apprentice. "Willowpaw," she meowed, "is it your wish to enter into the mysteries of StarClan as a medicine cat?" Whatever she believed privately, she knew the words for this ritual well enough—and sounded as if she meant every one of them, too.

Willowpaw's gray fur, turned to silver in the moonlight, was fluffed out in excitement and she held her tail high. Her eyes were filled with awe as she replied solemnly, "It is."

"Then come forward."

Willowpaw padded up to her until both cats stood on the very edge of the Moonpool. Mothwing raised her head to gaze at Silverpelt; Leafpool wondered what she saw there. Her voice was high-pitched and almost shaking as she went on with the ceremony; she looked more nervous than her apprentice.

"Warriors of StarClan, I present to you this apprentice. She has chosen the path of a medicine cat. Grant her your wisdom and insight so that she may understand your ways and heal her Clan in accordance with your will."

Leafpool's heart twisted with pity for her friend, recognizing what each word was costing her. Every day she lived a lie, but this was worse than anything else, to call on starry spirits she did not believe in where all the other medicine cats could hear her.

Mothwing waved her tail at Willowpaw. "Crouch down and drink from the pool."

Blinking, Willowpaw obeyed her. Her mentor and the rest of the medicine cats took their own places around the edge of the pool, and stretched out to lap up a few drops of the silvery water.

To Leafpool it tasted like liquid starshine, icy cold, piercing her to the bone. As the drops touched her tongue she sank into darkness; for a few heartbeats she seemed to float in nothingness.

Then her eyes opened and she found herself crouched on the edge of a pool whose waters glimmered with the reflection of Silverpelt. But it was not the Moonpool. It lay in a forest clearing; ferns and flowers grew around the edge and studded the grass, shining with a pale light.

Leafpool gazed upward, tasting the cold night air with the wild scent of wind and stars. She felt as if only the tiniest leap would carry her into the sky, to share tongues with StarClan in their own territory.

Then above her head she saw the three tiny stars that she had seen twice before. They seemed to shine more brightly than ever.

Beside Leafpool, Willowpaw was curled up asleep, and on the opposite side of the pool sat a beautiful tortoiseshell she-cat, her eyes glowing softly as she gazed at the apprentice.

"Spottedleaf!" Leafpool exclaimed.

She raced up to the starry spirit, drinking in the familiar sweet scent, and pressed herself against Spottedleaf's soft tortoiseshell flank. "I'm so glad to see you. Can you tell me about those three stars?" She pointed upward with her tail. "I would think they'd mean that three warriors have died, but I can't figure out who it would be!"

Spottedleaf shook her head. "The stars are a sign, dear one. But this is not the time for you to discover their meaning."

Leafpool opened her mouth to protest. But she knew that StarClan were wiser than she was, and they would tell her what she needed to know at the proper time. Swallowing her disappointment, she mewed instead, "At least you shared Mothwing's secret with me, about the moth's wing sign. Thank you."

"I thought it was time for you to know," Spottedleaf told her. "You're a good friend to her, and she will need your support."

"I haven't talked to her about it yet," Leafpool mewed. "Do you think I should?"

Spottedleaf gave her ear a warm, affectionate lick. "Not unless you want to—or unless Mothwing speaks of it herself.

Just reassure her that she can be a great medicine cat and that she deserves to keep her place among her Clanmates."

"That's not hard," Leafpool meowed. "Mothwing *is* a great medicine cat. No cat could care more for her Clan than she does. She *hates* what Hawkfrost is trying to make her do."

Spottedleaf nodded and a shadow touched her beautiful eyes. "Hawkfrost's destiny is in the paws of StarClan," she murmured. "He is not your concern."

She rose and padded around the pool with Leafpool following, until they stood over the sleeping apprentice.

"StarClan are grateful to you," Spottedleaf went on, "for the help you're giving Willowpaw. She will need you as much as Mothwing if she is to grow into a full medicine cat. I know you'll keep your part of her training a secret—you have already proved you can stay silent."

"Thank you, Spottedleaf," Leafpool meowed, grateful for the StarClan cat's trust. She hesitated and then went on, "I wish I could see Cinderpelt. She never comes to me, and I miss her so much! Are you sure she isn't angry with me?"

Spottedleaf nuzzled the top of Leafpool's head, making her feel like a kit again, secure in the nursery with her mother. "Quite certain. Stop worrying about Cinderpelt, dear one. She is closer to you than you know. Would you like me to prove it to you?"

Leafpool blinked. "Oh, Spottedleaf, if only you could!"

Spottedleaf bent her head to lap from the glittering water and twitched her ears to tell Leafpool to do the same. Awe shivered through Leafpool from ears to tail-tip. She bent her head and lapped a few drops. This was not the icy water of the Moonpool that would sweep her into dreams. Instead, it was cool and fragrant with the scents of healing herbs. Leafpool felt as though it were soaking into every part of her body, giving her strength and courage.

"Now follow me," Spottedleaf directed.

Leafpool padded in the other cat's paw steps across the clearing and into the trees. Suddenly she realized that she was back in her own familiar forest, with the thorn barrier to the ThunderClan camp looming up in front of her.

"Why have you brought me here?" she asked.

Spottedleaf did not reply. She led the way through the thorn tunnel and across the camp to the nursery. Close to the entrance, Daisy was lying among her kits, all of them curled up and deeply asleep. Leafpool edged past them lightly.

The former medicine cat led her to the far corner of the nursery, where Sorreltail was sleeping. Her four kits were nuzzling close to her belly. Three of them slept, but as Leafpool watched, Cinderkit raised her head and blinked open blue eyes, fixing Leafpool with such an intense, familiar gaze that she could not look away.

"Now do you understand?" Spottedleaf purred.

"It . . . it can't be true," Leafpool whispered. "Why . . . how?"

"It is true," Spottedleaf assured her. "Do you feel better knowing this?"

"Oh, yes!" Leafpool breathed out. "Thank you, Spottedleaf."

"Now we must go back," Spottedleaf mewed. "It's time to

make Willowpaw into a true medicine cat."

Cinderkit's jaws gaped in a huge yawn, showing a pink tongue and tiny sharp teeth. Her eyes closed again and she nestled into her mother's fur. Leafpool bent her head until the kit's fluffy gray fur tickled her nose and she could drink in her warm kit scent, then turned and followed Spottedleaf out of the nursery. *Good-bye, Cinderpelt*, she thought as the thorn branches closed up behind her.

Somehow, as they left the camp, they crossed the boundary again into the dream forest. Willowpaw was still sleeping beside the pool. Spottedleaf padded up to her and breathed softly into her ear. The apprentice blinked awake and raised her head, gazing up at the former medicine cat.

"You're a StarClan warrior, aren't you?" she mewed. "I can see the stars in your fur."

"I am, small one. My name is Spottedleaf. And here is your friend Leafpool."

Willowpaw scrambled to her paws. "Hi, Leafpool. Isn't Mothwing with you?" she added, glancing around.

"No, you will not see her in this dream," Spottedleaf replied.

A stab of discomfort pierced Leafpool at the thought that Mothwing wasn't here to see her apprentice taking her first steps in the world of StarClan. *But some cat must do it*, she told herself. *Mothwing can't and StarClan has chosen me.*

"Where are we? Why are we here?" Willowpaw asked. She whirled around, trying to take in all the clearing in one glance.

"We've come to share a sign from StarClan with you," Spottedleaf answered. "Are you ready?"

Willowpaw's eyes shone. "Yes!" She gave a little bounce, reminding Leafpool of the kit she had been not long ago. "Oh, this is so exciting! I never had dreams like this before I was apprenticed."

"You will have many more," Spottedleaf told her. "Wherever your paws lead you, you will never be alone."

Spottedleaf gestured with her tail for Willowpaw to lap from the pool. She crouched beside the apprentice, gazing into the depths; Leafpool took her place on Willowpaw's other side.

"What do you see?" Spottedleaf asked.

The water was flat, reflecting the stars above. Then gradually their light was blotted out, and Leafpool realized she could see gray clouds churning beneath the surface. A fierce cold wind sprang up, rattling the trees and gouging the surface of the pool. It buffeted Leafpool's fur until she dug her claws deep into the earth, terrified of being swept away. She heard Willowpaw let out a frightened cry.

"Don't be afraid!" Spottedleaf's meow rose above the rushing of the wind. "Nothing here will harm you."

Leafpool squeezed her eyes tight shut as the wind blew so hard, she felt her claws being tugged out of the ground. And then she was blinking awake on the edge of the Moonpool, her heart still pounding. Above her, the moon floated in a clear sky, with not even the faintest breeze to chase the clouds or disturb the surface of the pool. Willowpaw was crouched beside the water, her eyes closed, her breathing light and shallow. Farther around the pool, Littlecloud and Barkface still walked in dreams. Mothwing sat on the other side of Willowpaw, her paws together with her tail wrapped around them. She was gazing at the starry water with such anguish in her eyes that Leafpool thought her heart would break with sympathy.

"Mothwing," she murmured, pushing aside her vision of the storm.

Mothwing turned to look at her. "I'm so afraid," she whispered. "Do you think she'll have the right sort of dream? How can she be a medicine cat when her mentor doesn't believe in StarClan?"

Leafpool rose and skirted the sleeping apprentice to draw close to her friend and give her a few warm licks around her ear. "Spottedleaf came to her," she reassured Mothwing. "I was there. I saw her too."

Mothwing shook her head. "It was just a dream."

Leafpool pressed against her, trying to strengthen her with the certainty of her own belief. "You'll see. Everything will be fine."

Mothwing jerked away from her. "No, no, it can't be. Oh, Leafpool, I can't go on lying any longer! I have to tell you." She fixed huge amber eyes on Leafpool. "You think StarClan chose me, but they didn't. The moth's wing outside Mudfur's den wasn't a sign from them. Hawkfrost put it there, but I promise you, Leafpool, I *promise*, I didn't know about it until afterward."

Leafpool gazed at her. Warmth flooded through her at the thought that her friend trusted her enough to tell her the truth. Following it came icy terror. *Oh, StarClan, give me the right words!*

As Leafpool hesitated, Mothwing shrank back. "What are you going to do?" she whimpered. "Will you tell the others? Will I have to stop being a medicine cat?"

"Of course not." Leafpool pressed against her friend again, touching her nose to her ear. "Mothwing, I already knew."

Mothwing's eyes stretched even wider. "You *knew*? How?"

"Spottedleaf sent me a sign. And . . . and I heard Hawkfrost talking to you after the last Gathering."

"Hawkfrost!" Mothwing's tone was bitter. "He keeps threatening to tell every cat unless I do what he wants. He made me lie at the Gathering. I never had that dream—but you know that too, don't you?"

Leafpool nodded.

"I wanted to be a medicine cat so much! And at first I tried to believe in StarClan, I really did. When Mudfur took me to the Moonstone I thought I had a dream where I met some cats from StarClan, and they showed me things that were happening in the forest. Then when I got back to RiverClan, Hawkfrost told me what he'd done with the moth's wing. And I realized that StarClan must be just a story and that everything I had seen was only an ordinary dream. Because if StarClan really existed, they wouldn't let him do such a wicked thing or torment me like this!"

Leafpool stroked Mothwing's shoulder with the tip of her

tail. Her insides churned with anger, but she fought to hide it from her friend. Now she *knew* she had been right to mistrust Hawkfrost. He had destroyed his sister's faith, crippling her as a medicine cat when she had so much to offer with her healing skills.

"It's all right," she murmured. "Believe me, all will be well."

"How can it?" Mothwing protested. "I should have told every cat the truth right away. But I couldn't give up being a medicine cat. I love healing so much and I wanted to help my Clanmates. And now it's too late. If I tell them what happened, they'll drive me out, and I've nowhere else to go."

"You don't have to go anywhere," Leafpool promised. "Spottedleaf told me that StarClan want you to stay where you are and do what you've always done. She said you can be a great medicine cat and you deserve your place at the Moonpool."

For a heartbeat hope flared in Mothwing's eyes, as if she wanted to believe what Leafpool told her. Then she shook her head. "It's kind of you to say that, but I know it isn't true. Oh, I don't think you're lying," she added hastily, "but it was just a dream." She sighed. "But if you really think I should, I'll carry on. Only, how am I going to mentor Willowpaw properly? I don't know what to tell her about StarClan."

"But I do," Leafpool pointed out. "I'll teach her what she needs to know about them and walk with her in dreams. And you can show her all the herbs and how to use them. She'll be a wonderful apprentice."

Mothwing's head drooped. "I don't deserve her," she whis-

pered. After a moment she lifted her head again, a new determination in her eyes. "But I'm going to try. I won't listen to
Hawkfrost anymore. I'll remind him that no cat would ever
make him deputy if they knew he'd lied about a sign from
StarClan."

"That's a good idea," Leafpool meowed. "But be careful
you—"

She had to break off as Littlecloud, on the other side of the
pool, lifted his head, then rose to his paws and arched his
back in a long stretch. Barkface was stirring too, and
Willowpaw woke, sprang up right away, and pattered across
the moss-covered rocks to her mentor.

"It was so scary—but amazing!" she exclaimed, and added
more quietly, "I wish you'd been there." Leafpool's respect for
the apprentice increased as she saw how Willowpaw understood that Mothwing didn't meet with StarClan. She was also
very relieved that Willowpaw had been exhilarated by her
vision of StarClan's world, not paralyzed by fear.

"I wish I'd been there too," Mothwing replied.

"Maybe one day?" Willowpaw mewed.

Mothwing didn't say anything, but Leafpool could see she
didn't share her apprentice's confidence.

"Leafpool, what do you think the sign meant?" Willowpaw
asked anxiously. "Storm clouds! Do you think there's trouble
coming for our Clans?"

Leafpool flipped the end of her tail across Willowpaw's
mouth, with a glance at Barkface and Littlecloud to make
sure they hadn't heard.

"Medicine cats don't usually speak of their signs," she explained. "Not until they're ready to interpret them to their Clan. Yes, I think it means trouble," she added. "But it might be as well to say nothing to any cat yet. There's no sense in spreading alarm until we know more."

Willowpaw nodded seriously and Leafpool felt a pang of guilt that she wasn't being entirely open with the young apprentice. Littlecloud and Barkface showed no signs of troubling dreams, so Spottedleaf's sign must have been for ThunderClan and RiverClan alone. And there was one cat who connected both Clans: Hawkfrost!

As Leafpool followed the path that led out of the hollow she silently thanked StarClan that Mothwing had trusted her enough to tell her about Hawkfrost's false sign. But she couldn't be sure that Mothwing would have the courage to defy her brother, whatever she said. She had too much to lose.

A shadow fell across the hollow as Leafpool reached the top of the path. She looked up to see that a cloud had drifted across the moon. Her pelt prickled as a cold breeze swept through the circle of bushes and she felt once more the rushing wind of her dream. She was sure that terrible trouble was coming—and somehow Hawkfrost was involved.

CHAPTER 20

❧

Brambleclaw stood in the clearing and watched the hunting patrols leave through the thorn tunnel. The dawn patrol had already left, and the early-morning mist was beginning to clear. Above the trees the sky was a pale, distant blue, promising a warm day later. Soon the sun would rise.

The tabby tom glanced around, anxious to make sure that all duties were being covered. The fresh-kill pile was low, but the hunting patrols would take care of that. Daisy was yawning at the entrance to the nursery, watching her kits play-fighting in front of her. Leafpool crossed the camp to the elders' den, where Mousefur had just emerged, scratching her ear vigorously with one hind paw. Every cat looked sleek and well-fed; even slender Leafpool had grown quite plump. The famine in their old home had become nothing more than an unpleasant memory.

Behind Brambleclaw the branches of the warriors' den rustled; he glanced back to see Ashfur slipping between them and stopping to give his pelt a quick grooming.

Brambleclaw padded up to him. Whitepaw had gone with her mentor, Brackenfur, on hunting patrol, so the apprentices wouldn't be training together today.

"Where's Birchpaw?" he asked. "This would be a good time for a training session."

Ashfur narrowed his eyes. "I can mentor my own apprentice," he meowed. "I've arranged to give him an assessment today, actually."

"Yes, that's fine," Brambleclaw replied. "Remind him about the fox traps, just in case."

Ashfur stalked off toward the apprentices' den without replying. Birchpaw emerged when his mentor called him and listened to his instructions, paws working impatiently in the ground. Then he headed for the camp entrance, stopping for a brief word with Thornclaw as the brown warrior emerged from the tunnel with fresh-kill in his jaws. At last Birchpaw left, bounding away with his tail in the air. Ashfur gave Brambleclaw another resentful glare before he followed.

Brambleclaw told himself he could have been a bit more tactful; even so, if Ashfur's attitude didn't improve, he was going to find himself collecting mouse bile for the elders' ticks.

Suddenly he froze. He had become so caught up in his deputy's duties that he had almost forgotten about meeting Hawkfrost. Sunrise was not far off; he was going to be late. He headed for the thorn barrier, only to halt, groaning inwardly, when he heard Squirrelflight's voice behind him.

"Hey, Brambleclaw! Where are you going?"

Brambleclaw turned to face her as she came bounding across the clearing toward him. Squirrelflight hadn't been assigned to any of the early patrols. She wouldn't understand why he didn't want to spend time with her, since he wasn't going on a patrol either.

"Where are you going?" she repeated as she came up to him. "Hunting? Let's go together."

"I have to—" Brambleclaw began awkwardly. He broke off as Daisy's three kits, Berrykit in the lead, dashed across the clearing and disappeared behind the brambles that screened Leafpool's den.

"Those bad kits!" Squirrelflight exclaimed. "Remember the mess they made last time? I'd better check that Leafpool is there."

She raced off. Silently thanking StarClan, Brambleclaw slipped out through the tunnel and headed into the forest at a run, making for the lake.

The sun had risen by now, and the trees were casting long shadows over grass that glittered with dew. Cobwebs shone on every bush. There was no sign of other cats; he had made sure that the hunting patrols went to other parts of the territory.

He paused at the edge of the forest; he heard the gentle lap of water a couple of tail-lengths away and glimpsed its dazzling surface through the thick ferns. Opening his jaws, he tasted the air. He thought he could pick up RiverClan scent, and an unexpected trace of ShadowClan, but he couldn't see his half brother. "Hawkfrost?" he called cautiously.

No reply. Brambleclaw spotted a thrush a fox-length or so in front of him, dragging a worm out of the ground. It reminded him that he hadn't eaten that morning, so he dropped instinctively into the hunter's crouch. In the same heartbeat something heavy crashed down on him, sending him tumbling over. He let out a yowl of alarm and the thrush took off with a loud stuttering cry. Flipping over to face his attacker, Brambleclaw stared up at Hawkfrost, who was gazing down at him with a glimmer of amusement in his ice-blue eyes.

"Do you *mind*?" Brambleclaw spat. "Do you want every cat in ThunderClan to know you're here?"

Hawkfrost shrugged. "It doesn't matter. I'm allowed to be here as long as I stay close to the lake."

Brambleclaw scrambled to his paws and smoothed his ruffled fur with a couple of licks. Hawkfrost was right, but he would still have some explaining to do if any of his Clanmates spotted him talking to his half brother. He wished he had Hawkfrost's confidence, but he reminded himself that he was Clan deputy, and the RiverClan warrior's equal in every way.

"Come into the ferns," he meowed, flicking his tail to beckon Hawkfrost.

As they sat close together beneath the arching fronds, Brambleclaw picked up the scent of ShadowClan again. He wrinkled his nose. "You have ShadowClan scent on you," he mewed.

Hawkfrost narrowed his eyes. "I must have picked up their reek on my way across their territory," he growled. "Never mind that. We're wasting time."

Brambleclaw nodded and took a deep breath. He hoped he

could find the right words to let Hawkfrost know his doubts about Tigerstar's vision, without letting him think he was any less committed to becoming leader of his Clan. "This idea of Tigerstar's, that we take over ShadowClan and WindClan," he began, "I'm not sure it will work. StarClan have decreed there should be four Clans."

His half brother flicked the tip of his tail. "Like Tigerstar said, that was back in the forest. *Listen*, Brambleclaw. ShadowClan have always been a nuisance. Don't you think life would be better for all of us if they settled down under a leader who could make sure they stuck to the warrior code? Don't you think you could make a better job of leading WindClan than Onestar? Between us we could ensure that every cat in the forest was strong and happy. No more battles, no more quarreling over territory . . ."

"Well . . . maybe." Brambleclaw couldn't argue with the vision Hawkfrost set in front of him. It was true that strong leaders could rule the forest for the good of every cat. He remembered how the ShadowClan warriors had ignored Berrykit's cries for help when he was caught in the fox trap. *If I were in charge*, he thought, *no cat would ever watch a kit in pain without trying to help, no matter where that kit came from.* He wanted every cat in the forest to be cared for, but more than anything, he wanted what was best for ThunderClan. "But—" A faint cry interrupted him. "What was that?"

Hawkfrost shrugged. "Some unlucky bit of prey."

The cry came again. "No!" Brambleclaw exclaimed. "That's a cat in trouble. Come on!"

He dived out of the ferns and pelted along the shore in the direction of the cry. It came again, closer but fainter, a horrible choking sound. Brambleclaw leaped across the roots of a tree and found himself face-to-face with Firestar.

The ThunderClan leader lay on his side on a narrow path between close-growing ferns. His limbs jerked feebly and his eyes gazed at nothing. Foam flecked his muzzle. Around his neck, half buried in his flame-colored fur, was a thin, shiny tendril, leading to a stick driven into the earth. Firestar was caught in a fox trap!

Brambleclaw leaped forward to help him, only to be thrust aside by Hawkfrost's powerful shoulder.

"Mousebrain!" the RiverClan warrior hissed. "This is your chance, Brambleclaw. You're deputy now. If Firestar dies, you'll be Clan leader."

Brambleclaw stared at him in astonishment. *What is he telling me to do?* Then he realized that Firestar was trying to speak.

"Birchpaw told me . . . Blackstar waiting on our territory . . . Had to come alone . . ."

Hawkfrost's eyes gleamed with triumph as he padded across to Firestar and bent down to whisper in his ear. "But Blackstar isn't here. We are. You're a fool, Firestar. You were too easy to trap."

Brambleclaw felt the ground dip beneath his paws; he couldn't grasp the details, only that the absence of Blackstar, and the ShadowClan scent on Hawkfrost, added up to something murderously evil. "You did this," he said to his half brother. "You arranged for Firestar to be here, where there was a fox trap waiting."

"Of course." Hawkfrost sounded scornful. "I did it for you."

Firestar's sides heaved as he fought for breath. His gaze flickered from Hawkfrost to Brambleclaw and back again. Brambleclaw could see that unless he loosened the wire right away, his leader would lose a life—perhaps more.

Hawkfrost stepped back. "The brave ThunderClan leader," he sneered. "Not so powerful now, are you? Come on, Brambleclaw, finish him off."

Brambleclaw felt as though his paws were frozen to the bare earth. Every hair on his pelt stood on end as he heard Tigerstar whispering in his ear: *Kill him. No cat will know. You can be Clan leader. You can have everything you have ever wanted.*

He staggered as Hawkfrost gave him a vicious nudge, his tail lashing angrily. "What are you waiting for? This is what we have wanted all along, remember? Kill him now!"

CHAPTER 21

❧

"They're doing fine," Leafpool meowed, *stepping* back from Sorreltail's kits. "You must be very proud."

Sorreltail swallowed a bite of the thrush Leafpool had brought for her. "I am, but I'm sure they'll be into all kinds of mischief when they're a little bigger. Worse than Daisy's, even." Her amber eyes gleamed with amusement. "Cinderkit needs watching already."

Leafpool looked down at the kits, where they lay in a purring, drowsy heap. Warmth flooded over her as she remembered what Spottedleaf had shown her. How long would it be before the Clan realized the truth about Cinderkit? Leafpool longed to share the joy of her knowledge with them, but she knew that time had not come yet.

"You'll need to get all the rest you can, then," she mewed to Sorreltail. "And keep your strength up. Four kits at once are a big responsibility."

"I know. I'm really glad you're here, Leafpool."

Leafpool shut her eyes for a moment, trying to remember the feelings that had made her consider abandoning her Clan. It was like a shadow inside her, just out of reach. But now it swelled, filling her mind; she tried to shake it off, but the dark feelings seemed to build and build inside her, the guilt changing into a vision of blood and roaring, drowning the soft sounds of Sorreltail's kits and the warm, milky scents of the nursery.

Something terrible is happening—oh, StarClan, what can it be?

She stumbled blindly out into the clearing, ignoring Sorreltail's startled exclamation behind her. Once in the open, she realized that everything was peaceful. The clearing was almost deserted, with most cats out on patrol. Bright sunlight shone down from a blue sky streaked with a few fine wisps of cloud.

But Leafpool knew that something was horribly wrong—if not here, then out in the forest. She raced across the clearing, ignoring the puzzled looks from Cloudtail and Brightheart at the fresh-kill pile. Bursting out of the thorn tunnel, she almost crashed into Squirrelflight.

"Hey!" her sister exclaimed. "Take it easy. What's the matter?"

"Something dreadful," Leafpool panted. "Badgers—Twolegs—I don't know. Have you seen anything?"

"No." Squirrelflight rested her tail on her sister's shoulder to calm her. "Everything's fine. I've just been looking for Brambleclaw. The annoying furball went off without me. I tried to follow his scent, but I lost it."

"No, everything's not fine." The certainty of her terror rippled through Leafpool's pelt and struck cold into her bones. "ThunderClan is in great danger. Will you come with me?"

"Of course, but where are we going?"

"I don't know!" Leafpool's voice rose. "Oh, StarClan, show us the way!"

She had hardly finished speaking before she heard the sound of a cat blundering through the undergrowth. Fronds of bracken waved wildly as Ashfur dashed into the open. His fur stood on end and his blue eyes were wild with fear.

"Leafpool!" he gasped. "It's Firestar . . . he's caught in a fox trap."

"Where? Why didn't you get him out?" Squirrelflight demanded, her green eyes blazing.

"Because he's . . . Brambleclaw is there too." Ashfur was gasping for air as if he'd just dragged himself out of deep water. "And Hawkfrost is with him—a RiverClan cat on our territory. I couldn't take on both of them at once. I had to come for help." He pointed with his tail toward the lake. "That way. Hurry!"

CHAPTER 22

Brambleclaw stared down at his Clan leader. He still couldn't move. He knew that all he had to do was tighten the noose around Firestar's neck, and he would lose his remaining six lives at once. His gaze met Firestar's, where his leader lay helpless in front of him. But there was no pleading in the green eyes, only a fierce, proud question: *What will you do, Brambleclaw? It's your choice.*

Brambleclaw thought of how Firestar and Tigerstar had confronted each other, time after time. Each hated the other for what they stood for, the plans they had for their Clan. But Firestar had never needed to fight Tigerstar to the death. Scourge, the vicious leader of BloodClan, whom Tigerstar himself had invited into the forest, had killed him with a single blow.

This time it looked as though Tigerstar would win. Brambleclaw was aware of his father's spirit close beside him, urging him on. *Fool! Kill him now!*

Closing his eyes, Brambleclaw remembered the clearing at Fourtrees, the blood pouring out onto the grass as Tigerstar lost all nine lives at once. He saw Scourge looking down at his twitching body with cold triumph. Was that what Hawkfrost and Tigerstar wanted him to become?

"Six lives . . ." he murmured. Six lives stood between him and the leadership of ThunderClan.

"That's right," Hawkfrost hissed. "This is our chance to take revenge on Firestar for our father's death. He could have tried to stop Scourge, but he just stood there and watched Tigerstar die, over and over and over."

Revenge? Brambleclaw wrenched his gaze from Firestar to stare at his half brother. This wasn't about revenge. He knew very well that Tigerstar had willingly set his own paws on the path that led to his violent death.

All I want is to lead my Clan, he thought. *But not like this.* His loyalty was not to ThunderClan alone, but to Firestar too—the cat who had mentored him, accepted him in spite of his father, and in the end had trusted him enough to make him Clan deputy. He had thought that loyalty to the Clan didn't necessarily mean loyalty to the Clan leader. That wasn't true. Firestar *was* ThunderClan.

"No," he meowed to Hawkfrost, amazed to hear his voice come out strong and steady. "I won't do it."

He recalled how Brook and Squirrelflight had freed Berrykit when the kit caught his tail in a fox trap. Leaping over to Firestar's side, he began scrabbling in the earth, trying to dig up the stick that held the tendril taut around his leader's neck. "Keep still, Firestar," he panted as the earth flew. "I'll have you out of this in a heartbeat."

A yowl of protest battered his ears; he couldn't be sure

whether it came from Hawkfrost or from the vengeful spirit of Tigerstar. Hawkfrost sprang at him, slamming into his side and knocking him off his paws. Brambleclaw was pinned under him. Hawkfrost's ice-blue eyes glared into his.

"Coward!" Hawkfrost snarled. "Keep away and I'll kill him myself if I have to."

Never! Brambleclaw thrust his hind paws hard into Hawkfrost's belly, throwing him off. While his half brother lay winded, he hurled himself at the stick again, grabbing it in his jaws. His earlier digging had loosened it; now it came free altogether, and the tendril around Firestar's neck slackened. He heard his Clan leader draw a single gasping breath.

A fierce snarl behind him made him spin around to see Hawkfrost springing at him. Brambleclaw dodged to one side, letting the stick fall. He felt the sting of Hawkfrost's claws raking through his fur as his half brother leaped past him.

Spinning around, Brambleclaw faced Hawkfrost again, and saw a cold flame in the RiverClan cat's ice-blue eyes.

"Traitor!" Hawkfrost spat. "You're a traitor to everything our father planned! You were never strong enough to be like him."

"I don't want to be like him," Brambleclaw retorted.

"Then you're a fool," Hawkfrost sneered. "And stupid too. You never realized that this was a test. It was Tigerstar's idea. He said that if you really deserved power, you would do *anything* to get it."

"Even kill my Clan leader?"

"Especially that. But you're as weak as Tigerstar feared. We have great plans for the forest, he and I, and you could have been part of them. But we don't need you."

Brambleclaw understood exactly what his half brother was saying. He knew too much. Hawkfrost could not let him or Firestar live now; that must have been part of his plan from the beginning.

He took a step toward Hawkfrost. "Go back to RiverClan. You're my brother. I don't want to hurt you."

"Because you're weak," Hawkfrost taunted him. "You care more for kin than for power. But *I* don't."

He leaped for Brambleclaw again, carrying him off his paws and pinning him down. His ice-blue eyes blazed close to Brambleclaw's own. Brambleclaw felt sharp claws digging deep into his fur and saw teeth snapping at his throat. He struggled vainly to rake Hawkfrost's belly with his hind paws, feeling his own death a heartbeat away. To save himself, to save Firestar and ThunderClan, there was only one thing he could do.

Writhing from side to side, he spotted the stick from the fox trap lying half under his shoulder. He strained his neck and managed to grab it in his teeth. As Hawkfrost lunged down toward him he heaved the stick around and felt the sharpened end sink deep into Hawkfrost's throat. Hawkfrost stiffened with a horrible gurgling sound, then fell limp and heavy on Brambleclaw's chest.

Shocked, Brambleclaw struggled free of his half brother's body and let go of the stick. It fell to the ground, leaving a ragged wound in Hawkfrost's throat. Scarlet blood splashed onto the earth, faster and faster until it started to spill down toward the lakeshore.

"Hawkfrost!" Brambleclaw gasped. "I . . . I didn't want this."

Amazingly, his half brother pushed himself to his paws and staggered toward him. Brambleclaw braced himself, not knowing whether to expect another attack or an appeal for help.

"Fool!" Hawkfrost rasped; the effort of speaking made the blood pour even faster from his terrible wound. "Do you think I did this alone? Do you think you're safe within your own Clan?" He coughed, spitting out clots of blood, and added, "Think again!"

"What?" Brambleclaw took a step toward him, his forepaws splashing in the scarlet pool. Was Hawkfrost accusing a *ThunderClan warrior* of leading Firestar into this trap? "What do you mean? Tell me, Hawkfrost! *Who* do you mean?"

But the cold fire was leaving Hawkfrost's eyes. He turned away from Brambleclaw, staggered a few paces through the ferns, and collapsed beside the lake, his haunches trailing in the water. Tiny waves rippled over his body, and his blood spread out in a scarlet cloud.

Brambleclaw gazed down at him. There was so much more that he needed to know—but Hawkfrost was dead.

For a moment, his half brother's voice echoed softly in his ears: *We will meet again, my brother. This is not over yet.*

"Brambleclaw." Firestar still lay on his side, his neck fur

stained with blood from his own wound. Weak as he was, his gaze was unwavering as he looked at Brambleclaw.

"Firestar—" Brambleclaw broke off. There was nothing that he could say. Firestar had seen his own deputy struggling with the temptation to kill him. He would never be able to trust Brambleclaw again. How could he be ThunderClan's deputy now? He stood with bowed head and waited for the words that would send him into exile.

"Brambleclaw, you did well."

Brambleclaw looked up, staring at his leader in astonishment.

"Your path has been hard, harder than most," Firestar rasped. "But you fought a great battle here, and you won. You are a worthy deputy of ThunderClan."

His voice quavered on the last few words. Exhausted, he let his head fall again and closed his eyes.

Brambleclaw stood looking down at him, his half brother's blood sticky on his paws and the reek of it in his nostrils. *I won*, he thought. *But what will my father do to me now?*

CHAPTER 23

❧

Squirrelflight lashed her tail. "*Go back* to camp," she ordered Ashfur. "Fetch more cats to help."

Before she finished speaking, Leafpool was already racing through the undergrowth, not caring when trailing brambles clawed at her fur. Squirrelflight bounded along at her shoulder. Neither of them spoke. Ashfur's fear-scent was strong along his trail, showing them which way to go.

Leafpool's belly churned. Now she understood the premonition of danger that had flooded over her in the nursery. What could be worse than losing their Clan leader—Firestar, the father she loved?

Her mistrust of Brambleclaw swelled into a giant wave that threatened to crash down and swamp her. The tabby warrior was strong and brave, but Tigerstar's evil influence was surely too much for him.

Before the lake came in sight she began to pick up the scent of cats and, even stronger, the reek of fresh blood. Her heart seemed to stop for a moment. No cat could lose that much blood and survive.

She skidded around the roots of a tree and came to a halt

just above the water's edge. Firestar lay on his side in front of her, not moving. Brambleclaw was standing over him, his paws matted with blood.

I was right! Brambleclaw is a traitor. He murdered my father so he can be Clan leader.

Before she could speak, Firestar stirred and opened his eyes. "Leafpool," he whispered. "It's okay. Hawkfrost set a trap for me, but Brambleclaw killed him."

He shifted his foreleg, revealing the broken fox trap, and when Leafpool looked closer at Firestar, she could see that his neck, though badly scratched, was not bleeding heavily enough to produce this scarlet pool that lapped at her paws. The blood on Brambleclaw's paws was not her father's; instead, his claws were muddy and broken, which meant he must have dug up the stick and saved her father's life. Yet there was no pride or satisfaction in his gaze; his eyes were shadowed with horror, and he seemed to be listening to something no other cat could hear.

Squirrelflight flung herself past Leafpool and crouched beside her father, nosing him from ears to tail-tip. "Brambleclaw, thank you. You saved his life!"

Brambleclaw blinked as if he had only just realized she was there. "I only did what any cat would have done."

Leafpool padded past her father, feeling blood well up, damp and sticky, between her pads. *Where did all that blood come from?*

A trail led through the ferns to the lakeshore, leaving the stems flattened and broken—and stained with blood. Peering through, Leafpool saw Hawkfrost's dark tabby body lying unmoving in the shallows at the edge of the lake. Blood still spilled from a wound in his throat, clouding the water with a glaring splash of scarlet. Waves lapped heavily against the shore, turning the pebbles red.

"*Before all is peaceful, blood will spill blood, and the lake will run red,*" she whispered.

At last Leafpool understood. Brambleclaw and Hawkfrost were kin; blood had indeed spilled blood. Brambleclaw had killed his half brother to save Firestar. She had been right about Hawkfrost—he was too ambitious, too much like his father, Tigerstar—but she had never imagined that Brambleclaw would be the cat to stop him.

The prophecy that had haunted her paw steps for so long was finally fulfilled. Now the Clans could look forward to the peace that it had promised. And now that Hawkfrost was dead, Mothwing would be free of his attempts to control her. The secret of the moth's wing sign would be safe forever.

Leafpool turned away from Hawkfrost's body and went to join her father and Squirrelflight. Leaning on Squirrelflight's shoulder, Firestar had managed to sit up. Brambleclaw stood in silence beside them, still apparently stunned with shock, not even trying to clean Hawkfrost's blood from his paws.

"It's over," Leafpool told them quietly. She squared her shoulders and turned her face to the rising sun. "It's over, and peace has come."

The New Prophecy has been fulfilled . . . but there are more Warriors adventures still to come!

KEEP WATCH FOR

POWER OF THREE

WARRIORS

BOOK 1:

THE SIGHT

There will be three, kin of your kin . . .

Hollypaw, Jaypaw, and Lionpaw spring from a strong legacy: children of Squirrelflight and Brambleclaw, two of the noblest ThunderClan warriors, and grandchildren of the great leader Firestar himself. All three young cats possess unusual power and talent and seem certain to provide strength to the Clan for the next generation.

But there are dark secrets around the three, and a mysterious prophecy hints at trouble to come. An undercurrent of rage is rising against those who are not Clanborn, and the warrior code is in danger of being washed away by a river of blood. All the young cats' strength will be needed if the Clans are to survive.

. . . who hold the power of the stars in their paws.